I0563691

OTHER NOVELS BY DEANNA KING:
Jack West Novels
Twist of Fate
Lethal Liaisons
Vicious Vendetta
Trust No One
Gracie's Stories (eBook only)

Saving A Sioux Legacy

The Story of Blaze

Deanna King

Deanna King Writing

©2020 by Deanna King

All rights reserved. No part of this book may be reproduced, stored in a retrieval system or transmitted in any form or by any means without the prior written permission of the publishers, except by a reviewer who may quote brief passages in a review to be printed in a newspaper, magazine, or journal.

The author grants the final approval for this literary material.

This is a work of fiction. Names, characters, businesses, places, events, and incidents are either the products of the author's imagination or used in a fictitious manner. Any resemblance to actual people, living or dead, or actual events is purely coincidental.

Second Edition
ISBN:979-8-9856982-3-7
Cover by: Book Covers by Wilbert Stanton
Proofread and formatted by Staci Olsen
Published by Deanna King Writing
Deannakingwriting.com

For Honey Bear- daddy and I miss your funny antics- and your gauchos.
October 2003- December 2020

LIST OF CHARACTERS

PRESENT DAY
Blaze Clark- She Cougar
Meda Clark- Soft Dove
Payton Kangee- Paytah
Kanda Kangee- Wakanda
Blackie Kangee- Black Crow
Dakota Kangee- Wind Dancer
Sam Johnson- Running Elk
Pete Johnson- White Feather
Silver Moon
In the 1800s
Chief Black Raven
Chief Swift Eagle
Maka- Swift Eagle's Wife
Dark Cloud- (Warrior brave)
Captain Gene Ardenhert
Lieutenant T.H. Cooper
Major Bellamus

1

"Half-breed, half-breed!" I covered my ears, trying to block the voices out. It didn't work. I could still hear them taunting me.

"You're a squaw, that's what you are," a boy barked with laughter.

"Where's your feathers and animal skin dress, you stupid Indian?" another boy called out, and the girls next to him covered their mouths in giggles.

Tears streamed down my face, and I ran to the girl's bathroom to shut the world out.

***

"I DON'T CARE. I just want to move far away," I whispered into my hands.

"Blaze, this isn't a reservation. This is our land. We've built a community here. My father, Red Hawk, bought this land so we wouldn't have to live on a reservation," my father said.

"I don't care about the land or whatever—"

He cut me off. "Your ancestors lived on Standing Rock before the White man claimed it a reservation. I want our family to have its land again." His jaw tightened. "How can you be indifferent to your heritage? You are my only child. This is your home. No one looks down on you for being half White, not full-blooded Sioux."

"It is our land, Sioux land," he continued, voice steady. "No one controls us. Our community grows through marriages and friendships formed years ago. Each family is part of a close-knit Hunkpapa kinship."

"Well, I don't want the land, and I don't want to live the rest of my life being called a half-breed!" I yelled.

My mother reached for my hand. "Blaze, you should care about both sides of your heritage—Sioux and White."

"If knowing about my ancestors would change who I am, maybe. But it wouldn't. I don't care about my Indian heritage."

She patted my hand, and I jerked away.

"My Aunt Meda can tell you stories of our tribe, our history. We share bloodlines with high chieftains. You should be proud, whether Indian or White." My father's voice rose.

"I don't care about the past or a claim to fame. I want to live in the present—and I won't go back to that school."

"My parents found a school in Bismarck, two hours away. You can transfer next semester, come home on weekends. A private all-girl school. It will suit you."

I wanted to leap for joy. "You would let me?"

"Yes," my father said. "We know you're unhappy. This is a trial run. If it doesn't work, we'll bring you home."

I hugged him, laughing, then my mother. "Thank you, thank you!"

———— ❧ ————

THE NEXT FOUR YEARS were blissful. I'd never regretted the move.

Then tragedy struck. During my freshman year, the State Police knocked at my door. My parents had slid off the road on ice, hitting a tree head-on. Neither survived. I was eighteen, alone, stunned.

With Aunt Meda's help, I navigated the funeral. No siblings, no immediate family—I was the sole heir. Financially secure, but heartbroken.

Back at college, I moved on autopilot: classes, assignments, routines. I visited Meda on holidays but avoided the Sioux community. Other relatives? I never sought them. The family line ended with me unless I married. I had no plans to pass on the "half-breed" stigma.

Graduating from Augustana University with a business degree, I had no plans for work or graduate school. Money-wise, I was set. Yet boredom gnawed at me—an open door for men who preyed on vulnerability. One failed relationship after another... and then, wham. My heart shattered into a million pieces. That one man—and it had only taken twenty before him—had taken, used, and left me crawling to safety.

It was then I returned to North Dakota and Aunt Meda.

AUNT MEDA HAD BEEN in my life as long as I could remember. Her name meant prophetess in Lakota: "I know things. Sometimes I see the future, and the spirits talk to me."

As a child, I was mesmerized. As I grew, faith waned.

Back in the community, I kept my distance. No, that's a lie—I was a recluse, hiding in solitude. People thought me snobbish. I didn't care about the Sioux or their ways. I was an outsider.

The gap between me and the world widened until I barely existed. I stopped caring about myself—or life.

Then he came—out of nowhere. A stranger, not of the community. I felt alive again.

But it was short-lived. He vanished as quickly as he appeared, leaving me heartbroken. I retreated into a zombie-like state.

Aunt Meda guided me through the heartbreak. She knew my path. Soon, the fierce Iye Igmu'watogla—the warrior—would emerge.

2

Damn, it was cold—and getting colder. Rubbing my hands together, trying to warm them, even with gloves on, my fingers felt frozen. I inhaled through my nose, keeping my mouth closed, and hunched my shoulders, tugging at the fleece-lined jacket to bring it closer to my neck and block the icy wind. My toboggan pulled down around my ears, and a thick knitted scarf wrapped around my face. I wore tinted ski goggles, so all one might see were my frozen lips. Pushing at the bridge of my nose, I anchored the goggles closer, trying to keep the wind from sneaking in.

Why had I let Aunt Meda talk me into this ridiculous situation? Well, I knew why. Aunt Meda had that effect on me. So after her nagging, I'd relented and promised to trust her.

Aunt Meda had been badgering me for weeks. "Work for Blackie. It'll be interesting and fun. Besides, you'll get to do a little traveling. It's high time you did something besides hide out here and waste away."

Rolling my eyes, I thought, travel indeed. I would have rather gone to Greece or Spain—or some faraway place. Instead, I traveled from North Dakota to South Dakota. What a trip—from one cold state to another—and I was only six hundred miles away from home. Maybe a little farther with the winding roads and up-and-down turns. How I got here without getting lost surprised me. Yet here I sat, huddled alone in the cold, closing my eyes for a second to envision my dear Aunt Meda.

Living with my aunt on the land owned by her people—several miles outside the Standing Rock Indian Reservation—hadn't been an exciting life. Between the reservation and my aunt's small community, the noble Sioux Chief, Sitting Bull, lay buried near reservation land. Many people, mostly White men, denied he was buried there.

Opening my eyes, I glanced around. Small and uninhabitable. No one in sight. Who would camp here in winter? I'd done a little research and found that at one time there had been a mining town on this land. Huh. Not anymore. Now it was nothing more than a ghost town.

"Ghost town, schmost town," I muttered through chattering teeth.

I knew I was near the Black Hills, but not too near the national forest that stood as a boundless symbol in South Dakota. There were no signs anyone lived here, just this broken-down mill shed.

With closed eyes, I imagined the mining town as it might have been years ago: muddy roads, wooden buildings, a saloon, a dry goods store, a sheriff's office, and a small jail. Transport would be horses, wagons, or walking. Women in long cotton dresses with hoop skirts; girls in cotton frocks or flour sack dresses. Schoolchildren playing near a one-room schoolhouse. Men with rifles or sidearms and hats.

I could see it: active, dirty, alive during the Gold Rush. Miners flocking in, all chasing riches, all greedy. The White man's world.

Then I thought of the Indian world—my other half, my Sioux half. How sad, I thought. Losing land that was yours and being powerless to keep it. Greed—that was the key, then and now. I knew my Indian ancestors had tried to work it out with the

White man, but failed. Racism had always existed in some form. Both Indian and White men had suffered under greed. I wondered how life might have been otherwise.

When I was younger, I'd read through some of the Sioux histories. But I never found what I was looking for. Sure, I could have asked Aunt Meda about my roots—but why open that can of worms? I didn't want her to think I was interested in our Sioux history.

She could tell stories spanning centuries—our family tree, bloodlines shared with powerful Sioux chieftains. I wasn't interested in that past or my family's glory. All that mattered was living in the present.

I heaved a sigh; vapor from the cold flowed from my nostrils. How I wanted to leave. It was four o'clock. Even colder would come with night.

Blackie had told me two people were to meet around three o'clock. How did he know? He never said it was an affair—I just assumed. But I hadn't seen a single hotel, motel, or trailer for a tryst nearby. Only this decrepit, collapsing wooden shed. Absurd.

Who were these people? Important? Dangerous? Blackie could be mixed up in something illegal. It could get me hurt—or worse. Factoring in the bitter cold and my own stupidity, I felt duped. I did this for Aunt Meda, not for me.

So here I sat, huddled by this old mill shed, waiting for two unknown people—rendezvousing in the cold. Was it a joke? To heck with this; I'd tell Blackie I waited too long. Time to return to my rented Suburban, get warm, wait until morning, and drive back north.

Shrugging my shoulders, I stretched, letting warmth ebb away with every movement. Legs stiff from crouching, feet still warm inside triple socks, toe warmers, leggings tucked into Ugg boots.

Mostly, I'd weathered the cold. I sniggered. Yeah, I was getting punchy.

I crept upright, ready to move when I spotted them. Crouching back, stretching my legs behind me, I slithered into hiding. Peering around the corner, I flattened against the paint-chipped wood of the shed. My head stuck out too far, so I pulled back. Warmth spread into my veins as adrenaline pumped. Two more steps and they would see me.

Crunch. Snow under boots. Crunch, crunch. Silence.

"Now what?" I murmured.

Using sparse brush and tiny fir trees as cover, I inched closer. Checking my watch, sun dipping behind the mountains, taking light and warmth with it. Heart pounding, I spread brittle weeds for a better view.

The man was tall, scarfed, hat hiding his head, thick fur coat. The woman, taller, in the same coat. An affair? Ridiculous. They were overdressed for romance. She put hands on hips, shook her head, hat flew off. Hair braided, adorned with beads and a feather. He stepped back, arms sweeping the sky.

I didn't blink. Then she turned her back—her jaw jutted, lips grim. He sidestepped, shoved her hat toward her. She refused. Shrug. He dropped it. Unbuttoned coat. Pulled a wooden rod from an inner pocket, unstrapping it from Velcro.

"What the heck?" I whispered. Was he going to hurt her? I crouched, on all fours, poked my head out. Cover lost. Creeping backward, I grabbed a branch for partial cover.

They didn't see me. Not lovers. Body language said quarrel.

"Okay, think," I muttered, tapping my temple.

What were they up to? Blackie said: "Two people meeting where they shouldn't. Their futures and others' will be affected. Someone must intercede."

Sounds like an affair. Messing with futures = hurting people. Am I supposed to intercede? Blackie didn't make it clear. No photos, only a verbal report. How to prove anything?

They looked mad at each other. Good or bad? Freezing out here, waiting, wasn't an option. Danger? Heart raced, shivering—not from cold, from fear. Swallowing tears, I balled fists. One escaped; I swiped it away with a gloved hand. Feigned bravery.

"Auntie Meda, where is your Iye Igmu'watogla now?" I whispered. Puffs of smoke. Cougar instincts—fight, run. I might survive a few more hours. Could run, but not far. Eyes back to the pair.

Woman on snowy ground. Wind softened. Hat gone. Scarf fluttering. He stood close. Pushed wooden rod into snow. Didn't bend. Vast land, sparse trees, mountains in distance. I hid beside the shed—had to. Could have gone inside, but wind might collapse it. Trees to north? Not ideal. Too much open land to Suburban. Only option: stay or leave if they did. Fat chance—they weren't budging.

Hugging myself, teeth clenched: "Blackie, I'll get you for this if I make it out alive."

Frown. Eyes teared. Home, Aunt Meda, doom set in. Cramped, freezing, waiting. Sigh. Eyes shut. Might freeze and die. Thoughts rolled like a movie—past heartbreak, promises made, ending up here in this mess.

3

"Child, you will survive this. Your family line is powerful. I tell you there will come a time—"

I cut her off. "For what? Romance, love, marriage, and babies? Not for me—at least not in this lifetime." I was done with love and felt done with life.

Meda shook her head. "No. I do not speak of those things."

With a half grin, I rolled my eyes. "Aunt Meda, please don't go back into *your time* on me with that way of talking—telling me that is not of which you speak. I know you think you know my future, but let's keep it in the present. I don't want to look past today."

Meda was forever saying *one day, one day, one day*. One day what?

"Never mind," she said quietly. "It shall be so, and that is that."

Smiling, I kissed the top of her head and patted her soft, yet weathered face. Aunt Meda came from a long line of strong women, her lineage steeped in powerful Indian heritage. The whole *strong bloodline* jazz. But I lived in the here and now. There was no way I wanted to go back in time—especially not to those days.

All Aunt Meda had droned on about for months was *one day there will come a day*, blah, blah, blah. I was living day by day, never looking back, and absolutely never looking into the future.

"Buck up and learn that it's all right to be a woman without a man," Aunt Meda said with deep conviction. "You're a woman with strengths you haven't unleashed yet. One day, you'll have to rely on your own ingenuity. One day."

"Aunt Meda, I know you mean well. I'm just tired—tired of trying to have a relationship. And please don't go on about the eligible men in our tiny community. I'm not interested in a life with a man. Not one who's all into his heritage and stuff. They're nice men, but not for me. Let me just concede to the fact I will always be alone. And don't feel bad for me, because right now, it's fine. I'm fine without a man. And I'm not looking for a career, either."

"My *Iye Igmu'watogla*, you're never alone. I'm here, and so are others. I know you don't believe in the spirit world, but they are here, and they watch over you for many reasons, my child. They know you have a purpose."

I grinned at her use of the Sioux word for female cougar. "Why do you always call me *Iye Igmu'watogla*?"

"Because that is who you are. From your past to your present to your future, you will see. Over time, you'll understand," the older Sioux woman stated.

Each time I asked her why, this was her answer—every time, without fail.

"No disrespect, Auntie, but this is the twenty-first century, and my world differs from the world you came from. I've got to accept the things I have no control over, but as it is, I can't even control my own life."

I wasn't angry with my aunt, just agitated with myself. Here I was—a big, fat zero these days. A failure. Mistake after mistake: men, career choices, even my wardrobe felt wrong. Still, I kept those thoughts to myself. No need to act like the pathetic Pearl. Besides, it didn't suit me.

Aunt Meda stopped rocking and looked straight into my eyes. "No, you're not."

"I'm not what?" My voice was so low I wasn't sure she heard me.

"You're not a zero, nor a failure. You're my *Iye Igmu'watogla*, and one day you will see it is true. Now, no more of this talk. We will eat and relax."

That was that. No more talk.

It amazed me how my aunt could read my thoughts. Here I was, thinking I'd failed at life—no man, no family, no career—yet she saw something else entirely. It scared the hooey out of me, her unspoken wisdom and her uncanny ability to read my mind.

<hr />

I'D QUIT LOOKING FOR work since my parents left me well provided for. Still, I felt I needed something—though I didn't know what. That lack of direction caused a restless sadness in me. I tried to put on a cheerful face, but Aunt Meda saw through the charade.

"It is time," the old woman muttered, staring at me.

"So, you're turning your back on the world, eh?" she asked while stirring her homemade beef stew.

"What has the world given me? I'll tell you—nothing." Scooping corn masa, I dumped it into the bowl of flour and cornmeal. I stopped mixing and leaned my forehead against the cabinet door. "What's the point? I don't have to work since Mom and Dad provided for me after they died, so I have no daily purpose. My college girlfriends are busy with careers and men, or married with kids. None of them live anywhere near here. And I have no friends in this community. So what's the point?"

My face stayed buried against the cabinet.

"You!" Aunt Meda yanked the spoon from the pot and slammed it onto the counter, splattering stew everywhere. "You are not to stop living. You are to leave a mark in this world!"

I had never seen her like this. My mouth fell open.

"Close your mouth and sit down." She wiped her hands on her apron and pulled out a chair. "Sit."

Her sudden domineering tone shocked me.

"I know you don't wish to believe what I tell you, but you're going to listen. Once again, I tell you how powerful the line you come from is. There is no other line this strong—I assure you!"

Each word snapped with force.

I raised my hand. "If you'll stop being mad, I'll listen."

She exhaled, placing her hands flat on the table. "I know your heart, my child. I know you better than you know yourself. Now you must promise me. You must trust me. Do you understand?"

Something passed between us—energy, intention. Promise her what?

"Aunt Meda, I trust you," I said slowly. "But what am I promising?"

Without answering, she rose and stirred the pot. "Finish the cornbread. We'll eat soon."

"What—"

"Trust me. You start now."

She left the kitchen.

Amazing as she was, Aunt Meda was still weird. And I loved her for it. Still... what had I just promised?

The next morning, Aunt Meda was up early—breakfast, coffee, then more coffee. I stumbled into the sitting room just as she set the phone back in its cradle.

"Oh, here you are," I yawned, stretching before sitting on the small sofa.

She studied my face. "You favor my great-great-great-grandmother. She was the daughter of the Siouan Chief, Black Raven. You have her eyes."

I waited.

"Well, since I'm not full Sioux, I suppose I resemble my mother's family too."

"Hm. I suppose."

"Like my muddy-brown hair and skin tone?" I ran a strand through my fingers—skin like a fresh suntan, hair lighter than the raven black of full-blooded Sioux women.

"Yes, but you're more Sioux than you think. Your eyes see. Your heart is strong and wise. You are smart like a tracker, brave like a warrior, and you carry the ideals of a chief." She pointed at me. "And don't mock an old Indian woman. Believe."

The room was small but cozy, morning sun warming it. Her ancient rocker sat in the corner, an old Indian-style blanket draped across it. On the walls hung photographs I didn't recognize. I never asked.

Books on Native and Sioux history filled a lone bookcase. I'd never felt compelled to open them. I'd had enough history.

I wanted the future. The past was where you came from, not where you were going. And right now, I'd done nothing but screw mine up.

"Are you ready, Blaze?"

"No. First I need to eat, then shower, then—"

I stopped. Her eyes darkened.

"What is it? Did I do something wrong?" I sounded six years old.

"No. Are you ready for what I need from you? Remember what we discussed last night? Are you ready to trust me with your life?"

4

FROZEN STIFF, I COULDN'T feel my body, much less my brain working. Had I just recapped my life to present day, getting me to this dreadful situation?

I looked at my watch. Fifteen minutes had passed. I'd closed my eyes for that long? Blinking to focus, I raised my head and stretched my neck, working out a frozen kink. It didn't feel as cold—or maybe I was so cold I couldn't feel the cold any longer. That was a scary thought. So cold you didn't feel cold. Just peachy. I thought of one word—and only one: dead.

Had the man and woman left? Hunching, I pulled away from the side of the mill-shed and leaned out, peering around the old building. Nope, they were still there. Why on God's green earth were they still here? Why didn't they leave? They were doing nothing but keeping me from a nice, warm place with a hot bath and food. I got angrier by the second. This anger fueled energy—not for warmth but enough to thaw my brain, though I couldn't feel my feet anymore.

Huddling next to the old shack, I tried to get warmer, if that was possible. The sun was fading. I still had to get back to my vehicle. The rented Suburban was parked half a mile back in a thick nestle of trees. I was trying to be sneaky, and now I regretted not parking it behind the dilapidated shed. But they would have seen it, and that would have blown my cover.

I'd try to make a break for it if I got the chance, praying my frozen limbs would move. Getting to my vehicle was one thing;

starting the engine in this freezing weather was another problem entirely.

The man and woman were about thirty yards from me, and I knew my destiny was to freeze to death. Maybe I was already dead, and this was hell. I felt giddy. My situation wasn't funny, but I chuckled.

The sun continued its descent, and the temperature would follow it, getting colder than it was now—if that was even possible. The wind stopped its low whining, and I strained my ears. They had resumed talking. I wanted to get some idea of what to do next.

"It will be done. It is possible one more time. I know it is, Kanda. I feel it here," he said, gesturing to his heart, then pointing to his head.

"Payton, this is dangerous. We have no idea of the year or the place and the situation. I'm scared—terrified that you will get me there, and I too will be stuck with no way to return."

Okay, perfect. Now I had names: he was Payton, and she was Kanda. But who was going where, and how would they get stuck? This was ludicrous. I focused on their names. Kanda was unusual—one I'd never heard before. Payton sounded familiar; an old Indian name, I realized. Clamping my teeth together, I wondered why Indian things always seemed to sneak into my life.

Who was I kidding? I was half Sioux, my aunt full-blooded Sioux, and my present employer, Blackie Kangee, was Sioux. Kanda was Indian, and the man likely too. Were they Sioux? Out here in South Dakota, they could be Kiowa, maybe Cheyenne. If Blackie had me spying on them, they were likely from the Sioux tribe. What miffed me was that I'd clarified to Aunt Meda and Blackie my intentions: no involvement with Indian affairs. Yet here I was, right in the middle of it.

The man turned, removing his scarf from his lower face and his hat—a massive one with earflaps. His rich, dark hair fell long and thick, braided on one side with a feather hanging at the end. His facial features were sharp, his lips thin, high cheekbones, dark eyes, and a crooked nose—likely broken once. Full-blooded Indian, I realized.

Payton lifted the rod he carried and stuck it into a small hill of snow. It stood erect, unwavering. Kanda stood ramrod straight, hands in fists, jammed into her pockets.

"How can you make me do this when you know I'm terrified? I miss Dakota too, but why will you let me go into possible oblivion, never to return home? Don't you love me? Don't you worry you'll lose your wife?"

Payton came up beside Kanda, arm wrapping around her shoulders. His other gloved hand touched her pink, cold cheek. No sound—no wind, no crackling—just their breathing.

"You're our one hope, Kanda. You are the one to bring him home. It is the prophecy, and you possess the magic. Wakanda—your name—means possessor of magical powers. A strong woman shall go, and that woman is you."

His arms gathered her closer, their foreheads touching. I was mesmerized, eyes failing to blink. They pulled away, still locked in a stare.

Kanda unbuttoned her coat and withdrew a leather bag, looking like animal hide with drawstrings. She set it down, re-buttoned her coat, and hesitated before reaching in. Payton nodded. She opened the bag and removed twigs and dried grass.

Twigs and dried grass? Were they building a campfire? Making s'mores? I continued to watch. She poured a powdered substance from a vial, flicked a lighter, and smoke billowed upward. Time stood still.

Ducking my head, I closed my eyes, then reopened them. The embers of their makeshift fire glowed. How was it still burning in this cold? Who were these people?

Payton slipped off his coat, revealing a buckskin shirt and leggings. He placed three feathers in his hair crown. Kanda sat with her head bent, hands folded. Standing, Payton's face painted as a warrior completed the authentic Sioux look. Kanda revealed a buckskin dress adorned with beads and shells.

Oh, for heaven's sake, I muttered. Was this a mating ritual? Here, in this godforsaken, snow-covered, cold, middle-of-nowhere place?

Payton placed tiny twigs on the fire, took Kanda's hand, and kissed her lips. She stood rigid. He whispered to her, enfolded her into his arms, stroking her hair. She shivered, wiping tears.

If I'd been sure there wasn't a knife or gun in that bag, I'd have jumped in to find out what was going on. Pepper spray would've been handy. Blackie had said I'd be in no immediate danger. Huh. I'd run-of-the-mill him when I saw him again, I muttered through clenched teeth.

Payton pulled the stick from the snow. Untying the leather pouch on his belt, he took out a leather strap adorned with shells, beads, and feathers. I rubbed my arms and legs, trying to restore circulation. Lord, help me—I was about to freeze to death alone.

The mountains faded as night fell. The moonlight helped, but I'd left the flashlight in the Suburban. Would I make it back if the vehicle didn't start? Crap. This hadn't occurred to me until now.

Peering around the shed, I watched Payton place the rod in the center of the fire. Kanda held an uncapped vial, moving closer as he circled her, head lowered, chanting. She followed in a singsong, dazed way.

They moved too slowly. I wanted them to hurry. Could I walk up and ask what was going on? Funny later, maybe. Right now, infuriating. All this Indian stuff, Blackie's plan, Aunt Meda's tales of strong magic bloodlines—it was making me furious.

Kanda raised her arms, chanting at the moon. The wind whipped, cutting into my skin. Were they controlling it?

Scrunched like an inchworm, I rolled tighter, keeping my head down, eyes up. They stopped chanting, and Kanda lifted the vial, sprinkling the dust of the past over the tiny flames. The fire stayed lit.

Kanda looked at Payton. "I cannot deny this sign."

Payton replied, "In minutes, the gods of past lives will descend, taking you to another realm. What if the magic misfires? You will be lost, and Dakota too."

Their words were gibberish to me. The moon was a perfect, ominous sphere. My gut tugged; something was happening.

Payton poured his vial's substance into the fire. It grew redder and hotter, smoke billowing in colors. Indian phrases reached my ears. The ground trembled—or was it me? Kanda joined him, chanting louder.

I forgot the cold, mesmerized by the smoke and chanting. The rod jabbed into the fire. I closed my eyes.

Suddenly, the smoke faded. The embers died. Payton opened his eyes. The moon darkened behind clouds. Darkness crept in. He gathered their belongings, checking Kanda. She was still there, head bowed, fists bunched.

"What happened?" she whispered, tears falling.

"We did it as before. We didn't make a mistake. We failed," he wailed, dropping to his knees.

Kanda placed her hand on his head, offering silent reassurance. "We have to leave. Our window is gone for now. Next full moon, we try again."

He collected the items, handed her the leather bag, lifted her coat. They stood for a minute, staring at the cold fire, then walked back, hand in hand, crunching snow beneath their boots.

5

THE COUNCIL MET IN the abandoned church on land owned by Sam Running Elk Johnson. They had repaired and painted the exterior and refurbished the inside. Twenty old wooden pews sat in the vestibule, scrubbed, re-stained, and buffed to a reflective shine. Women of the community had also polished the hardwood floors, while woven grass mats at the entrance let visitors dust their feet before stepping onto the gleaming wood. Four sets of plate-glass windows lined either side of the main room, each covered with wooden shutters painted with colorful hieroglyphics depicting Sioux history. When closed, the shutters told a story of the tribe's vibrant past.

The walls displayed pictures of Sioux history, past and present, contributed by each family. There were real-life photos of ancestors and vivid paintings by Running Elk, adding authenticity to the room. Indian relics adorned the walls: fragments of a war bonnet, necklaces made from bear claws, a worn buckskin shirt and leggings. A shadow box held an old peace pipe and tobacco pouch made from deer hide. Squaw dresses decorated with flat shells, glass beads, and dentalium shells hung nearby, dove feathers lining the shoulders.

Behind the podium on the back wall was another deerskin shirt, trimmed with ermine, a tomahawk, and an ancient spear decorated with beads and flowing eagle feathers. Glass cabinets along the walls held Indian pottery and artifacts, items that might seem like junk to outsiders but represented the lives of ancestors.

This building was a place of tradition and pride, filled with Sioux heritage. Those who gathered here still followed some of the old ways, trusting council leaders—Soft Dove, Black Crow, Running Elk, and White Feather—to guide them as the chiefs had long ago.

The four leaders sat on the platform facing the crowd, waiting to explain why the council had called an assembly of the family heads.

"A year ago, I found an ancient book," Meda Clark—called Soft Dove—began. "It is made of thin buffalo-hide paper, bound with braided buffalo hair. Each spring I plant my garden in the same place I have for years, so it is a mystery why I only discovered it then. It was buried between two tree planks and wrapped in split buffalo horns to keep it from disappearing into Mother Earth. This artifact has survived many years. The writing and drawings were difficult to decipher, but I discovered a mark from one of my ancestors—Chief Black Raven. You have heard the legends of his powerful magic."

She scanned the room, nodding as murmurs rippled through the crowd.

Pete Johnson continued. "Meda asked me to examine the diary, written in Lakota. The drawings made little sense at first. It was a complicated puzzle that took many months. When I finally understood it, I brought it to the council. It spoke of magic—powerful magic—used as a time warp to travel back into history."

A few people snickered. The idea seemed preposterous. Every tribe had its tall tales, and centuries later, that was all they were—myths and legends. The old mystic beliefs no longer guided daily life. Facts and realism belonged to the new generation.

"And just what does this mean," Little River asked, "since time travel isn't possible and never will be?"

"It is possible," Blackie Black Crow Kangee replied. "My nephew, Dakota, was sent back in time. I know it can be done."

"You're saying he's in another world—back in time?" Red Wing scoffed. "That's impossible."

"I agree with Red Wing," Little River said, looking around the room. "I loved the old stories, but that's all they are—stories, not truth."

"Red Wing, Little River—you are the youngest here, perhaps too young," Sam Running Elk Johnson said, waving a hand toward the elders. "We are older. We have seen more, and some of us still remember when our people were first forced onto reservations." He gestured toward Silver Moon and Tall Grass.

Winona, First-Born Daughter of Wild Fox, spoke. "So you are telling us Dakota left this realm and traveled more than a hundred years into the old Sioux world—and I don't doubt you, Black Crow—but why would any of us need to go back?"

"The journal was not clear," Running Elk said. "From what we can piece together, it is to change something—or perhaps to alter our future. The writings were vague."

"My father, Wild Fox, used to speak of a time of great magic," First-Born Daughter said. "Most thought him a crazy old man. He dreamed of the Paha Sapa—and of change."

"Your father rambled," Deer Hoof retorted. "He was ancient even then, before he walked into the spirit world. He was not a visionary—just an old Sioux longing for the past."

"You understand very little, Deer Hoof," Winona snapped. "My father lived ninety moons. He was in tune with the old ways and understood our magic."

"I know our history," Deer Hoof shot back. "So why would going back in time matter to our people?"

Black Crow's glare silenced him. "It worked—and I will tell you what happened."

All eyes turned to him as his voice echoed through the old church.

"I was there. I saw it happen. You know I would not lie—I would not suffer the Sioux punishment for dishonor. No one here wishes to be mocked for the rest of their life, never trusted again."

His stare locked onto Deer Hoof, who slumped in his seat, head lowered.

"I watched Dakota's earthly body fade until it became a thin, cloudy spirit," Black Crow continued. "The spell worked. Never believe that sorcery does not exist, that visions are not real, or that our ancestors' spirits do not live on within us."

An old woman spoke, and the room fell silent.

"No more grumbling. No more questions. Let Black Crow speak."

Silver Moon sat ramrod straight, her silver hair in two long braids, her face wrinkled and weatherworn. Small as she was, she had outlived many, and no one knew how many moons she had seen. She rarely spoke, always listening, telling tales of long ago and keeping the town's children entertained. Most thought her ramblings were the tales of a senile old woman. Her faded eyes scanned each face. Though not the head of a family unit, she was the matriarch of the group. Even those who doubted mystic magic held a quiet respect—and a certain fear—for her.

Black Crow continued, "My nephew, Dakota—known to you as Wind Dancer—was chosen for his devotion and steadfast will. Pete translated the journal as best he could. It told of a man who would travel back, one from a powerful line, the firstborn in his family. Dakota's great-great-great-grandfather, Rushing Waters, fought General Custer. He was brother to my great-great-uncle. Dakota's great-great-great-grandfather was Chief Wahkoowah, Charging Bear—you know the stories of him."

"This strong medicine sent Dakota to the Black Hills, back to when the land belonged to the Sioux, before uprisings and wars, before the government forced our people onto reservations—a time when all Indians knew freedom, before our people lost their lands.

"As time passed, the older ways of the Sioux and other clans died. With them, the real spirit of the Sioux faded. The youth no longer embrace who they are. Our people are poor without the wealth of the land we once controlled," Black Crow finished.

Deer Hoof, frustrated, could not contain himself. "You called us here to explain old magic? To tell us what we already know? To explain how poor we are and what we lost? You're kidding, right?"

Pete White Feather Johnson stepped forward before Black Crow could answer. "Deer Hoof, you would do well to listen before making assumptions. You don't know everything."

White Feather's scowl deepened. "Once Black Crow finishes, I will share other news—news that should both satisfy and scare you."

He looked over at Red Wing and Little River. "In addition, you two shall listen as well. It seems your tribal sisters—Swan Maiden and First-Born Daughter—though close to you in age, are far wiser than you young pup braves. My advice is this: be more open-minded about what you think is impossible, because in reality, it is possible."

White Feather's ears reddened, his nostrils flaring. He rarely lost his temper, but when he did, it was fierce. Sam placed a hand on his brother's arm. Pete glanced at him, exhaled, and relaxed. He knew exactly what Sam was thinking. *Our mother should have named you Smokestack… or Fire Head.* Pete held back a grin and pressed his lips together. Sam wasn't wrong.

Meda took the opening. "There is no way to communicate with Wind Dancer, so we followed the journal's next step. Another was meant to be sent back—someone from a strong bloodline, possessing mystical power, to complete the circle of travel. When the moons were right and the sun gods aligned, the ancient ritual took place. That ritual happened three nights ago."

"Wakanda has gone too—" Running Elk began.

"No," Soft Dove interrupted, her voice quavering as she glanced at Black Crow. "She has not gone."

"What do you mean?" Running Elk asked, his eyes narrowing.

"After Wind Dancer was sent back, Black Crow and I went through the diary again. Pete's interpretation was that one who possessed otherworldly enchantment must travel. We believed that meant Wakanda—her name itself means *possesses magic*. But we... missed something." She looked at Black Crow. "Something important."

"And what was it I missed?" White Feather asked, leaning forward.

"Wakanda has magic," Meda said gently, "but she is of Wind Dancer's family—joined by marriage to his brother. No one from the same family line can be sent back."

"Then who?" White Feather crossed his arms. "Paytah and Wakanda are already at the base of the Black Hills performing the ritual. Who is there, Meda?"

"Blaze—She Cougar—my niece," Meda said. "She has gone into the spirit worlds of the past."

The Johnson brothers stared at her in shock. Before Sam could speak, Pete did.

"How can you be sure?" Pete asked, pacing. "And how could you have convinced her? She's more of an unbeliever than—" he glanced at the others—"Red Wing, Little River, and Deer Hoof."

"Meda," Sam said carefully, "she isn't familiar with our history. She never cared. And she isn't even full-blooded Sioux."

"She doesn't understand her heritage," Pete continued, agitation rising. "Her focus has always been the future, never the past. She'll be lost in that world." His voice faltered. "What if she—" He couldn't finish. "She might not make it. As a seer, you must understand that."

All eyes turned to Meda. She drew a deep breath.

"My niece is not full-blooded Sioux, but you all knew her father—Gray Wolf, a true Sioux. Her lineage runs deep, as all of ours do, though not all were written into history. Have you forgotten whose journal this is?" Her gaze settled on Pete. "Chief Black Raven's. Blaze comes from his fierce bloodline—the same magic that made this journey possible."

She paused, steady and resolute. "She never involved herself in our rituals. She wasn't interested. But she has endured much—losing both parents at once, surviving with no siblings, no family but me. Her sorrow is no less than any of yours. I know her better than any of you. And I know who she is."

Meda fell silent, studying each face. She had witnessed the births of the younger generation and shared both hardship and triumph with the elders.

"I have been a seer for as long as I can remember," she said softly. "I cannot say when it began. You all know my gift. I have seen sickness before it came, fears before they were spoken. I do not claim to know everything—but when something is true in my heart, it is simply true. Blaze is stronger than she appears. She has faced loss and survived it. Her heart is strong, her mind is sharp, and she will endure."

"Meda, that may be true of her present life," White Feather said more calmly, his earlier anger fading, "and yes, like many women, she has endured heartbreak—losing her parents most of all. We have all known such sorrow. But I must ask—how did you talk her into this?"

"In my niece's defense," Meda replied, "she might not have chosen this path had we told her. She would have thought my crazy Indian mind had gone berserk. Black Crow and I planned this without her knowledge. It has been years since she last saw most of you. She has never met Wakanda, and the last time she might have seen Dakota or Payton was at her parents' funeral. Her life shattered then, and she would not remember faces from that time. You all know—especially those close to her age—that she pulled away. She chose a quiet life with me."

Everyone knew Blaze as standoffish, withdrawn, almost a recluse. The world beyond the reservation was vast, and this place was only a small corner of it—a tight-knit people who kept mostly to themselves. Blaze had uninvited herself from them long ago, though if she chose to return, their arms would be open.

"What do you think will happen to her," Deer Hoof asked, doubt softening into concern, "since she doesn't know what has happened—or why?"

"Yes," Swan Maiden added. "How will she survive without knowing what lies ahead?"

It warmed Meda's heart that even the skeptics feared for her niece's safety.

"She is *Iye Igmu'watogla*—strong, smart, and braver than she knows," Meda said. "I have told her for years she has a destiny. She never believed me."

"That's comforting, Soft Dove," Red Wing said, "but she will be at a disadvantage. She doesn't even know our language."

Black Crow let out a deep belly laugh. Red Wing shot him a sharp look. "What is funny about that?" he snapped.

"You are," Black Crow replied. "You speak of Sioux ways, yet you yourself claimed our magic was only myth—stories old men tell. You don't believe in our powers, so why worry about what she does or doesn't know?"

"If magic brought her there," First-Born Daughter said quietly, "then magic will help her survive."

Little River snorted. "We can only hope. Still, I wonder what she can do. Even with knowledge, she is a weak woman. Dakota will have to carry her as a burden."

"Oh?" Swan Maiden's eyes darkened. "So now you believe in the power—and think women are nothing more than burdens?"

"Enough," Tall Grass said sharply. "This arguing is foolish. You young men know women—then and now—are strong. Look at our history. Look at our village. Tell me again women are burdens." He shook his head. The three young men ducked their heads in shame, knowing the women among them were often the bravest—and the wisest.

Meda seized the moment. "Blaze is a fighter, even if she doesn't yet know her own abilities. She will embrace her heritage and learn who she is—I feel it in my heart. Once she asked me what the point of life was. I told her *we* are the point. Her destiny will touch all of our lives. She Cougar, descendant of a mighty chief, will awaken with the heart of a true Sioux. Her destiny is to save the one person who will continue the Sioux legacy."

She raised a finger, forestalling questions. "No—we do not know who that person is. The journal says she will know when the time comes."

"We shall see," Deer Hoof muttered. Red Wing barely suppressed a laugh.

Pete White Feather had had enough of the young men's attitudes. It was time to reveal what he knew—truth not rooted in mysticism, but in fact. Out of fear, he had kept it hidden, though no matter how often he reviewed the records, they never changed.

"I told you all that once Meda finished, I had a story to share—one I have told no one until today." Ten pairs of eyes turned to him. "Our people are disappearing through sickness, poverty, and rising crime. Do you know how many Sioux have gone missing in the last ten years? They are not dead. They were never born. I've tracked family trees and bloodlines, and there is no explanation."

"Are you sure?" Sam asked.

Pete continued, "I'm sure—because I've been tracking this for over five years. I kept a journal, and now"—he held up his empty hands—"it's nothing but blank pages. No names. No births recorded. I've checked and rechecked. There's no faded ink and no sign of tampering. Our history is fading—places, people, events. At first the changes were trivial, but now they have never happened."

He turned to Silver Moon. "This isn't a surprise to you, is it? You've known for years, haven't you?"

Silver Moon sat with narrowed eyes and lips pressed into a grim line. No one spoke. Every gaze settled on her, waiting.

"Yes," she said at last. "I have known for many years. The changes began quietly—noticed by no one but you, White Feather. The moon has now entered the right phase, and the correct year has come. Time has waited for those bound to this magic to fulfill the destinies the spirits designed for them."
She paused. "As Soft Dove explained, if one spirit's life ends, the Sioux Nation will fade, and our history will change."

Her gaze shifted to Meda, Blackie, Sam, and Pete. "You four will meet at the next full moon and follow the instructions in Chief Black Raven's journal."

Then Silver Moon turned to the three younger men who had scoffed earlier. "Deer Hoof. Red Wing. Little River. You may not believe, but I have known this day would come. Do not mock what you do not understand. You are here to represent your bloodlines—bloodlines that will fade and become nonexistent."

Her eyes hardened. "Everyone here must believe. There can be no doubters. Is this understood?"

If there was one person the younger tribal members feared, it was Silver Moon. She affected lives in ways no one understood, and her words were never fancy or myth.

The three young men lowered their heads. None spoke. No one—including them—took Silver Moon's words lightly.

After a long, awkward silence, Little River cleared his throat. "I think I can speak for the three of us." He glanced sideways at Deer Hoof and Red Wing. "We agree Silver Moon is the wisest among us. If she says there can be no doubt, then we will trust her wisdom."

"Good," Silver Moon said. She then addressed the rest of the group. "You will all hold your tongues about what was spoken here. Until our people are returned to their rightful time, we will not disrupt our daily lives."

Her words ended the council. In silence, the eleven departed.

Just inside the doorway, Silver Moon turned to Meda. "The next full moon is in three days. Be ready."

That was all that needed to be said.

Three Days Later

Twenty miles from Standing Rock Reservation and far from most of the larger towns in North Dakota, the members met. Each was an elder of the community, between the ages of sixty-two and seventy-two, and each was full-blooded Sioux—heart, soul, and body.

The night of the full moon arrived.

Soft Dove, Black Crow, Running Elk, and White Feather—Meda Clark, Blackie Kangee, Sam Johnson, and Pete Johnson—sat outside at the back of their council hall. A small fire glowed nearby as each sat on the ground in a tight circle, legs crossed.

The men wore buckskin breeches and leggings with buckskin shirts adorned with shells, elk teeth, eagle feathers, and ermine tails. Meda wore the dress of a prophetess—long, fringed, and made of buffalo hide, tanned and beaten to an almost translucent white. It was decorated with tiny alabaster-colored shells, rinsed in black paint and wiped clean so the ridges remained outlined in dark contrast. Clusters of shells were sewn at the bodice and lined each side. A single soft dove feather was woven into her braided hair, and a leather band rested across her forehead.

The men painted their faces, each color representing a direction: yellow for the East—beginnings and inspiration; white for the North—purity, spirit, and fire; red for the South—change, family, and emotion; and black for the West—harvest and the return to the earth.

Somber and anxious all at once, Meda's heartbeat remained steady as she brought out the ancient diary and began.

"Black Raven was a man of vision, a man who lived two lives," she said. "He lived in his world and saw ours. He knew he could not change the future himself, but he believed we could go back and change one thing—one life—to ensure the Sioux Nation did not cease to be."

She opened the journal. "In his drawings, Black Raven sketched what looked like many stars. Beneath it, the same image appeared again, but with fewer stars. He then drew a single figure and placed a star beside it. We believe the stars represent our people."

Pete nodded. "From the census I have kept of the Seven Sioux Nations, many names no longer appear where they once did. I compared photocopies I made years ago to the originals, and they no longer match." He looked at each of them in turn. "I also examined records from the Trail of Tears. It is not only the Sioux who are affected—other tribes may suffer as well."

Black Crow stood and placed more wood on the fire. "It is time to begin."

Meda reached for the pouch hanging from a thin leather strap at her waist. She opened it and began chanting, the others joining her. Reaching inside, she drew out a handful of dust and cast it into the flames.

The fire crackled and sparked. Smoke surged upward, billowing briefly before settling back into itself.

Each of them fanned the smoke toward their faces, chanting louder and louder until the voices softened into whispers—then fell silent. Only Meda continued, her voice steady as the others rocked gently back and forth, inhaling the power of the crushed, burning peyote—the vision enhancer.

Each saw visions meant only for them: caves and men in ragged uniforms led by greedy hands; Sioux people drifting between worlds. Sacred lands appeared, thunder rolling through the Paha Sapa, and figures falling in battle. Four shadows emerged—two traveling up the mountain, two descending.

Suddenly, the wind rose from nowhere.

The fire vanished. Not a single ember glowed. No smoke curled into the sky.

Meda smiled, knowing Blaze was on her journey—a journey to her people, her birthright, and her future.

No one spoke as they departed, one by one.

6

My Journey Begins back into the 1800s.

I FELT GROGGY AS I lay flat on my face, my eyes squeezed shut. I tried to brace my foot against the mill shed for support. Nothing. There was nothing there.

With my legs stretched out, I shifted the lower half of my body, inching sideways, trying to find the building. Still nothing. Panic fluttered in my chest. Had I rolled away from the old mill shed and ended up in the open where those two men could see me? I squeezed my eyes tighter, afraid to look.

I shrugged my shoulders and felt no jacket or scarf around my neck or face. My hands were cool. I wiggled my fingers—no gloves. Where had they gone? It felt as though all my winter clothing had vanished. Was I a spirit now? A weightless figure, unbound by fabric or warmth? Had I frozen to death and become nothing more than drifting air?

If I opened my eyes, what would I see? Other spirits? My parents, who had gone before me?

My head felt thick with cobwebs. The thought that this might be my fate made my chest ache. Worse, if I was dead, there was no changing it—unless this was only a dream.

I rubbed my cheek against the ground. No snow. I wiggled my toes. No socks—but I wasn't barefoot. I had been wearing several pairs of warm socks and my Ugg boots. Had I lost them? Or was I so dead I could no longer feel cold or clothing?

I cracked my eyes open, just a fraction. Light seeped in, hazy and unfocused. Okay. I opened them wider—still cautious, bracing myself for whatever waited. Everything looked smoky.

Great. Had I been such a terrible person that I ended up *there*? At least it wasn't hot or flaming. No screaming, no moaning. Whew. Not Hell.

If this wasn't a dream, then stretching wouldn't change anything—but I did it anyway. With my eyes shut again, I extended my arms and legs, flexed my fingers and toes, arched my neck, and took a slow breath in and out.

Could spirits feel this? Muscles stretching, lungs filling, a heartbeat pulsing steadily? One thing reassured me: sensation flowed through my hands and feet.

I stayed flat on my stomach. Before this, I had been huddled against an old, rickety mill shed in the dead of winter. Rolling onto my left side, I stuck out my foot, waving it, trying to touch the wood.

Nothing.

Only empty space.

Fear clenched tight. I didn't open my eyes. A tear slipped free, and I brushed it away with the back of my hand.

Still keeping my eyes shut, I placed my palms against the surface beneath me. My fingers dug into hard, gritty dirt—real dirt. Warm dirt. My hand swept side to side: dirt and grass, no snow.

That meant I wasn't floating on some heavenly cloud.

What if I stayed here like this, unmoving? Would another spirit come for me? Did they do that? No one ever explains death to the living. The unknown terrified me, and I prayed—fervently—that I wasn't dead.

Enough. I had to be brave. I would open my eyes and face whatever this was—afterlife, dream, or nightmare.

DAKOTA WATCHED FROM A brushy rise as the woman stirred.

Her hair was dark—muddy brown, not the coal black he re-membered—and she looked smaller, shorter. It wasn't Kanda. They had said someone would be sent in a year, and he had assumed it would be Wakanda, possessor of magic.

If this wasn't her, then who was this woman? And why was she alone on the desolate prairie?

He lifted his gaze to the sky and whispered, "What now?"

The past year had been nothing but waiting—drifting from one purpose to another, wondering why he was here at all. No signs. No guidance. Nothing dramatic. The only reason he'd returned to this exact spot, on this exact day, was Soft Dove's words:

If in one year's time you have not vanished back to the present, return to where you began, and another will be sent.

He had been certain it would be his sister-in-law. Payton wouldn't have stopped Wakanda—she was strong, devoted to their people and their history. So what had changed?

Dakota kept watching the stranger, unease settling in his gut.

⚬⚬⚬

OKAY. I NEEDED TO get a grip.

I opened one eye. Dirt.

That wasn't so bad.

I opened the other. More dirt. A dried brown twig.

Inhaling deeply, I lifted my head. Tall, prickly grass sur-rounded me. I lay in a small clearing, just wide enough for my five-foot-four frame. The ground beneath me was flattened, dry grass and dirt, worn down as if something—or someone—had been there before.

I turned my head left. Right. Behind me.

Flat land stretched in every direction. No mill shed. No mountains. Just scattered trees and grass swaying as a gust of wind rolled through, then faded into stillness.

I pushed myself up a little, inching forward like a worm into the taller grass. A shiver ran through me as I hoped—desperately—that there were no snakes. Pressing up farther, I gained a better view of my surroundings.

Trees stretched ahead, scattered rather than clustered. Some were tall and narrow, others more like bushes—short, round, and bristled. This wasn't a forest; the trees were spread across the land with barren stretches between them. In the distance, mountains rose so far away they barely looked larger than hills. The ground was covered in sparse, dead-looking grass with patches of brush here and there.

It all felt strangely familiar.

Farther off, I spotted a small thicket of short trees, again surrounded by open land. If I'd been lying by the old mill shed, my head would have been facing east. I swiveled my neck left—north. That should have been where I'd hidden the Suburban.

Nothing.

I turned slowly, scanning every direction, and grew more disoriented by the second. North, south, east, west—none of it made sense anymore.

I rose onto all fours and twisted my head left, right, then back over each shoulder. Everything looked the same. When I stopped moving and listened, there was nothing but my own breathing and the wind gusting, dying, then rustling the weeds softly.

Holy guacamole—I wasn't in Kansas anymore. Maybe not even South Dakota.

The feeling reminded me of Dorothy in *The Wizard of Oz* or Alice tumbling into Wonderland. Like I'd fallen through some invisible looking glass or been swept up by a wild, unseen force. If I were truly dead—if this was the spirit world—wouldn't I be floating? Wouldn't there be others?

If this was the netherworld and I was alone in this desolate place, then yes—this would be torture. My own personal Hell.

I glanced down at myself and gasped.

My clothes were no longer winter wear, and definitely not from a mall. I wore a buckskin dress with three-quarter sleeves, leather fringe trailing down each arm. My boots were buckskin too, trimmed with animal fur, and leggings made of some kind of hide covered my legs.

I shook my head, trying to loosen the knots forming in my brain. Earlier, I'd felt weightless—naked, like a spirit. Now I was keenly aware of the weight of the material draped from my shoulders to my toes.

How was that even possible?

Pressing my fingers to the bridge of my nose, I tried to remember what had happened before I woke up. There had been two people... a fire... a man holding a rod with things dangling from it. Then—nothing.

Had I passed out?

"What on earth is going on?" I demanded aloud. "Who dressed me like this?"

The idea that this was some elaborate joke made my temper flare, but there was nothing funny about it. Panic clawed at me.

I stood with my hands on my hips, stubbornness masking fear, and searched for something—anything—familiar. The mill shed was gone. Everything looked wrong. There were no signs of other people, no movement, no life.

Inside, I wilted. Crying threatened, but what good would that do? I walked about fifty yards, staring out across miles of open land—prairie, I supposed. Alone. Completely alone.

Crossing my arms, I imagined what I must look like: brooding, confused, and scared out of my mind.

———— ⚜ ————

DAKOTA SHOOK HIS HEAD as he watched her. Whoever she was, she had no idea where she was—or why. That much was obvious, and it unsettled him.

If he couldn't return to his own time, how was he supposed to help her? Not that he was eager to go back—at least not yet. He still didn't understand the purpose of his journey. No signs, no guidance.

Was *she* the sign?

Lord, he hoped not.

One thing was certain: he couldn't let her jeopardize his life. If the council had sent her instead of Kanda, she would know, wouldn't she? He caught only fleeting glimpses of her face. Even dressed like this, she might belong to this era—abandoned, rejected by her people.

Until he knew who she was and why she was here, he would play dumb.

Another thought struck him. Did she speak Lakota? If she came from another tribe, communication could be impossible. That would be dreadful—at least for her.

"All right, Wind Dancer," he muttered to himself. "If this is who they sent, I'll find out."

Tapping his heels against his horse's flank, he guided the animal forward.

———— ⚜ ————

MY MIND WAS SPINNING, too tangled to notice anything else. I didn't hear him approach. Hunger gnawed at me; my mouth felt dry, my temper brittle. I had no idea how long I'd been here when a horse whinnied and twigs snapped.

I whipped around.

My ears rang as I searched for the practical joker—hoping this nonsense was finally over.

Instead, I found myself staring at a full-fledged Indian warrior on horseback.

Real. Terrifying.

Every instinct screamed at me to run, but he was mounted, and I wasn't stupid enough to think I could outrun a horse. It was just me, him, and his horse—no one else in sight.

He spoke in his native tongue. I understood none of it. I spoke English. That was it.

Heaven help me—I couldn't help myself.

I turned and ran, screaming my foolish head off.

Running at breakneck speed—for me—I didn't want to look back, but I did and lost my footing. As the strange Indian man and his horse bore down on me, I stumbled and slammed to my knees with a loud *whap!* I scrambled upright without brushing myself off and tried once more to outrun them.

It was pointless.

Dakota shouted in Lakota for her to stop, telling her he would not hurt her. She didn't understand. That told him one thing clearly: she didn't speak Lakota. If she were the one sent, she would have been better prepared—at least knowing the basics. Still, he had to give her credit. She was a fair runner.

Taking the reins, he slapped his pony's flank to urge it faster, then swung off the horse.

Damn it. He was going to have to chase her on foot.

I glanced back again, and even giving it everything I had, I was no match for his long, powerful stride. He swooped in, grabbed me around the waist, hauled me down, and pinned me to the ground.

Terror seized me. This wasn't a dream. This was real.

This was how I died.

What was the scalp of one woman worth? My thoughts spiraled darker—what if he took me... against my will? Oh my God. Tears burned behind my eyes. I would rather die than—no, I couldn't even form the words.

He stared down at me, and I stared back, wild-eyed, scanning his face. As my gaze drifted upward, I noticed three feathers fastened at the back of his crown.

Three feathers.

Where had I seen that before?

Dakota saw the tears and thought he'd hurt her. If she would just stop fighting, he could ease up. He needed to think of something—anything—besides tying her up and terrifying her further. But he couldn't reveal who he was until he knew who she was.

He studied her closely. Was she familiar? Someone he had known... later?

The thought of the feathers vanished as I squirmed beneath him. A cramp tightened in my left calf. He was heavy, and I needed air. Wedging my arms between us, I shoved at his chest.

"Get off me!" I bellowed. "I won't run!"

He paused, looking at me with confusion, as though trying—and failing—to understand.

"As if I *could* outrun you or your damned horse," I muttered.

He loosened his grip, shifting his weight off me.

I scrambled up, dusting off my backside and tugging my buckskin dress straight. Inside and out, I felt twisted. Rolling my eyes toward the sky, I spread my palms upward.

"What have I done to deserve this?"

He studied me, questions plain in his eyes, then uttered a single sound. "Hunh."

"Yeah, yeah," I snapped. "I hear you grunting. It's the only thing I understand."

He snorted—and laughed.

That did *not* amuse me.

Apparently, I was funny. Comic relief. Wonderful.

Crossing my arms, I cocked my head and glared at him. Useless, but satisfying. I asked anyway, in English, knowing full well he wouldn't understand.

"Now what do we do?"

Maybe he'd understand my body language. I was tired of this game and had a sinking feeling I wouldn't like the next part.

Despite being scared out of my mind, I forced myself to stand tall, feigning bravery and clinging to pride. I pointed to his horse, then gestured for help getting up.

The look on his face was priceless. I almost laughed.

Hands on my hips—the universal sign of an irritated woman—I said, "Well? Are you going to stand there like an Indian statue? We'd better get moving."

I mimed again for him to pull me up. I sighed. Talking to myself.

He didn't understand a word.

Dakota turned his head and grinned.

He understood every word. She just didn't know it.

Then his grin faded. No argument? No struggle? She wasn't trying to escape. Yes, he understood her—but he didn't understand *her* at all.

She was more than she appeared.

Paytah, he thought, *what have you done to me?*

Acting indifferent, he mounted his horse without ceremony and stared down at her.

I lifted my arm. With one hand, he grabbed me and hauled me up behind him as if I weighed nothing.

I swallowed.

Okay... that strength was impressive—but I kept that thought, and several others, firmly to my The ride was long, and I grew stiffer and sorer by the mile. One thing was certain—I would never have made a respectable equestrian. My backside and legs ached mercilessly. How much farther until we reached civilization? That was a hoot. Civilization. I saw no camp, no tribe, not even a town for miles.

What lay before us were hills, trees, and more hills and trees, the mountains buried beneath blankets upon blankets of greenery. High and low, wide and thin, the land stretched endlessly. It was beautiful—untouched, wild, and natural in its purest state. As I admired the scenery, I drew in deep breaths of fresh air, feeling oddly invigorated.

"Paha Sapa." The Indian swept his arm outward, encompassing the land. "Paha Sapa," he repeated.

If it meant *beautiful*, then yes. I nodded and echoed him. "Paha Sapa."

Paha Sapa—the Lakota name for the Black Hills. Dakota considered trying to explain it to her through drawings, but that would have to wait. They needed to keep moving. Light was fading fast, and soon it would be too dark to travel.

He had a destination in mind. His tribe—especially with this woman—could not find him on the sacred grounds. They accepted him, but they did not trust him. After all, they had found him much the same way he had found her—more than a year ago.

He had not been with a tribe and hadn't known what to tell them. He had played sick, which was not entirely a lie. He'd lain semiconscious for two full days, without food or water, dehydrated and half-crazed. They had nursed him back to health, though never without watchful eyes.

Being able to speak Lakota proved he was Sioux. The problem was that he couldn't say from which Sioux Nation he came. So he'd claimed amnesia.

The Indian stopped his mount, dismounted, and with a jerk of his head and a grunt, motioned for me to get down. My chin jutted out in rebellion as I slid off—far from gracefully. He loomed over me, amusement dancing in his eyes. He fought a smile, and I could tell.

Sometimes words weren't needed.

I dusted myself off, shrugged, and snubbed my nose at him.

A loud *ha-ha-ha* burst from his chest. I bristled, huffing as I summoned every ounce of bravery I had. I'd be danged if I showed fear—hoping confidence might drown out the quake inside me. My unnamed captor tugged the reins, and like a sheep, I followed behind.

Huh. Maybe I'd fear him later, but right now bears and mountain lions seemed the more immediate concern.

The trees thickened as we began a steady uphill climb to wherever he was taking me. *Dad-gum it,* did he not realize I wasn't a mountain goat? I grabbed branches to haul myself upward, lungs burning. I wasn't sure I'd make it to the top, while he moved with ease.

"Humph," I groused. "You just had to make this difficult, didn't you?"

He offered no response. One—he had to keep up the act of not understanding her. Two—getting soft on her wasn't safe. If she was to survive here, she had to toughen up. The climb was hard work, even for him, though this was nothing compared to other mountains. She hadn't trained for this life, but that wasn't his fault either.

Dakota had expected someone else to make this journey. Now he was stuck with whoever they'd sent—if she truly was the one sent. He pressed on, navigating toward caves he knew were uninhabited by man or beast. He needed shelter before nightfall.

Later, Dakota watched as she slept. He knew how exhausted she was—he'd experienced it himself. Once sleep claimed her, it would be deep and heavy. She would wake disoriented, still tired, believing this was all a dream—just as he once had.

She didn't look comfortable on the hard ground, but it was all he could offer. He slept little, keeping watch. She was pretty. Even with her brow furrowed in troubled dreams and her face drawn tight, she was beautiful.

Her skin tone was darker than he'd first assumed. Her hair was deep brown with an almost black sheen—natural or colored, he couldn't say. Studying her features more closely, he saw her Indian heritage. Not dominant, but present.

He disliked labels like *half-Sioux, half-white*. People never said *half-white*. They said *half-breed*. Her heritage was not her choice.

Dakota loved being full-blooded Sioux and wondered if she liked who she was.

Closing his eyes, he thought about how he would explain her to the tribe. He would have to lie—and be creative.

The sun began to rise, beams of light slipping through tall trees in shimmering prisms. Greens fractured into brilliant flashes against the sky. He loved the Black Hills for more than just their sacredness. He was one with this living land, a place echoing his past life.

If Kanda had come instead of this unnamed woman, he would have brought news of Dakota's family—of the year Dakota had missed in his own world. But that was not to be, and he accepted it.

I woke blurry-eyed.

What an awful dream. A nightmare, really. Someone had found me half-frozen and carried me home—to Aunt Meda's.

But the ground beneath me was rock-hard. When a horse neighed, my insides flipped.

Not a dream.

Reality.

My living nightmare.

Forcing myself to move, I sat up. I couldn't stay there forever, no matter how badly I wanted to close my eyes and wake in my own bed. I was starving. There was no fire, no food—nothing. I stood and watched him working with his horse.

He turned, stepped toward me, and handed me a sack—some kind of water container—nudging it into my hands when I didn't immediately take it.

self as I tried to size him up.

With reluctance, I took the sack. It sloshed in my hands, but I was so thirsty I didn't care what it contained. Wet was wet, and I drank my fill. Handing it back, I murmured, "Thank you," knowing it fell on deaf ears—he didn't understand me.

Dakota sensed her presence behind him and knew she was hungry. He'd felt the same way on his second day, starving and desperate. With a heavy sigh, he hopped onto his pony and extended his hand. She let him pull her up. At that moment, she had surrendered to her fate—there seemed to be no other choices left in her life.

7

THE SUN WAS AT its highest when I saw the village. It was a marvelous sight—a village. It had taken us forever to get there. Nonstop travel, and I had stopped counting the days. Time no longer mattered. We traveled, ate, and slept. What I ate, I never turned my nose up at. Small rabbits, and whatever birds he caught—I wasn't sure how, because I never saw him hunt or kill them—became my meals. I supposed he thought I was a pansy, a fraidy-cat, and I was okay with that. Who was I to act brave? I kept my head down, mouth shut, and hoped to live long enough to wake up from this atrocious nightmare.

People watched as we rode in. Men, women, and children were everywhere. Horses ran free. The scene was surreal, like a movie. Children played beside their mothers; women carried baskets, and some held waterproof bags dripping with water. Men walked or sat in front of their tipis, enjoying the sun.

As soon as the people saw us, they ran toward us, yelling in a language I did not understand. Gone was the gorgeous picture; now fear flooded me. Tightening my grip around my companion, I looked from side to side as more people surrounded his horse, everyone talking at once. His laugh sounded bawdy as a few of the men said things to him, looking my way. I didn't understand their words, but laughter spoke clearly—I wanted to slap a face or two.

I removed my arms from his waist, jutted my chin up, and scooted away as far as I could. If I went back too far, I'd fall off the horse onto my rump. I had to maintain dignity.

He dismounted, half pulling, half dragging me off, and I lost my footing, pawing at him to stay upright. He brushed my hand off to greet another man—who I assumed was the chief. Somehow, I stayed upright.

Women swooped in, examining me, stroking my hair, checking my clothing. One woman turned me around and tapped my backside, laughing at her companions. I was mortified, prodded and scrutinized as if I were a living cadaver. Panic rose in my throat.

Dakota kept an eye on the interaction. He explained to the chief and council that he had found me lost and frightened on the small patch of prairie near the Black Hills.

"You must take her in hand, Wind Dancer, if that is what you wish. You will be her guardian for now," Chief Swift Eagle advised, then moved on to another subject.

I could take no more gawking. When one younger woman poked me again, I instinctively snapped, growling low in my throat, baring teeth to show anger.

"Iye Igmu'watogla," he said, patting my back firmly. All the others hooted, but I stood stunned. She Cougar. He called me She Cougar—my Indian name, given to me by Aunt Meda.

He did not know me, yet he knew my name. A chill ran up my spine. He guided me toward a tipi, pushing open the flap. I followed, mind racing.

Inside, his living quarters: a buffalo-hide bed, clay pots, straw bedding, bow and arrows, weapons, extra clothing, a breastplate made of tubular shells with feathers, a pouch, and a spear decorated with colored cloth and feathers.

This was a disaster waiting to happen. One bed, two people. Had he made them think I was his woman? I refused. I scanned him and the sleeping area. He gestured with both palms and shook his head—no, I was not sleeping with him.

I plopped onto the buffalo hide, exhausted. He handed me a small pouch, gesturing for me to drink. I drank, gritty but wet, then took a tiny bite of dried meat—buffalo.

Pointing to the bed, he indicated I should sleep. I lay atop several hides, covering myself with a thinner one. My hands rested at my breasts.

With one finger, I lifted a silver chain from my neck, pulling out the charm Aunt Meda had given me: a small circle within a larger circle. Aunt Meda had said the two circles represented two lives—the past and present.

"Keep this with you always. It is blessed, and it will be lucky for you one day," she had whispered years ago.

I hoped the charm and this journey through time were a positive omen. My eyelids grew heavy, and I drifted into a dreamless, heavy sleep.

Dakota left, still considering how to communicate without giving himself away. He could not speak to me in English, not yet. Another burden on him—how was I to help him? I was a greenhorn in this time. He went to Swift Eagle's home and waited outside.

Chief Swift Eagle spoke, "It is land for the Sioux, not the White man. We must guard what is ours. Has there not been talk of an agreement, one that is in the White man's paper?"

"What does a piece of paper do for our people? You can't trust something that can blow away in the wind," Dark Cloud replied.

"It is a parchment holding our people down. The White man steals what is ours," Teton added.

"We will not let the White man take our lands and kill our buffalo, and we will not let them destroy our tribe," Dark Cloud declared, towering over the others. "Each of us knows the truth, but knowing is not how we save our people. Are we to hide behind our women and act like cowards? Is this the Sioux warrior's way? We shall fight to keep what is ours."

"It is the yellow rock of the Black Hills the White man wants. That rock lives within Sioux lands. How do we stop them from destroying our lands and people for a yellow rock?" Dakota asked, thinking of gold.

The chief pondered. Never one to rush, he always reflected before making a decision. "I will think on these matters as each of you shall. Now stop talk and we smoke."

The men passed the pipe. Dakota bided his time, needing to know his mission and the role I would play.

Waking, I felt more rested than I had since day one. I turned to the flap of the tipi and saw him sleeping. I had not heard him come in—I must have slept like a dead woman.

I lay on my side, propping my head on my hand, watching him sleep. His soft breathing was faint; he looked majestic, not menacing. His chest bare, breastplate removed, moonlight highlighting dark eyelashes, a firm jawline, and full lips. Holy cow—I was attracted. I shook it off. It had been years since I'd felt attraction, and I would not allow it.

He stirred slightly, and I held my breath, hoping not to wake him. He grimaced in sleep, and a bead of sweat formed on his forehead. I berated myself for thinking about love, closing my eyes again.

Real Time, Twenty-first Century

Meda sat in the dark, with the diary on her lap, holding the charm of two circles. On the chain hung a small circle, which lay inside a larger circle, attached with a thin piece of silver. Closing her eyes, she rocked as she lifted the charm and held it next to her heart; it soothed her fears as her niece's face appeared behind her closed eyes.

"I'm with you, my Iye Igmu'watogla, always. I'm with you."
Her voice was calm.

She put the long chain around her neck and closed the old
diary, putting it back into the leather pouch, securing the leather
ties. Still sitting, she closed her eyes, half-thinking, half-dream-
ing, and could see her niece Blaze, unsure of what was happening. Meda could feel the child's fear. The poor child, frightened
out of her wits, and as Meda felt the younger woman's fears, she
also felt a sudden surge in her power—Blaze's power. Meda Soft
Dove Clark knew in her heart it would work out. Even though
she'd not felt Wind Dancer as strong as Blaze, she was sure at this
very moment in time they were both safe. Opening her eyes, she
was no longer as fearful as she had been, and in less than a week,
another full moon would be upon them. They would try the
visionary ceremony again.

8

MONTHS HAD PASSED SINCE my arrival into this less-than-civilized era. My skin was dry, my hair a mess, and I wanted some darned Chap Stick. What I wouldn't give for a hot shower with body wash and a blow-dryer. Instead, I washed in icy streams and used buffalo fat to moisturize my skin. Was I living high off the hog or what? Running my fingers through my dry, brittle hair, I tied it back with a leather strap, making do with what was at hand. Boy, this was worse than roughing it. Once I got back to my real life, I vowed I would never complain about anything again.

In my other life, I had experienced some awful days, but here I was building my repertoire of terrible days. I had been with the tribe eight or nine days when a small buffalo wandered away from its herd. Three braves took it down. It took several braves to hang the smaller calf by its hind feet in a nearby tree so the tribal women could begin the skinning process.

Had it been a full-sized buffalo, perhaps I would have reacted differently. But when a woman took a long flint knife and cut the animal's throat to drain the blood, I turned green around the gills, trying to stay upright. Another woman pushed me back, steadying me, then patted me on the back, giving a walloping thump as she pointed to the buffalo blood.

Gesturing at the blood and miming eating, the Indian woman said something in Lakota. I could not understand her. All I saw was a dead animal and blood. I closed my eyes, hoping to remove myself from the sight, but the smell was worse. One fear was losing my stomach contents in front of everyone. I needed fresh air.

Just as I thought I had regained composure, another woman took an even bigger bone knife and sliced the buffalo from jaw to anus, splitting it open completely. I fell flat on my face in a dead faint.

Lying in the beast's blood, Dakota wasn't sure if he should move me. The other women worked around me, stepping over, nudging my arms aside. This was women's work; men just watched, waiting for the spoils of the hunt.

Feeling a pang of pity, Dakota grabbed my legs and dragged me out of the blood and out of the way. He would not make a scene. All eyes were on him as he took a clay pot, filled it with water, and splashed it squarely in my face.

Sputtering and coughing, I wiped my face, madder than a wet hen.

"Hey! What the Sam Hill was that for?" I sat upright and looked at him, towering over me, then glanced at the women still tearing apart the buffalo.

"What happened? Oh, cripes, I fainted."

"Humph." My keeper waved me to get up and rejoin the women.

With as much dignity as I could muster, I dusted myself off and half-walked, half-stomped back. "I'll not faint again. It took me by surprise, that's all," I muttered.

The chore was long. Mercy, they used every part of the buffalo. I questioned each woman in English with hand signs: Why keep that? How do you use it? What's this for? It was amazing as I figured out little things.

Horns became scraping tools, cups, or spoons. A woman took me to her tipi, showed a bow and bowstring, then held a piece of bone shaped like a spool. I pointed at my clothing, mimed sewing, and she nodded with a big smile.

I didn't need to ask about hides or buffalo bladders. Ornaments, necklaces, and charms came from teeth. When she showed me the brain, I felt queasy but reminded myself: I won't faint, I won't faint. She used the sun and the brains to tan the hides.

Next, I pointed at the hooves. She showed me how to create glue, dipping a stone in a clay pot, sticking it to buckskin, and blowing on it. I smiled and said, "Glue." Makawee repeated the word, grinning.

Dakota watched quietly. Even though I spanned a century of language and culture, I had somehow communicated with most of them through sign language and facial expressions. I helped crush corn, worked in gardens, and carried water in buffalo bladders. This wasn't my choice of life, but I adapted.

Dakota felt relief that Makawee, Swift Eagle's wife, had taken me under her wing. She ensured no one would harm me. It was strange how quickly kinship formed, but Dakota never prided himself on knowing women's hearts. He knew their fears and pleasures, but not in the way love required.

Not once had Dakota let his heart get involved, and he'd never been serious about a woman. "There is no such thing as true love. Staying single is my plan," he had told his friends.

They laughed. His brother Payton snorted, "You'll never see it coming, pal." Dakota refused to believe it.

His heart tugged faintly as he watched Makawee with the woman now called Iye Igmu'watogla. She was learning their ways, trying to fit in, yet she didn't belong. How could he explain her presence when he didn't know why he was there? Without understanding their language, how could she help him solve the time-travel mystery?

Makawee picked up a small clay pot, a tiny stone, and a piece of torn buckskin. Dipping the stone in the pot, she stuck it to the buckskin, blowing on it. The hoofs of buffalo contained properties that acted like glue. I smiled and nodded, saying in English, "Glue."

Makawee repeated the word with a smile. It was a bonding moment—a connection between me, Iye Igmu'watogla (She Cougar), and Makawee, Mother Earth.

9

FOR MONTHS I HAD worked hard in the village. I was tired—and still frustrated. If this was my life now, then so be it, but *what if?* I tried not to think about the what-ifs, but it was hard. Even though I'd grown very fond of these people, the language barrier was wearing me down. Lakota was a hard language, and Lord knew I had never been a promising linguist. Shoot, I'd barely passed Spanish just to graduate.

Makawee handed me a tall, deep clay pot and a bone fashioned into a crushing tool. She poured dried corn kernels into the pot and gestured for me to pound them. I did so without thinking, frustration building as I hammered the poor kernels into pulp. Of course, that was the point—I was making cornmeal the old-fashioned way.

I was not cut out to be a pioneer woman or a Plains Indian maiden. I smiled at Makawee—Maka, as I'd taken to calling her. She was a wonderful woman, and I genuinely liked her, but I hated this life. These women were used to it; it was their time. Both my shoulders ached from hauling water, pounding corn, and working in the small gardens alongside Maka. I needed a moment alone.

When I finished the task, I used my improvised sign language—two fingers walking, pointing to myself—to show I was stepping away. Somehow, Maka understood. She nodded and shooed me off, speaking softly in her language. I assumed she was telling me to go, to reflect, that it was all right.

I wasn't sure how far I'd walked before I found myself in a grove of trees near a narrow stretch of the stream where they drew water. I sat down and leaned against a tree, staring out at the vastness of the land. A heavy sigh escaped me as I wished I'd been transported somewhere—anywhere—else. Maybe the Roaring Twenties. Somewhere I could converse, take a hot bath, ride in a Model T, and attend a ball in a gown fit for Scarlett O'Hara.

It felt like I'd lived two lives in just a few months, and I was exhausted and homesick. The tears came. Pulling my knees to my chest, burying my face in my hands, I folded in on myself and cried. I cried alone because I never wanted them to see me this way, never wanted them to know I had been reduced to tears. I deserved this cry—long and hard—to cleanse something inside me, if that were even possible. Sorrow and fear poured out, followed by anger and defeat. I cried until my body shook.

Dakota was not far away, watching. Even if he hadn't been concealing himself, she wouldn't have seen him. The woman was crying, and it saddened him deeply. He needed to tell her who he was—to comfort her—but he knew how furious she would be when she learned there had never been a language barrier. He wasn't ready to face that wrath.

He could have spared her so much misery, but too many things had stayed his hand. What he had needed was to see how she would cope—how strong she could be without him as a crutch. She had endured trial after trial and passed each one with quiet resilience. He could use that truth to justify his silence. Yes, that would be his reasoning. It was close enough to the truth that it might appease her.

Back home—far into the future, in another century

In her own world, Meda Clark sat in her rickety rocking chair, fingering a necklace as she rocked, hummed, and chanted softly. The old diary rested on her lap. The next few pages were difficult to decipher—the writing crude, the drawings rough—but she believed she understood their meaning. This was magic of understanding.

She read and reread the pages. The diary did not specify what form that understanding would take. It could mean Blaze would comprehend the Sioux language—or finally grasp how she had been pulled back through time.

The charm in Meda's hand mirrored the one Blaze wore: two circles hanging from a long chain. Meda prayed it hadn't been lost in the warping of time. The diary foretold a transfer of magic, a sending across time and dimensions. Once more, Meda chanted the encrypted words tied to the ancient charm of understanding. She lifted it to her face, studying the circles—one life within another. Past and present fused, inseparable. Without one, the other could not exist.

She slipped the chain over her head and pressed the charm to her heart.

"My She Cougar," she whispered, "I am here. I will guide you. Open your heart to my words. Let your mind meld with my knowledge, your spirit with mine. You are Sioux. You are blood of my blood, kin to my tribe. Hear me in your heart. Your day has come. With all you have endured, you will understand. You will become one with my spirit."

Meda closed her eyes and envisioned Blaze.

———— ❦ ————

On the hill, at the base of the tree, I sat dry-eyed now, hollow and alone. I straightened my legs, crossing them at the ankles.

It felt as though I had cried for hours. Exhausted, I let my body relax against the trunk. Using my sleeve, I wiped my eyes, hoping my face wasn't too red or blotchy—though any woman, Indian or Eskimo, would know I'd been crying.

I decided to wait a few minutes. It wasn't like I was on a time clock.

Without thinking, my hand drifted to my throat, fingering the chain beneath my dress. Pulling it free, I looked at the two circles nested together. One side was wide enough for an inscription, though I didn't need to read it to know the words by heart:

To Blaze, on your 16th birthday.
This is your connection to me
Love, Aunt Meda.February 1996.

My connection to home.

"Aunt Meda, I miss you so," I whispered to the charm. "I wish you were here with me—to help me." Another tear slipped down my cheek. "You are wise. I am not. Help me."

Holding the charm tight against my breast, all I could think of was Aunt Meda.

A clap of thunder cracked sharp, loud, and long.

I jumped, heart racing, and looked up. The sky was perfectly clear—no clouds, no hint of rain. It was strange, but so was my situation, so I ignored it.

———— ❧ ————

SOMEWHERE YEARS IN THE future, Meda Clark jumped too.

She rose quickly and went to the window, staring out into a cloudless night, stars bright overhead, no hint of rain. Her heart lurched. This signified something—something good.

———— ❧ ————

DAKOTA LOOKED UP FROM where he hid when he heard the thunder.

Nothing.

He looked back toward She Cougar, still sitting there, staring into the clear evening sky. The sun had set, yet there were no signs of rainfall. Odd. That was not rain thunder. It was different—deep, resonant, vibrating—like Zeus had hurled lightning and struck solid rock. Almost as if a volcano had erupted and then stopped.

Dakota watched as the woman spoke to herself, flailing her arms, stomping her feet, acting half crazed.

It was time.

Wanting her to know he was approaching, he deliberately crunched twigs beneath his feet and called out her Sioux name.

Thinking again about the thunder, I stood and scanned the sky once more.

"Hell's bells. If I'm stuck out here in a cloudburst, that'll just make my day. And Lord knows I've just about had enough."

No longer sad, no longer worried about rain, I was angry—angry at myself, angry at my situation, angry because I missed my old life. As dull as it might have been, I wanted to go home.

"Iye Igmu'watogla. Iye Igmu'watogla."

My head snapped around. "What?" I yelled. Of course he wouldn't understand me—but he could hear, right? He was saying something and didn't seem to care whether I understood.

"I want to go home! I want a shower! I want fast food! I want a feather bed! I want to go to the mall, get a pedicure, and see my aunt!" I screamed, not caring if he thought I'd lost my mind.

Eyes wide, he raised his hands, motioning for me to calm down. In Lakota, he spoke evenly.

"I understand. This is different—unexpected. I realize you're homesick. So am I. I—"

He stopped when he saw my face.

For a split second I was speechless. Then I said, "You're home-sick too?"

An eternity passed.

He had spoken in Lakota—and I had understood him.

He stared at me, dumbfounded. I had answered him in Eng-lish. What was happening?

Neither of us spoke. We simply gawked at each other. This was nuts.

He spoke again in Lakota. "Yes. I am homesick. I have been here over fifteen moons, on a mission." He watched me closely, waiting to see if I understood.

"You've been here over a year? On a mission? What mission? If this isn't your tribe, I don't understand."

I knew I was speaking English. I was also enunciating every word carefully.

How had she understood him?

This was impossible. No one learned fluent Lakota in the time she'd been here. He himself had studied for over two years before making the journey—knuckling down, perfecting the language to fulfill his destiny. This wasn't a scripted movie. There were no teleprompters, no language apps, no translation books.

"If you understand me," he asked slowly, "can you speak my language?"

He was beyond amazed.

She concentrated. "I learned a few words from Maka—but not enough to have a conversation. No, I can't speak Lakota. But if you understand me, can you speak English?"

This was his moment to tell her. But should he? He didn't understand how this was happening.

"So?" I pressed. "I need an answer."

He shrugged and nodded.

"Just now," I demanded, "or have you understood me all along? I need to know."

He motioned for me to sit. I shook my head—I was far too keyed up. With a sigh, he sat instead, waiting.

Huffing, I dropped down and turned to face him. "I'm waiting for an answer. I think I deserve one, don't you?"

My anger was barely contained now, simmering just beneath the surface.

He muttered an expletive in Lakota, and I bit my lip to keep from smiling. It wasn't funny—but it was, because I understood him.

"I'll explain," he said, "if you'll listen and not interrupt."

"I'll have questions," I warned, "and I don't promise not to get mad."

"No yelling. No one can hear you, but if you lose control, our lives could depend on this. Do you understand?"

Our lives depended on it. That was ironic. My life already felt like a nightmare. I might be dead—or worse, whisked into yet another century.

I crossed my arms and squared my shoulders. "Fine. Now tell me what in the Sam Hill is going on."

"Two years ago," he began.

When he finished, I didn't know what to believe.

His name was Wind Dancer. He didn't know why he'd been sent back—only that he had been. Nothing dramatic had happened yet, nothing obviously altered. According to him, I had been pulled into a time warp of ancient Indian magic to help him fulfill a purpose neither of us fully understood.

What I thought was that this was insane.

Either I was in the worst nightmare of my life—or I was dead. Or maybe this was voodoo magic and I was trapped in perdition.

"By the way, Wind Dancer," I said slowly, "what's your future name?"

"Dakota Kangee," he replied, pride clear in his voice.

My breath caught.

He was related to Blackie.

"How is that possible?" I whispered. "You're Blackie's son?"

This was impossible. I'd been working for Blackie when all this madness began.

"No, I'm his nephew." He interrupted. "And you—who are you? I call you She Cougar, but I'm sure you have another name."

"Blaze. Blaze Clark." I stuck my hand out.

He took my hand in his, holding it for a long moment before speaking.

"Clark. Meda Clark's niece."

It wasn't a question—it was a statement.

"You're saying my Aunt Meda took part in this ceremony to get you here—and then again to get me here?"

He nodded. "Yes. She was a big part."

"That isn't true. My aunt was nowhere near... some man and woman were in the snow doing God knows what. Blackie sent me there to spy on them, and I was reporting back to him."

"That was a ruse," he said this time in English.

He had told me he spoke my language—and now he was proving it. Once again, my hackles went up.

"All this time, you understood me, could speak to me, and you let me flounder around like a fish out of water, like a—ooh!"

I was mad. Mad, mad, mad—and ten mads more. All the times he had laughed his butt off at my previous confusion and drama.

"Calm down. I did not know who you were, or who your aunt was. You could have been just a person I found on the prairie—and I could've left you there to die. Get it through your thick skull that we—you and I"—he poked at my shoulder, then his own chest—"we're now a team. And that's that."

Now he was getting angry. I could see his neck hairs stand on end.

"I'm telling you again—my aunt wasn't with me."

"Did you hear the names of the two people who were there? Payton and Kanda?"

"Yes. That was their names... how did you know?"

"Payton is my brother. His Sioux name is Paytah, meaning Fire. His wife is Kanda; her Sioux name is Wakanda, which means 'possesses magical power.' She was supposed to be sent here. I have no clue why you're in her place. Kanda was to come on a special moon phase. Meda—our seer, the prophetess—understood the old diary, at least most of it."

"Understood what? You're not sure what you're supposed to do, and now you've got me here, not knowing a damn thing about a damn thing."

I tried to get up, but he stopped me, hand on my arm, keeping me pinned. I looked at his hand holding mine—and then into his eyes—and saw desperation.

"Okay. I'm not leaving."

Dakota relaxed his grip. "I didn't mean to hurt you."

"You didn't." Looking down at my arm, I saw his handprint. Slight, but visible. I chuckled and rubbed at it. "I'm all right. Tougher than you think." One thing was certain—I would not let him think I was some kind of pansy, not after everything that had already happened.

He smiled.

"Look, I don't profess to understand this magic, but I have some vague clues about what I'm searching for."

He held up a hand to keep me from speaking. "Not going into that right now. I just need you to trust me, and I need to trust you. You were sent back to help me so I could get back home—but this isn't the time."

"So I'm not dead, not in a living hellish nightmare, and not going to float around in time forever?" I giggled. It did sound preposterous—but this entire ordeal was preposterous. "Can you tell me how I fit into this plan? I mean, I'm only half-Sioux, nothing special, not mystic, and I've never been involved in all the tribal... stuff. Yet here I am, in a place I should not be, with a man I've never met."

A startled look appeared on Dakota's face. "I remember when and where I've seen you before. But you don't remember me, do you?"

"No. Should I?" I looked at him, trying to place his face, trying to remember where we might have met before.

"You were sixteen, and it was at a council meeting. I believe you'd just gotten your driver's license and wanted to drive your parents' car."

Ah, I remembered that night. I was home for summer vacation and had passed my driver's test. I wanted to drive, but I asked my parents to sit in the back seat since I couldn't be up front without a licensed driver.

"Yes, I remember."

"I was the angry young man at the front of the council, making an ass of myself that night."

"That was you? I tried not to laugh, but it was funny. The spear hanging on the wall went crashing down on Sam Johnson's head. It was an accident, but you had backed up and hit it with your elbow just as Sam pointed his finger at you. You looked like a young Indian brave on the warpath as you snatched the spear and held it up before it bounced again on Sam's head!"

Recalling the scene, I laughed harder. "Back then I had a little crush on you after that night, but I never went to another council meeting. I just wanted to drive that night; I wasn't interested in the meetings. But I thought about you—even though I didn't realize who you were. The crush lasted until I went back to school. Funny that if I had a crush on you, seems I would have shown up at all the council meetings hoping to see you." My face went pink.

"So why didn't you?" Dakota grinned at me.

"Like I've said, I didn't want to get into all that tribal stuff, really; I kept myself separated from the rest of the community. It was how I was." I shrugged, not apologetic—it was just me.

Dakota did his own facial shrug. "I was an angry young Sioux, hell-bent on tribal matters only. Girls, and, uh, relationships—well, I've never had time for them, and I still don't."

He cleared his throat and fidgeted as his cheeks turned pink. Was he embarrassed that I had had a crush on him?

Still rambling, he continued without a prompt from me.

"I was mad at the white man's world and how they treated us. I was furious because no one wanted to take a stand."

"We agree on one thing," I replied.

"We do?" His forehead crinkled.

"Uh-huh. The man-woman thing—we have that in common. Neither of us wants a relationship. Not my thing either."

Boy, I was relieved. That was a dead issue. Minor, compared to the bigger worries—like what we had to do to get back home.

"How did you know about Iye Igmu'watogla?"

No one knew me well, and I hadn't spent much time with the rest of the clan. Moving away, I finished ninth grade at an all-girl private school. In high school, I knew none of the kids in the community. It wasn't until my parents' deaths that I came back for the funeral—and then headed straight back to college for four years. Even then, living with Aunt Meda, I kept to myself.

"No one told me about your Indian name. I mean, how could they? I didn't know it would be you here. You acted like a wildcat that day you met the entire tribe, and I guess that's how I saw you. The memory is still vivid in my head."

"My aunt christened me with that when I was a kid. My father and aunt were the only two who called me by my Sioux name."

It made me wonder if my father would have gone along with this whole time-travel plan. My heart said yes—he loved his heritage and may have condoned this—but now he was dead, and I would never know.

"We must go back to camp. We've been gone awhile, and remember—you will understand them, but they won't understand you. You must play along with this charade. We'll figure it out. Can you do this?"

It wasn't a question. It was a command—but I was up to the challenge. Lord, look at what I'd already been through.

"Yes. I can keep our secret. Now, do you know how I'm to help us get back?"

I stood still, facing him.

"No. Two circles are all I know, but I can't explain what it means. Other than that, I guess somehow, some way, our present future selves will guide us."

I put my hand to my chest, feeling the chain holding the charm underneath. Two circles—well, how about that? I didn't know what it meant either, but fair was fair. He'd kept secrets from me, so I'd just keep this information to myself, at least for a little while longer.

10

MAKA SAW THEM COMING, and she smiled. She watched them together, seeing a difference she could not explain— not yet.

─── ❧ ───

It was hard for me to keep from reacting to certain things now that I understood the language. Though I desperately wanted to cry out my understanding—every word, whether cruel or compassionate, and answer them—I held back, honoring my promise to Dakota.

One day, though, after hearing a snide remark from one of the girls I was helping lug water to her tipi, I decided she did not deserve my help. When she'd commented to another woman that I was just a scrawny half-breed, wondering what Wind Dancer saw in me, my mood turned black, and I dropped the buffalo stomach filled with water and walked away, even though I wanted to throw the water in her face. I understood her, so I stomped off, catching the tail end of the woman's words.

"She no likes to help me, never!"

Humpf, yep, sister, that will be the last time I ever help you, I thought as I walked past Swift Eagle's lodge. I stood there, arms crossed, glaring at the woman.

I wasn't trying to eavesdrop, but I heard my name in the conversation in Swift Eagle's lodge.

Acting as if I had a pebble in my moccasin, I bent, untied it, and took it off. I sat down, rubbing my foot, listening.

"*Iye Igmu'watogla*, she is a good woman. Maka likes her very much, Wind Dancer. You like her very much."

"She does not talk lot, works hard. I am glad Maka likes her."

"No, how do you feel... like a man feels about woman?"

Dakota was taken aback, as it was not in Swift Eagle's nature to ask these sorts of questions. He weighed his words.

"As a man, I see her as a woman who is nothing more than a woman. I have no desire to take a woman." He had a small feeling deep in his gut that had grown, but that was his secret, for now.

"Mmm, I see more, Wind Dancer, and so does Maka. In time, you shall see it too. She Cougar is a brave woman. As a stranger, she has fit in, but she not planned to be here, with us, with you. Does she have people?" Swift Eagle continued, asking questions.

"Yes, but she does not know where they are or how she got separated." He hated to lie, but he had no other choice. "Is she not welcome, Swift Eagle? Do I need to take her away?"

Dakota now worried that perhaps they wanted her back on the prairie and away from the tribe.

"No, she is welcomed. In time, She Cougar will realize that we are her people. To be alone is not good."

Dakota nodded. He understood Swift Eagle and knew the old Indian chief thought he should take the woman as his own, but he knew this would not last forever and they would both end up back in their world, each to go on with their lives in different directions. That thought was not a pleasant one. Even after this amazing journey, would they still keep in touch, continue to be a part of one another's lives in the future? The uncertainty of the matter swam in his head.

I slipped my moccasin back on, tying the leather straps so I could hurry off. Swift Eagle wanted to know if Dakota was going to take me as his bride. I also supposed that, being an unwed maiden, maybe the tribe thought I should be chaste. Oh, Lord, I'd passed go on that account long ago, but that was none of their business, nor Dakota's business either. Not that I'd had many lovers—two, to be exact. However, I was not that kind of girl, and I wasn't looking for love—not here, and not now. It was time I had a talk with him about this because leaving his lodge was out of the question.

The flap to Swift Eagle's tipi opened as I was walking away.

"*Iye Igmu'watogla,*" Dakota called out.

I turned, stopped, and slanted my head in the now-what-do-you-want? look, as my brows dipped in question.

He motioned me over, so I obeyed, as he signed to me and said in Lakota, "We walk, we talk." He made the sign to walk with his fingers and a gesture to his mouth for talking. With a shrug, I nodded, although I understood his Lakota, and we walked away.

⚊ ⚊

MAKA WATCHED THEM TOGETHER. She felt a ripple in the air, a spark. Good, very good. She was not sure how, but she knew they communicated as if the barrier had been a pebble wall washed away by a swift flow of moving waters.

Out of earshot of the others, Dakota spoke to me in English. "How long were you outside of Swift Eagle's lodge?"

"Long enough. I was just walking by and heard my Indian name in the conversation. Being a woman, I figured I had better listen since I can understand what everyone is saying. I suppose everyone here thinks we're sleeping together?"

"Yes, er, no, just living in the same lodge,"—he eyed me—"nothing more."

"I don't care what everyone thinks, except I care what Maka thinks. What she thinks of me seems to matter, but I can't explain why."

"Do you care what I think?"

"Not much. You already know the truth, all of it."

"I must go away for a few days."

"Alright, when will you be back?" I was upsetting his manhood, I think, because I didn't wail or whimper about being left alone.

"No argument that I shouldn't leave you here alone?" His eyebrows came up, quizzical, wondering why I was no longer afraid to be alone without him. "I won't be alone unless the entire tribe is moving off or going with you."

"She Cougar, you're a funny woman, such a paradox. Do you want to know when I'm going to leave?"

"No, just that you're coming back. It's all I need to know."

"Really, that's all you need to know, not where or why? Don't you care?"

"I care, but look, just think, what good is crying going to do? Will you stay and hold my hand?" I narrowed my eyes at him in defiant question.

"Well, you need to know where and why in case something happens to me. We're going to look for buffalo, and then we'll—" He stopped talking when he noted a certain look on my face. "Are you okay? I mean, you look, well... you look sad."

A tremendous sigh escaped my lungs. "Look, Dakota, if you don't make it back, I'll survive. I can understand them, and given enough time, they will think I have learned their language. I'm too tired to be afraid any longer."

"Don't you want to get back to your own time?"

"Well, what can I do to change it?"

"Come on, I think it's time we had another long talk about some important things. Let's get further out. I don't want anyone to accidentally overhear us."

Dakota walked in front, and I followed.

He knew the time had come, and she was ready. He saw it in her face, her eyes, and in her body language. She stood upright, ready to face whatever she had to face. He had not given her the credit she deserved for withstanding all she had over the past few moons. It was time he filled her in on some facts.

After taking a seat on top of a large boulder, I crossed my arms and looked at him.

"Okay, Dakota, I don't think anyone will overhear us, or that anyone even cares we have gone off. So, what is so important?" I was tiring of this conversation; it was going nowhere fast.

"Blaze, do you know what part of the Sioux tribe your family is from?"

"No, not really. Does it matter?"

"I mean, do you know your bloodline?"

"No, I don't, and what does that have to do with anything?" Tired of all the mystery and games, I looked out across the stream, wishing he would just tell me.

"I need to tell you something and apologize for keeping you in the dark. You've proven to be a very worthy member of our duo, and you've befriended a chief's wife. Almost everyone in the tribe trusts you."

"I think—"

He held up his hand. "Let me finish."

Nodding, I let my eyes wander the hillside and the beauty of the open prairie, but my ears were listening.

"You have worked hard and joined in, making it easier on yourself, and I admire you. Most women would've been trying to find an escape and end up on the prairie—dead or in the hands of another tribe, most likely not a Sioux tribe. This would be a fate worse than death."

This thought caused a shiver, because I'd considered this before and did not like the conclusion then any better than now.

"I know you're wondering where this story is going."

"Yes, I am. I thought maybe you were recapping my brief life here for no reason, so just what are you trying to say?" Sarcasm dripped from my lips.

"I'm proud that you're here, proud that I had realized who you were in this scheme of things when you had introduced yourself to me that day under the tree." He stopped to let her recall the scene.

Yeah, the day I went stark raving mad and threw a personal hissy fit over my situation, crying my eyes out. He had found me all a mess of tears, and then a loud clap of thunder changed everything, and by magic, I could communicate with the man. Don't think I wasn't still mad at him a little when all this time he could have told me he spoke English, and we could have communicated from the beginning.

"Tell me, Wind Dancer, just who is it I am?" I turned so I could see him.

"You are Blaze Clark, daughter of Charles Gray Wolf Clark, great-granddaughter to Bob Thunder Cloud Clark, and great-great-granddaughter to White Owl and his wife Macha, which in Sioux means Aurora."

"Fine. We've established my lineage and all who sit in my family tree. I am sure I'm the bat—the crazy one hanging upside down. By the way, how do you know my family tree, and why does my family tree even matter, Dakota?"

When I said his name, he rubbed the back of his neck and gave himself a little shake, as if throwing off thoughts he didn't want.

"I was getting to that. Macha is the daughter of Chief Black Raven, and her sister is Maka."

It took a few minutes for it all to soak in, then a light came on.

"Are you telling me that Maka is my great-great-great—however many greats— aunt?" I had to whisper. My voice caught in my throat.

Dakota slid in closer. "That's what I'm telling you. I don't know why I didn't figure it out sooner. When you told me Meda was your aunt, it hadn't crossed my mind that Gray Wolf was your father. Meda had all kinds of adopted nieces and nephews; everyone calls her Aunt Soft Dove, or in your case, Aunt Meda. I'm sorry, there has been a lot on my mind, and..." His voice trailed off.

"So? I still don't get it. I mean, yes, it's more than exciting that I'm meeting a skip all the greats—aunt that went on to the spirit world long before I was born. That within itself is astonishing, and I suppose that's why we bonded like we did. But I can't see anything else that is so earth-shattering about your news." I did not understand what one thing had to do with the other.

"No, I guess you wouldn't understand." He shook his head.

"Cripes, what in the hell is that supposed to mean? Hell's bells, I don't understand any of this." Not only did my tone get louder, it went an octave higher, too.

"Don't get into a snit, and I'll explain. Holy cow, woman, your hair should be red, not the dark brown it is, and you should have freckles instead of that golden-brown skin, because you have that kind of temper. If they had matches here, I would have named you match head."

I could not help it, and I giggled, and then he joined in.

"Oh, alright, I will calm down. Please go on with this tall tale." Half-bowing, I swept my hand, palm up, in the air. "By all means, please continue."

"We don't speak of Black Raven; it is ill manners to speak of the dead. He hasn't been seen in over two years. They've sent warriors, but no one's found his body. Some fear him captured by soldiers, but most think him dead. Without him, Swift Eagle became the new chief."

"Are they brothers?"

"No, not brothers, but something like second-removed cousins, raised in the same lodge all their lives, so they were thought of as brothers."

"If they were considered brothers, is him being married to Maka odd, not to mention the age difference? Maka is a lot younger than Swift Eagle."

"Indian tradition says a woman is ready to marry when... you know, the first time she has, a—you know." Dakota flushed.

"Her womanly period, is that what you mean?" I chuckled at his embarrassment.

He cleared his throat. "Yes, that."

"Come on, it is a bit late to have that trivial information embarrass you." I tried not to laugh outright.

Dakota cleared his throat, glad to move off that subject, and continued his story.

"Anyway, they're younger when ready to marry. A man can have many wives, but for a strange reason, he had taken none before her. Swift Eagle waited. And this is strange. He has been devoted to her and is much older by, I figure twenty-five to thirty years. A lot of Indian men father children late in life; but they have no children. He could've tossed her aside for being barren, but he didn't. This shows true love and courage, because this means he will not continue his line."

"Maybe they couldn't, oh, goodness. I mean, he is pretty old, and, well, maybe sex wasn't his thing, know what I'm saying?" Now it was my turn to be embarrassed, trying to say Swift Eagle was too old for sex. My face felt flushed.

Dakota laughed, loud and hard, doubling over, pleased at my apparent embarrassment.

"Oh, to hear him talk, he is energetic and enthusiastic about his copulating." Dakota hooted, and I blushed so hot my cheeks felt like they were on fire.

"In answer to his age, he won't tell his age, but he is near his early sixties. It's a little hard to tell. Maka is maybe in her mid-to-late forties, but again, it's difficult to tell."

"They appear to be a lot older." Then he added, "I guess this life will wear on me soon too."

A little annoyed, I huffed. "I still have no clue where all this useless information is going, or are you just filling me in on the local color?"

He shot me an arched eyebrow look. "Woman, you are the most impatient person. I was just giving you some background, but I was trying to get to what I believe, which is... I don't think Black Raven is dead."

Well, my annoyance vanished. "Wow, maybe you were sent here to find him, you think?"

"No."

"Why not? I mean, that's one reason to be here, correct?"

"Yes and no."

"Yes and no? What are you saying yes to, and what are you saying no to? You're confusing me." My exasperation was growing again because I figured Dakota was being cryptic for no reason except to make me mad or confuse me.

A frown creased Dakota's brow as his inner turmoil about how he felt about me waged a war with his head and his heart.

"You're frowning. Are you angry with me?" I asked. "I'm really not sure what is up and what is down. Besides, I'm not trying to make you mad, but for the life of me, I can't keep up with your erratic mood swings."

She sat down next to him and looked at him. "Dakota, you're always skirting around, never giving me a straight answer. Why are you getting mad? I have not said or done a thin—"

He had meant for it to be a short, quick smack on the lips just to shut the woman up. That was not what he got. As soon as his mouth met mine, Dakota felt a spark ignite, and when he felt this spark, he deepened the kiss and let his hand slip up to rest at the back of my neck.

After the immediate shock of this kiss passed, warmth enveloped me, causing me to lean in for more. But as wonderful as it felt, it was over as quickly as it had begun. Disappointment flooded my inner being when Dakota pulled back.

"Uh, I apologize, I don't know what came over me," Dakota stammered. "I never act this way with anyone." He moved farther away.

So, he regretted kissing me, and this was embarrassing. I played the kiss off, even though my heart was racing, and I sure as heck didn't want him to know what that one kiss had done to my knees—turning them to jelly.

"Not to worry, really, just chalk it up to a crescendo of the moment. I've already forgotten," I lied, smoothing out the material of my dress, not looking at him. "By the way, about Black Raven, what does this, or he, mean, you know, to our time travel?"

"It's Chief Black Raven's diary that got us here, but he didn't write, er, draw it in this past. He wrote it in this future," he explained, looking a little upset.

"What in heaven's name does that mean?"

"It means that he's alive somewhere, writing this diary as we sit here. I saw the diary, She Cougar—"

"Blaze," I corrected him.

"What?"

"When it is just you and me, please call me Blaze." I wanted him to know me as me and not just the woman he called She Cougar.

"Fine. Blaze, I saw the diary at Meda's house. It was the mark of Chief Black Raven, at the end of the journal—diary. Dated eighteen hundred and something; the numbers had faded, all but the one and the eight, so we can assume the eighteen hundreds."

I did the math in my head. "That would be like one hundred forty or more years from our time. Holy shit. Oops." I covered my mouth.

"Yeah, no doubt about it, holy shit," he repeated my sentiments.

"Do we know what this means? Do we go hunting for him?"

"We?" Dakota asked, as if surprised.

I nodded.

"First, we go back to the village. Let me think on this," he said.

"Alright, whatever you decide, I will go along with it, because, well, I have no choice, you know."

"True, but we're in this together. I promise it'll all work out," Dakota reassured me.

"You can't know that. We do not know what will happen in the future. I mean this future, not our future-future. Oh, you know what I mean."

"Yeah, I understand what you mean," he chuckled. "Hey, just think, we could have one best-selling story—fiction to most—but we'd always know the truth."

He reached over and helped me to my feet. We walked toward the village, and he was still holding my hand. I didn't know why I let him. I had ignored the kiss, but not holding his hand? Odd. After that kiss, being alone with him in his lodge should scare me, but it didn't. It made me think perhaps he was lonely without a woman. It had been more than a year since he had arrived here back in time.

What I knew was we had to ignore any feelings that might heat between us. Oh sure, we shared a nice kiss, one I had thoroughly enjoyed and needed to forget—there was a but coming here—but I didn't want to forget it. The reality was we did not need complications, and kissing—and what that led to—would most definitely be a complication.

My thoughts went to every action I'd made. I would need to make sure not to play the helpless female—Sorrowful Sally or Pitiful Pearl—which might goad him into thinking he had to protect me or whatever. Nope, I would stand steadfast, and whatever the cost, not get caught up in a fairy tale in my mind.

Dakota felt rejected and put out by my wiping my hand. Was he so repulsive she had to wipe off his touch? Maybe it was better this way, and besides, she was not his type.

As we began our walk back to the village, he wondered, do I even have *a type?*

11

WITH COLORS CHANGING AND a brisk new coolness in the air, fall was setting in. I had been here with these people for almost six months now—or at least that was my closest guess. The people were worried; no one had spotted any buffalo herds. Scouts had gone out for weeks on end and returned with no news. Swift Eagle was concerned for his tribe and their survival through the coming winter.

"I saw visions," Maka said in her native tongue.

Outside the old woman's tipi, I was shucking corn, readying it to pound into cornmeal. To maintain the ruse of my limited Lakota understanding, I pretended to catch more of the language than I actually did, noticing words and feigning comprehension. Understanding them was, in itself, a lifesaver.

"Visions? Visions of what?" I continued grinding the corn kernels into the clay pot.

"Tatanka. Many Tatanka."

"Buffalo? Where?" I raised my head, hoping to glimpse the animals. Maka reminded me of my Aunt Meda—always knowing, always wise. We were of the same bloodline, so I guessed it was natural, though still strange.

"Far, over that mountain," Maka said, pointing. "Soon we will be going."

I trained my eyes on the mountain, wondering what lay beyond. For the past six months—or however long—I had been as far as nowhere since I arrived. We'd never traveled back to where Dakota found me, or to the Paha Sapa. Danger lurked everywhere, but at least for now, with these people, I would come to no harm.

"We all go? All of us?"

"Yes, we go," Maka answered.

My heart rate quickened. Dakota had told me we were not going when the tribe left. This was a small disappointment. Even if there was an unseen door back to my real life, I wasn't ready to leave—not yet.

"Wind Dancer changed his mind, says he will go; you come with him." Her English was stilted, but she had spoken to me in my language.

"Maka, you spoke to me in English."

The older woman beamed. "I learn from you, She Cougar," she reverted to Lakota. "After the hunt, Wind Dancer told Swift Eagle he has something important to do before winter comes, and you will go with him. Wind Dancer needs a woman, and you, She Cougar, are a fine woman." Maka was inquiring without inquiring.

I ducked my head, looking at the unshucked corn in my hands, trying to hide the blush that washed over my face. Maka was aware that Dakota and I would be alone, and well... things might happen.

"I'll miss you and the rest of the tribe." It was all I could think to say. There were so many things I wanted to tell Maka, but I couldn't. I knew the truth: I was Maka's flesh and blood, from many moons in the future.

Sitting cross-legged in our lodgings, I asked, "So, you changed your mind about the buffalo hunt, Dakota?"

"Yes. I can't pass up this once-in-a-lifetime opportunity. It will be the most exhilarating experience I've had since I arrived. I know there are more significant reasons I'm here, and it's not just for a buffalo hunt. But being part of this hunt is an adventure I'd only see in a movie—and it might be my only chance."

He rambled a mile a minute, and I laughed. It was nice to see him enjoying this opportunity. Since the time warp and our meeting, he had been staunch and serious, worried why he was here and what he was supposed to do.

"Why are you smiling like that?"

"It's nice that you'll get to do something that makes you happy."

He smiled back.

"Your Lakota is getting better. You learn fast."

"Necessity deems I must, to survive."

"I'm acting like a schoolboy with this hunt, huh?"

I held up my thumb and forefinger about a half-inch apart, wide-eyed. "Oh, just a smidge, I daresay."

"I'll try to rein in my enthusiasm; I don't want to seem like a newbie hunter. But I'm glad I can share these feelings with you. It's nice to confide in someone for a change." He placed his arm around my shoulders. Somehow, it felt natural, and I didn't move to shrug him off. We walked like this out of our lodge.

"The tribe will soon move to where the herds have been spotted, over that mountain," he said, pointing. I followed his finger; it was where Maka had said they would go.

"After the hunt, we'll have to leave, but I couldn't pass this up. I told Swift Eagle we'd search for your people once the hunt is over."

"You know I have no people."

"Yes, I do—but it was the best lie I could come up with."

"Where are we headed?"

"Deeper into the Black Hills. It's where my gut tells me to go."

"So, that's the where... what's the why?"

"To find Black Raven," he lowered his voice to a whisper. "It's what I saw in my dream."

"Do you have the gift of vision?" I thought this odd, but who was I to question what was happening?

"No, but I dreamed this, so I'm going on my gut instinct."

"Maybe I put that thought into your head a few weeks ago. Could that be why you dreamed it?" I hadn't intended to plant thoughts in his head—except maybe about me—but he hadn't thought of me in that way.

"I don't dream."

"No dreams or nightmares ever?" I recalled nights watching him sleep and knew he had.

"Sure, I dream, but not like this—so vivid, so real. That kind of dream." He took my hand. "And no, I'm not telling you about it."

"Good. I don't interpret dreams. I wondered if I had a gift like Aunt Meda or Maka, but it turns out I don't. I dreamed of possessing their gift for understanding the world."

"You have many gifts that are God-given. Maybe not visions or magic, but a gifted heart."

"What is a gifted heart? Or are you just placating me?"

"You've fit in here better than any other woman from our time would have. Helping with chores, learning to communicate with these people... before you say it, you had some... magical help. Plus, you've shown genuine interest in the culture and ways of the Sioux. You don't give off haughty airs because you're from a different time, and you've befriended the chief's wife. She has grown to love you."

I sat wide-eyed. "Lordy, I did all that? Perhaps I should run for president when we get back to our time, you think?"

"She Cougar, you're a funny woman." He nudged me with his shoulder.

Maka watched, more pleased than ever with our togetherness. Good. Her heart felt a kindred spirit with the woman they called She Cougar. She could not explain it, but it was as if she watched her family grow within me. She had prayed for visions or answers, but none came. Instead, she hoped Wind Dancer would not lose this woman. They needed more time together for it to flourish.

Maka wished Black Raven were still amongst them. He would have liked She Cougar; she would have made him laugh. Though she thought of him, she never spoke of him. He was her father, and she missed him. She saw him in night visions—pleasant memories, not visions to aid the tribe. Somehow, she knew Black Raven's spirit traveled with them and had already accepted She Cougar.

Maka went into her lodge.

"You're smiling again, my dear wife," Swift Eagle said as she ducked under the flap.

"They are together," she murmured. "And it is good. My heart says She Cougar is the one for Wind Dancer."

"Huh, but there's still strangeness with these two I can't describe. It's like a secret only they know."

"Maybe it's love, you old goat, or have you forgotten?" She sat beside him, pulling up the blanket over her feet.

"Old woman, I have not forgotten, and if you will let me—"

"What am I, an old goat, you say? I'll show you." Maka laughed.

Swift Eagle, though not as young as most warriors, was still virile. In minutes, he pleased his wife.

THE SUN ROSE, AND it felt as though I'd just laid my head down. Cripes, did these people never sleep? Never in my life had I known people to move so quickly. I'd moved four times in my life: as a baby, when my parents relocated; at twelve, to boarding school; then college; and lastly, home to Aunt Meda. Each move had been chaotic. These people dismantled lodges, packed belongings, and were ready to leave the next day. Horses—packhorses—worked better than trucks and air conditioning.

Maka walked up, bridle in hand, leading a packhorse.

"Can I help you with your work?" I stroked the mare's soft gray muzzle.

"No, we will leave as soon as Swift Eagle says. You are happy, She Cougar, here with my people?"

"I'm happy." What would have made me happier would have been to tell her everything, that we were kindred spirits—but I dared not. Even if I did, Maka might think I'd gone loco.

"And Wind Dancer... he makes your heart smile?"

The language barrier seemed eons ago, and I was almost as fluent in Lakota as Dakota.

"You're a matchmaker, huh? Maka, stop wishing this. I notice it every time I see you watching us." I shook my head and finger at her. "Don't push."

"Humph, I know what I see. I may be old, but I am not blind. I know what I see—even if you don't." She tried to sound angry, but it didn't work, and I hugged her.

"You remind me of my aunt."

Maka's brows shot up. "Your family? You remember your people, and I remind you of someone?"

Darn it, now why had I said that? Silently, I berated myself. Don't open a Pandora's Box.

"Yes, you do, but it was a long time ago. She isn't in this world any longer."

Okay, not a real lie, just a small white lie. Aunt Meda wasn't in this world now, was she?

Maka nodded, understanding no one spoke of the dead. "I understand." She patted my arm.

"We go."

Wind Dancer walked up, leading three horses. I made to mount, but he shot me a warning look.

"We walk, lead horse. Wind Dancer rides ahead with hunters."

Maka saw his look but said nothing. Dakota handed us the reins to the horses—one packed with his belongings, his lodge strapped to two poles behind the other steed. I had nothing to pack, and without him, I had no home. If he hadn't been here, I shuddered to think what might have happened to me. Walking while the men rode seemed unusual, but I was young and healthy; I could manage.

———— ᴍ ————

Two miles later, in the hotter part of the day, I wondered if we'd get there at all. I hadn't realized how large the village was—the lodges spread out in rows, some large, some small, housing two or three families. Even with the many lodges covering the flatlands across from the stream, I hadn't grasped how many people lived there. They were in groups, but still part of the tribe.

I hadn't met everyone, and until this move, I had never seen all the people at once. The Sioux were many, and I was now part of this tribe's higher ranks, linked with Chief Swift Eagle and his spouse. As a friend to the chief's wife, I felt honored. If I hadn't grown close to Maka, the tribe might have treated me worse. Some people still scared the bejesus out of me.

Wind Dancer rode up beside us.

"Perfect day for travel. It will be a successful hunt, you think?"

"Yes, I see many Tatanka in my dreams for our people. Winter will be good," Maka replied, shading her eyes.

I had no comment—I wouldn't know a first-rate hunt if it came up and bit me.

"She Cougar, you are well?"

As if he cared. Heavens, he was comfortable on horseback, while I was on foot.

"I'm fine," I said, Lakota rolling off my tongue like a second language.

"You do well with Lakota words, She Cougar," Maka remarked.

"Yes," Dakota agreed, then rode away as quickly as he had come.

Drat the man, I thought, tossing my head as my braids flapped against my back.

"You see what I mean?" Maka's eyes sparkled with glee.

I had no earthly idea what she meant. If it was because Dakota made me mad—yeah, I saw that—but that was all I saw.

12

THE SUN WAS SINKING behind the mountains, and the cooling effect was a relief. When, in the devil, were they going to stop and pitch camp? One of the hunters finally hailed them to halt. The entire village stretched over more than an acre of land, and they stood still, waiting for the next command. Children were restless, horses tired, and I was spent—sweaty, sore, and irritable. My feet throbbed, my legs ached, and I was ready to collapse. But I stayed steadfast, not complaining. Even though I wasn't conditioned for this type of trek, I wouldn't cave—not now, not in front of anyone, especially Dakota.

The tribe parted to let Chief Swift Eagle ride into the center. "We stop now; this place, right place. Over that ridge, our scouts saw many buffaloes. We stay until the hunt is over. Hunters go now, we wait for the kill, then we celebrate."

Whoops and hollering erupted from every direction. Women moved packhorses, arranging the camp. Men who were not hunting helped set up the lodges. Children scampered, giggling; dogs barked, and horses whinnied. I was in awe once again at how quickly these people came together to forge a village from nothing.

In no time, the camp looked ready, as though it had always been there. These were extraordinary people. And then I realized—I was part of them, being half-Sioux. Perhaps, deep down, a part of me was remarkable too. Nah, I wasn't—they were truly remarkable—but me? I was from another time, a person called Blaze Clark, nothing inherently special.

⸻

THREE AND A HALF more days of travel had taken us over twenty-two miles. These people were not merely amazing; they were beyond comprehension, with stamina and fortitude that people in my present time would never understand.

A few tribesmen helped me raise our lodge since Dakota had been called elsewhere to assist the chief. It fell to me to set our lodge in order. By the end, I was exhausted, my feet blistered. Dakota found me sitting on the ground, quietly contemplating my fate. The only reason I'd survived this ordeal was because of him—and Maka. Without them, perhaps I would have given up and perished alone on the prairie. Perhaps fate—or pure luck—had brought me to them.

Alone, we watched the others working: arranging lodges, chasing children, dogs dashing here and there. No one paid us any mind; they were immersed in their tasks. Dakota glanced sideways at me and then back at the others.

"Blaze, what are you thinking about?" he asked.

"I was thinking of my journey here... how it might've been nice to have had a choice," I admitted.

"You're not sorry you're here, are you?"

"No. I can't change anything, even if I wished to. But no, I'm not sorry. This has been eye-opening. I've realized these are my people, and I'm one of them—maybe from long ago, maybe from far in the future—but still a Sioux Indian."

"Yes, you are, She Cougar." He smiled, nodding toward my feet. "How sore are they?"

"They look worse than they feel," I said, inspecting the blisters.

Rising, he ducked into the tipi. "I have something to take the sting out," he said.

Outside again, he dipped a cloth into a clay pot of water and applied it to the bottom of my foot.

"This will help."

His gentleness surprised me. I hoped Maka wasn't watching; she'd likely read far too much into it.

He chewed tobacco from a pouch, then applied the mush with a bit of cactus flower juice to my feet.

"Tobacco with peyote mixed in?" I wrinkled my nose.

"You know about peyote?"

"I wasn't born yesterday. More like a century and a half from now."

He laughed. "You're a first-rate woman, Blaze."

Maka, observing from afar, hid behind the bustle of children. She couldn't see Dakota and me clearly, but she felt the tension and the unspoken connection. Her feelings for Wind Dancer were more than just like—She Cougar might hold hers in, but when it burst forth, it would be unstoppable. Maka hummed to herself, carrying kindling back to her lodge to prepare the evening meal.

⚊ ᴟ ⚊

IN THE EARLY HOURS of dawn, Dakota nudged me.

"Blaze, wake up."

"Hmmm, I want to sleep. Stop poking me," I groaned, pulling the buffalo skin over my head.

He shook me harder. "Wake up!"

"Is the camp on fire? Are you sick? If not, let me sleep," I murmured. My body ached from the previous day's travel. I'd been unable to keep my eyes open, yet the tribe had been in a festive mood, and I'd joined in despite my exhaustion.

Whoosh!

He splashed a clay pot of freezing water on my face.

"Wake up!" he commanded.

"Oh my God, that's cold! What's so urgent?" I bolted upright, wiping water from my face.

"Blaze, lower your voice," he squatted, eye to eye with me. His smirk made me glare back.

"What? Why wake me up?"

"To see the herd at night. You'll never see anything like it again—maybe in pictures, but never in person."

"Most Sioux women never see this. They stay in camp until the hunt is over. I'm letting you come."

"You're allowing me?" I bit back a laugh.

"You aren't much of a morning person, are you?"

"Oh, morning, my behind," I said, throwing off the buffalo hide.

He tossed me my moccasins. I slipped them on, following him outside.

The sight stole my breath: a million buffalo, standing, lying, grazing. The land was painted brown with humpy bodies, black and white horns piercing the dusk. They were enormous, intimidating. I'd read about buffalo once, in school, but this was nothing like what I'd imagined.

We lay flat, side by side, peering over a jutted ridge.

"You've been here over a year; why haven't you hunted before?" I whispered.

"In a word, trust. They didn't know me. I've earned the honor now."

I understood why he had postponed leaving. This hunt was rare, an experience few ever had.

"Can they hear us? Be quieter?"

"No. Their eyesight and hearing are poor; smell is their strength," he said.

"Downwind, then?"

"Yes." He didn't pull away from my body.

I shivered, wondering what dangers the hunt might bring. What if something happened to him? Would I be stuck here? Would I even survive?

Back in our tipi, I was no longer sleepy. I wanted to talk, to savor being with him.

"I'm awake now. Chat a bit?"

"I need rest for the hunt," he murmured, closing his eyes.

I lay down, smiling at him calling me She Cougar. Was it intimacy, or just his way? A small moan escaped me as I wished he were holding me.

STILL DARK, I HEARD him moving.

"Are you leaving?" I asked groggily.

"Yes. Go back to sleep," he murmured.

"Are all the others up?"

"Yes, everyone's ready for the send-off."

I stretched, wiggling my sore muscles, donning my moccasins. Dakota wore face paint, a wolf's head on top of his head. His hair fell to his shoulders, feathers at the base of the crown. His lean, rugged form—painted in red, yellow, and dark blue—was striking.

"Is that the hunters' gear?" I asked.

"Yes. Camouflage for some. We hunt with bows, arrows, and spears. Guns aren't used. There are other Sioux methods, but time won't allow explanation."

He opened the tipi flap, spear in hand. "Are you coming?"

I nodded, following him. Around us, men mounted horses, boys held bows, young wives watched, the tribe buzzing with energy. Maka stood beside Swift Eagle, who would not join the hunt this season. Those left behind would protect the camp.

Swift Eagle addressed the tribe: "It is time for hunters to gain their Tatanka victories, led by Dark Cloud. I step down to let him claim his place."

Watching Dakota ride off, I swelled with pride. He and the other hunters were leaving to provide for winter, their lives intertwined with survival.

Maka appeared beside me.

"It is good. Soon our people will have supplies for winter, and you... soon, life will be set for you."

I touched my lips, wondering if that small kiss from Dakota meant more than luck.

"Come, make ready for when the hunt is over," Maka said.

I followed, wondering if it was more than that—this life, this moment, this connection with Wind Dancer.

13

THE HUNT

THE GROUND WAS SILENT except for the plodding of horse hooves, soft nickers, and the occasional snort of the horses. No brave spoke as they waited for the signal from Dark Cloud, who led the hunt. Two miles out of camp, Dark Cloud raised his spear and then lowered it—the signal to stop.

The men dismounted, anxious and ready. Some horses stayed tethered to nearby trees for those who would hunt on foot. Dakota wore the wolf's head. The hunters would come in from the bottom of a nearby hillside, forming a line to drive the herd back, shooting arrows and tossing spears into the mass of animals.

Many braves wore wolf heads atop theirs, a camouflage to sneak up on the unsuspecting herd. The others on horseback would run the herd straight, shooting arrows as they went.

Four miles up from the hunting site lay a small ravine. The plan was to drive as many of the buffalo off the cliff as possible, sending them to certain death. It didn't seem sporting, but it was their way, their way to survive the winter—or any survival at all.

The sun was just waking, its golden rays dim as it began creeping over the mountains to the east. The herd had stirred, moving at a leisurely pace, oblivious to the danger that awaited.

Then Dark Cloud gave a loud whoop, screaming the command to begin. Chaos erupted. Dakota, in the middle of over a hundred braves with bows and arrows ready, charged with the others.

The herd snorted and picked up speed, startled. Arrows flew, piercing thick hides. After several arrows struck the same buffalo, it fell—two tons dropping to the ground. Other herd members, trampling their own kind in panic, aided in the ultimate death.

The massive beasts ran as one, a pack locomotion impossible to stop. Dark Cloud and the others on horseback yelled and whooped as they shot arrows and tossed spears. Braves on horseback forced part of the herd southeast, toward the ravine, hoping to increase the kill.

As the colossal beasts scattered, Dakota marveled at how he and the braves on foot avoided certain death. They had stopped when one brave grabbed him by the wrist, and each man down the line did the same. Forming a human chain, they advanced into the herd. He admitted later it had terrified him. He pictured Blaze's face in his mind, determined that it would be the last image locked in his brain before death.

Somehow, it worked. The herd turned away from the puny men. Bison eyesight was poor, and with the wolf-skinned heads, who knew what they perceived? Thunderous hooves beat the ground, sending dust into the air. The grunting and snorting of the buffalo seemed a mere whisper compared to the pounding of their hooves. Some braves ran headlong into the angry herd, spears in hand, striking the mighty animals. Knives from leather belts ended the suffering of the injured. It seemed inhumane, but an injured buffalo was far more dangerous than a bull or cow trying to flee.

The dust was thick, nearly choking, yet the hunters pressed on. The buffalo ran at breakneck speed, trampling grass and small bushes like a woman pounding corn into meal. Their weight dug trenches into the prairie, their heads down, eyes blind to the world, only charging forward. Men on horseback forced them one way or another, riding close enough to touch the animals with outstretched hands.

Over twenty buffalo were driven toward the small ravine. The horsemanship amazed Dakota. The hunters moved as one with their mounts, so fluid that one could stick out a hand and touch a massive beast. The animals ran headlong toward certain death, one by one plummeting into the ravine. Not all went down, but enough.

The horseback hunters circled as half the herd turned from the cliff, then pursued them again, shooting arrows with precision. Dakota's group, having done all they could on foot, charged back for their horses. The hunt was over, and it was time to reap their spoils. They had never killed more than necessary; greed had no place here.

I felt the tremors of the herd's passage, the ground shuddering for miles. One could die on a hunt like this. I prayed no one did, especially Dakota. Once again, I helped pack horses and move belongings, readying for another move closer to the fallen buffalo. The tribe brought the supplies to the people, not the other way around.

Maka had me working like a madwoman, tying long limbs together with leather straps to make several travois—platforms dragged behind horses to carry large portions of meat and hides. Buckskin bags were readied, filled with meat to be carted. The villagers gathered for another journey to reap the spoils, after which celebration would begin.

Looking back at the area we were leaving, I thought I saw something—but fatigue made me shrug it off.

***

HE WATCHED FROM ABOVE. This woman was special, he knew, and she felt his presence. Like his daughter Maka, he needed to remain unseen. Maka could sense his life force, so he stayed distant. This woman was vital to his future.

Black Raven, thought dead by most of the tribe, lived on in spirit. His chains could not hold his life force. While his earthly body lay motionless, his spirit soared across the plains of his people, unseen by those who believed him imprisoned.

***

I HAD NEVER, NOT even in picture books or on TV, seen so many dead buffalo. Yet it was enough to feed a village for months. Lordy, they were enormous, bigger than I had imagined. I recalled the first buffalo I saw gutted after arriving with the tribe; I had fainted then. Now, I smiled at the memory. I had not fainted again.

Dakota approached, beaming, speaking a bit about the hunt in Lakota.

"More talk later, happy hunter," Maka said, walking up and smiling. "We have work. Leave us. Go rest until the celebration."

Two hundred women and younger maidens entered the shallow ravine, gathering buffalo fallen to their deaths. A few braves helped with the heavier lifting. It was hard, grueling work—removing innards, peeling hides—but it was fluid, precise, a coordinated team effort.

It was an amazing sight. Men and women worked together seamlessly, for survival, not greed. If only the future had such ethics. These people lived as a tribe—falling, surviving, working together with no politics or jealousy. I was proud to be part of them.

Night fell, and the work done, the celebration began. Fires burned high, dancing, merriment, gambling, and storytelling lasted long into the night. I had eaten my share of buffalo meat and was bursting at the seams. How they stayed thin with such feasting, dancing, and chanting was a mystery.

I watched Dakota gnaw on another rib.

"Was a satisfying day for the tribe, huh?" I asked, tired but content.

"Yes," he mumbled, chewing.

"I'm tired." My eyelids grew heavy. "The sun will rise soon. Do these people ever sleep after a hunt, or just keep going like Energizer bunnies all night?"

"Energizer bunny? Sometimes you make me think of the future," he said, chewing and swallowing. "Do you like buffalo meat?"

I yawned. "Yes, it was good. Now I'm tired. I want to sleep."

"Okay, you rest. I'm headed to Swift Eagle's lodge to party Indian style." He performed a quick dancing jig.

I watched him walk away, happy, perhaps wanting to stay here, not return to his own world. I trudged back to our lodge, sleepy, the thought making me sad: him here, me back in the future—was that what I wanted?

14

BLACK RAVEN'S SPIRIT TRAVELS

The chief had been gone for twenty-four moons, and he had finally perfected this out-of-body experience. At first, it had been short-lived, only allowing him to leave his shackles and move around his immediate surroundings. The old chief had grown weary as they moved him from prison to prison; his spirit needed stability, not a nomadic existence. He guessed they had been in this abandoned Army Fort for three moons, but that had been long enough to settle his spirit.

He had transformed fully from a spirit trapped inside his body to one that could move freely outside it, gliding farther and farther from his captors. The more he practiced, the stronger he became—until this day. He had traveled miles from his physical body; it felt exhilarating to ride high and free, even for a brief time.

Black Raven had never considered himself magical, but the gods had indeed blessed him. His wisdom intimidated most men, as did his bravery. Fear had brought him to this magical place—not fear for himself, but fear for his people, a nation that needed to multiply and be fruitful.

A few years before his capture, he had written in a journal. He had kept his thoughts to himself, never confiding in Swift

Eagle. Many would have thought him mad for his words and drawings: visions of the future and the magical notion of time travel. These dreams and visions were so vivid he could not contain them. On the thinnest buffalo-hide parchment, he recorded them—things known only to him and his heart. Bound and hidden, the journal was meant to survive for his people's future, for the Sioux Nation and its legacy.

Chief Black Raven did not hear his jailers—men now outlaws and deserters of the 6th Regiment of Dragoons. Only the chains held his body as his soul roamed, watching over his people. To reveal himself would risk upsetting the balance of time; his people might seek him out, which could not happen. He needed to observe, to witness the power of his dreams and visions, knowing the prophecy was ready to unfold. This magic would secure his people's past and future.

His spirit lingered near a small nest of brambles, observing the tribe as they concluded the long celebration of a successful hunt. It was a blessed day for him and for the Sioux he called family. Each member passed this spot to reach the nearby stream. They would not linger; winter approached, and soon they would move to the mountains for shelter, off the flatlands, until spring awoke.

The man they called Wind Dancer was not alone. Black Raven remembered a powerful woman from the tribe's move—a woman with strength who shared his spirit. The old chief knew this woman, called She Cougar, had a magical kinship with him, and she would be the woman Wind Dancer would take as his own.

NEXT TO THE BRAMBLE bushes near the stream, where I had stopped for a private moment, the hair on my neck tingled. Glancing over my shoulder, I expected one of the children trying to sneak up to scare me. No one was there. I chalked it up to fatigue and punchiness, needing only sleep.

Slipping under the flap of the lodge, I fell onto the hides, exhausted. I sighed. I had not been this tired in a long time. The last time I felt this emotionally drained had been at my parents' funerals. No—scratch that—it had been the first night Dakota found me. Gees, I was too tired to remember exactly when. How ironic. My eyes closed, but sleep refused to come. It was chilly, so I pulled up a deerskin for warmth.

Cold, tired... crud, now I remembered when I'd been this exhausted. That day in the bitter cold, waiting as a private investigator for Blackie. I guessed the joke was on me now.

If I had to be here, at least these people liked me enough to protect me. And then there was Dakota. If we were stuck here together, would we become a *we*? My sleepy brain struggled to comprehend. With a weary groan, I rolled onto my side and fell into a deep, unbroken sleep.

A few hours later, Dakota found me as he returned to the lodge. It had been one of the most exciting days of his life, one he would cherish forever. The hunt had invigorated him; he felt he could conquer the world. He didn't know if this was all part of some plan, and he didn't know why Blaze had been sent, or why so soon. Nothing made sense—he was tired from the day's hunt and the night's celebration.

Without a sound, he left the lodge. He had drunk enough of the special cactus juice mixed with berries to relax, and he needed a moment alone at the stream. Heading to a darker, secluded spot, he passed the bramble bushes woven with spirit energy.

BLACK RAVEN FOCUSED ON the man called Wind Dancer. He was strong, but not as powerful a force as the woman he had encountered. There was no doubt the journal he had buried hundreds of years ago had been found, and his magic had worked this miracle.

The chief did not understand why the spirits of time revealed visions instead of instructions. Deep down, he sensed many reasons this magic had to unfold as it did, unaltered.

His time was ending; his spirit grew faint, his vision blurred. The older chief felt the rise of his physical eyelids. His spirit no longer floated above the bramble; it returned to his chained body. Once strength returned, he would allow his spirit to roam again.

BLACK RAVEN, THE PRISONER—BACK at the Makeshift Army Camp

The old chief looked at the slop they called "food." Tonight, his spirit had glimpsed cooking buffalo meat and could almost smell its savory aroma. What they served him was no better than watered-down gruel. A scrap of meat might come his way, but not tonight. He sucked it up, drained the liquid, and drank dirty creek water. He had to maintain strength, no matter the cost to his palate.

Captain Gene Ardenhert had banded together soldiers who were little better than outlaws. Greed drove them—they wanted out of structured military life. Promises of fine horses and a life exploring the western prairie lured many men to enlist during fall, ensuring food and shelter through winter. Higher-ranking officers treated lower men poorly, exposing dreams that didn't exist. Those unwilling to conform became rebellious deserters.

"What's on your mind, Sergeant?" the captain asked, walking beside the man.

"We haven't much time. Major Bellamus isn't far behind, and he's heading into the Black Hills with the government's blessing."

"So, you suggest we advance a few days early?"

"Yes, sir. We've lost half a dozen men to dysentery and other maladies. There's no way to fight Bellamus' troops. And hanging isn't exactly appealing."

Captain Ardenhert knew returning wasn't an option. Court-martial or hanging—they were all destined for death. His plan: seize the Black Hills gold before anyone else and dispose of the prisoner. Black Raven was a powerful chief, a visionary, a shaman. Ardenhert did not believe in such "Indian hogwash," but he kept the chief shackled, indifferent to the consequences. Once he had the gold, he would discard the old man and his ragtag men.

Ardenhert had spent his life following orders, risking his life for causes he did not care for. Now, the Black Hills gold promised a way out, and he would not let the government claim it first.

BACK IN 2020—FOR A Moment

Meda switched on the small table lamp, set her drink on the short round table, and settled into her rocker. Taking the dog-eared diary from its deerskin pouch, she traced her fingers over the smooth leather. Made from buffalo hide many years ago, its texture had softened in places. She imagined the stories it could tell.

There was more to this book than ceremonial magic enabling time travel. She had decided, after so much time and no phenomenon—or one they hadn't yet observed—she must reread it from page one. This time, she pushed feelings aside and focused entirely on Black Raven's words.

"What do I need to know? Will you show me?" she whispered, imploring the old chief's spirit as she reread the diary, absorbing each word as if her life—and the lives of her loved ones in another world—depended on it.

BACK IN THE 1800S—AFTER the Hunt

Dakota shivered, though it wasn't cold. His belly was full, the special cactus-and-berry juice having relaxed him. Unlike alcohol of his time, it was milder, yet potent if overindulged. He felt content, but something spooked him near the brambles. A quick glance over his shoulder revealed nothing. He was alone; the camp had settled into silence. Still... someone—or something—was there.

"My imagination," he muttered, shaking it off.

Dakota pulled his loincloth back into place and stretched, grateful for no alarm clocks. He liked this life: slower, serene, a different rat race from his world. The real battle would come when he saw death or had to take a life. Yet for now, he mused, staying here wouldn't be so bad. His world was filled with murders, wars, and chaos—the savagery was just different here.

Could Blaze feel the same way?

He entered the lodge and sat beside her. She slept, breathing deep, not quite snoring, yet completely unconscious. His She

Cougar looked peaceful, angelic even. If he stayed, would she stay with him? That was his last thought before lying down. His head barely touched the fur pile of hides before sleep claimed him.

15

I WOKE FEELING MUCH more refreshed and sat up, glancing over at where Dakota had slept—but he was gone. Alone in the lodge, it crossed my mind that he'd let me sleep in, as I could hear activity outside, though not as boisterous as the day before. Pulling on my moccasins, I ran my fingers through my tangled hair and decided that a soak in the stream would feel relaxing.

As I stepped out of the tipi, something felt off. Everyone was working—cleaning up or helping preserve the fresh meat, stretching hides, and performing other odd chores that came with slaying so many buffalo—but they were all very solemn, too hushed.

I'd only walked a little way downstream when I found Dakota crouched on his hunches, staring across the water.

"Why does it feel gloomy this morning? The celebration was wonderful, and everyone should be cheerful." I squatted beside him, dipping my hands in the cold water, splashing my face, and wiping my eyes. "Dakota?"

Still, he didn't respond, so I flicked a few drops of water toward him. "Earth to Dakota."

"He was here."

"Who was here?" I sat back on my heels to slip off my moccasins, then pulled my dress to my thighs and stepped into the cold water. A shiver ran from my toes to the top of my head. I began rinsing my feet and legs; I'd do the rest when I was alone.

"Are you listening to me, Blaze?"

"Hmm, yes. Who did you say?" Right now, I was wishing for scented soap and shampoo, my mind wandering to the luxuries of my future.

"Black Raven. He was here." Dakota's voice was low.

"I thought he was, uh... you know, with the spirits." Speaking of the dead was taboo, and I didn't dare utter the word.

"Maka doesn't believe he's dead. She felt him last night during the celebration. Oddly, I could've sworn last night, when I came out to the stream, I felt someone with me—but I was alone." He spoke softly.

"Maybe Maka had too much celebration. And why was she the only woman drinking the special juice?" I babbled, but he didn't seem to catch it.

"What was that? I didn't hear you."

"That you didn't offer me any juice, so I'm not worthy—or women don't partake of this drink. Kind of like women don't smoke the peace pipe either. I consider this sexist." I huffed and pouted.

Dakota chuckled. This woman was indeed a card-carrying feminist. He made no comment and continued. "Back to what I was saying. Maka is strong, in mind and spirit. She drank the juice to enhance her visions."

My eyebrows shot up, and I gave him a look.

"It's not drunken visions like in our time. Don't think she does this for a buzz or weird hallucinations."

"I wasn't thinking that. I was thinking,"—I emphasized the word *thinking*—"since I come from a line of seers, maybe I could have visions too."

Dakota tilted his head, a thoughtful look crossing his face. "It might be possible. That never crossed my mind."

"Since you mentioned feeling someone with you last night, I had a strange sensation before going back to your lodge. I was going to walk to the stream to wash but changed my mind. I could have sworn someone was sneaking up on me—but when I looked back, no one was there. Don't you think it's odd that we both felt like someone was watching us?"

Stepping out of the stream, I resumed my place next to him, uneasy about the strange sensation of an unseen watcher, but I dropped the subject. I couldn't fight what I couldn't see. I wanted to ask why the people were quieter than normal; the successful hunt should still have them joyful.

"Everyone working in silence? I didn't see Maka either. Is she all right? Did she see a vision after all that cactus juice?" I asked, moccasins back on and tied.

"No, it's not just that." He sat, pensive, silent.

"It's not just what? A secret, or a guessing game?" I poked his side. Heavens to Betsy, the man could stretch a brief conversation forever.

"They believe it's disrespectful to speak of the dead, especially a revered chief. Swift Eagle is unhappy with Maka."

"I don't understand. She is Black Raven's daughter. She has a powerful gift of sight, so why would he be mad at his own child?" My emotions flared. I cared for this woman who had taken me under her wing, like a daughter.

"It's stirred the people up. They're divided."

"I thought they stuck together, like a real family. This shouldn't divide them. They're a deep-seated unit." I had assumed the tribe would never go against one another. But I had to remember—they were human, and this era was different from my world. People throughout time had changed.

"Some feel her vision of him alive is truth, and they want to start a search," he said.

"So what's the harm in that? Why not search for the man? How could they know he's dead if no one saw his body?"

"Swift Eagle doesn't want men hunting for a spirit. It's complicated. And Blaze, somehow, I wonder if you and I caused this."

"Why, Dakota? Why would you think that? No one here can be controlled by us, and even if we weren't here, would it have changed anything?"

"Who says we're supposed to be here?" His voice wavered with doubt.

"I guess our ancestral genes, our beliefs, our destinies—whatever. We're here, and we can't change that, can we?" I almost barked. How funny. Here I was, trying to reassure him.

"Don't get snippy. I'm just trying to figure this out."

"While you sit figuring this out, I'm going to find Maka. Let me know what you come up with." I snapped again.

I tried not to be angry, but I couldn't help it. Maka possessed remarkable insight and was a wonderful woman. She knew how I felt about Dakota, although I wouldn't admit it. I liked him... more than liked, but now wasn't the time. I would worry about that bridge later; for now, I needed to focus on befriending Maka.

Maka sat in front of her lodge. Different clay pots of paint sat nearby. She had braided horsehair attached to a thin buffalo-bone brush. Short, bristly, and precise, it rested in her hand as she stretched tanned deer hide over two thick branches, creating a blank canvas.

"I didn't know you were an artist," I said, sitting on the ground beside her.

"No, but sometimes when I await a vision, I paint what the gods let me see. It's the only time I can translate words into pictures. Your Lakota is good. She Cougar, you learned fast—too fast, as if by magic."

I didn't answer her implied question. "I have smart teachers," I replied with a smile.

"You hear talk, is that why you come here? Speak with gentle voice to me?"

"Yes and no. I hear talk, but only from Wind Dancer. I worry about you and Swift Eagle."

"He is displaying warrior madness. It will pass soon."

"How long will he not speak to you?" I worried that animosity was brewing; I wanted things to remain as they were.

"He speaks soon, or no dinner, and no arms in the night to keep him warm." Maka laughed.

One thing was for sure: women here were just like women in my future. Stay mad, go hungry, sleep alone.

I laughed with her. "I understand, I understand."

We sat quietly. Maka, brush in hand, eyes closed, and I watched the others working nearby. Women tanned buffalo hides, laying them fur side down, driving sharpened bones into edges to hold them flat. With flint rocks, they scraped the undersides, thinning them for drying. Others cut meat into strips, hanging it in the sun to dry as jerky. Children, women, men—all were busy.

Sitting in silence with Maka, I felt like I was in another world, yet I was still somewhat an outsider. Though they no longer distrusted me, I wondered if I could learn to love it here, forever. I'd grown less fearful, felt part of the tribe—but I missed my aunt, my only family. My eyes flicked to Maka. She was my family too, though I couldn't tell her that.

"You grow bored watching me, my child. Go find Wind Dancer." Maka never opened her eyes, but she knew me.

I smiled at the older woman, reminded so much of Aunt Meda. "I'll see you later. We will talk."

This woman was amazing. I hoped one day to make her spirit proud.

Sitting with the men, reliving the hunt again, I saw Dakota standing silently, not far from the group. I listened, not wanting to interrupt. Stupidly, I tried willing him to know I was there, connecting my thoughts to his, linking our spirits.

I wasn't all-powerful—not a visionary—yet I aspired to be more Sioux, like my future Aunt Meda and past Aunt Maka. A few minutes passed. I concentrated harder. Still, the men talked and enjoyed the hunt's victory.

⁂

Dakota felt something tugging at him from inside, as if unseen forces called. It was an odd, unfamiliar sensation. His urge to rise and leave was almost irresistible. A deep breath, and he let the feeling pass. What had come over him?

The pull returned, stronger. He stood.

"Not finished with the story yet," Dark Cloud said firmly.

"I, uh, need to go tell She Cougar something."

The men smirked and guffawed, teasing him for letting his woman run him—but it was all in fun.

He couldn't admit that something tugged him toward her. Stupid, he told himself. Could his feelings for her be that strong? No. Impossible. He had to clear his head, resist letting her into his heart.

⁂

Oh crap, I'm an idiot, I thought, closing my eyes, and almost collided with Dakota.

Grabbing my arm, he marched me away. "I need to speak with you alone. How long were you standing there?"

"I don't know. Five minutes. Why?" I wanted him to let go but said nothing.

"Never mind."

I kept my brief experiment of willing him to me to myself. He would have thought me a huge idiot. I'd let all this Indian mystic stuff get to me—but then again, I'd traveled through time... or was having the most absurd dream.

He walked me to the stream where a large boulder sat. I took a seat, pulling my knees to my chin. He sat beside me, but not too close.

"I was with Maka a while ago, and something occurred to me. Maybe we've disrupted our future—or their past. Our being here might shift not only these people's lives but our own and our families'. What if we've altered history, with no way to stop it?"

"That's a lot of what-ifs and maybes. We can't change history. We're here. We can't turn back the clock." The words escaped before he thought.

"Don't you think we've already turned it back? Geesh, Dakota, think about it. I didn't prepare for this. I wasn't planning this journey! So tell me the history for the here and now. I might understand, but I can't understand what I don't know. You had the time to read the diary, but not me. Someone tossed me into this vortex without preparation! Enlighten me. I can read, I'm smart enough." My eyes bugged out, and I stuck out my tongue.

He tried not to laugh; a small snorting chuckle escaped.

"I know you're smart. You've proven it by how fast you learned the language."

"Don't give me all the credit. Somehow, I understood what I heard. That still puzzles me. How do you think it happened?"

"It's a moot point. It did, and you can. There's no way to explain it. Look, I'm not sure what year this is. My closest guess is early-to-mid 1800s. I haven't studied Black Raven's diary. I'm as much in the dark as you. My uncle and your aunt deciphered the Sioux hieroglyphics, each drawing a word. They still don't understand all of it. Black Raven was a powerful shaman—he saw the future."

"Have you asked anyone about Black Raven? I know they don't speak of the dead, but someone told you something." My eyes narrowed. "Was it Maka?"

"No, Swift Eagle did."

"Did he volunteer this, or did you ask, Dakota?" I gave him a hard stare.

"When I came to this tribe, I told him I wanted to see their chief. I guess they'd have skinned me if I hadn't been adamant. They knew I was Sioux, though not of their tribe."

"How many Sioux tribes are there?"

"Seven Sioux nations. Each nation has many tribes. Being Sioux from another tribe doesn't mean you fit every tribe. You're half Sioux. Why don't you know this?"

"Let's not discuss my lack of Sioux knowledge. Go on."

"They didn't trust me. Then I kept asking about Black Raven. Swift Eagle told me he was in the spirit world, warned me not to speak of him again."

"Did you find out what happened?"

"I did, but Maka didn't rat me out. She told me the story. Black Raven went with a small band to the Black Hills. White trespassers appeared, trouble broke out. The Sioux killed three of eight hunters. In the chaos, Black Raven separated from his men. Two of twelve Sioux braves died. The rest searched. They weren't worried—they hadn't seen his body. Black Raven had to be alive."

"Maybe he isn't dead," I countered.

"After all this time, he'd have returned," Dakota barked.

"Maybe he can't get back. That doesn't mean he's dead. Look at us—we're here. Maybe he's alive. And don't snap at me." I flung my arms up.

Dakota exhaled in frustration, taking it out on me.

"They haven't seen him since. At least two years, I think."

"That's it? Didn't they send braves to look?"

"No, that's it. Not much to go on."

"Didn't they tell you more about the diary, why we're here? Or did you jump the gun, hothead that you are, always in a hurry?" I waited, poking him to answer.

"It might be to find Black Raven, or stop something. I'm not sure."

"You're telling me they didn't tell you why you traveled back 150 years? No clue? Nothing? Mercy, I thought at least you knew something, keeping me in the dark. We—you and I—are here, flying blind. We have no clue what to do, how to do it, or if we'll ever get back."

Frustrated, I stood—and lost balance, toppling onto him. Dakota grabbed my hand, but momentum pushed us over the boulder. We landed chest-to-chest, nose-to-nose. Neither moved. A gnat couldn't have gotten between us. He held me close.

"My Iye Igmu'watogla," he whispered, taking command of my lips.

I couldn't resist. I needed this. Arms slid under his neck, pulling him closer. Lips scorching, nibbling, teeth nipping—wild animal instincts. I realized I had to stop.

Pulling away, I said, "No, this isn't good."

Dakota's eyes widened. "Hell, woman, what do you mean it's not good? You've got me worked up!"

"I don't mean it's not good. I mean it's the wrong time. We're here for something—something we don't understand—not for this." I tried to roll off him; he held firm.

"Are you afraid?" he asked, licking his lips, studying mine.

"Uh... no, er, yes. We need to see where our lives go—here or back in our century—before bringing another problem into the mix."

"Sorry. It felt like you wanted it, too. I apologize." Abruptly, he let go.

"Don't get angry, Dakota. We have other complications. Sharing your lodge as a single maiden is distressful enough—I don't want it awkward later. I'm not a one-night-stand sort of girl."

Without looking, I brushed grass and dirt off my leggings, straightened my dress, and looked up. He stared at me.

Right before walking away, he said, "Who said this was a one-night stand?"

My mouth gaped as I watched him return to the village.

16

I SLEPT RESTLESSLY, HAUNTED by dreams of searching alone in the dark for something or someone. There were shadows and fog, and I called out, but no one heard me. Waking with a start, I felt the sweat on my brow. It was only a dream, but it felt so real, like I was going down a black hole.

The pallet where Dakota slept was empty. Judging the time, it had to be more than several hours before sunup. I shivered. The weather was changing, so I put on my moccasins, wrapped myself in a hide, and went to look for him.

It was quiet, and most of the fires had burned out. As my eyes grew accustomed to the darkness, I scanned the area for any movement. Nothing moved except for a few horse tails, swatting at a fly or two, and the slow, steady swish of a light wind. Not one dog growled, and no one whispered behind a tipi flap—the silence was loud. I felt alone for the first time in a long time. Where could Dakota be? It was too dark for me to wander very far, especially alone.

Wide awake and in tune with the night, I felt as if I were witnessing time at a standstill. I can't describe the strange feeling I had. It was like the eye of a storm—still, but waiting for the right time to explode. Why was I always expecting the worst?

The truth is, I was doing all right, still healthy, even though I was in a different time zone, and I'd felt safe for most of it.

I breathed in and out, reminding myself I wasn't alone and had nothing to worry about. There were people here who would protect me, including Dakota. I was afraid of the unknown, worried about heartbreak, and scared that it was all just a dream.

After getting back to the lodge, I huddled outside under a buffalo hide. I closed my eyes and imagined him, confident that he would come back. We were from the same future, and this was our connection. Though I felt a greater bond between us, I found it impossible to focus as my eyes grew heavy. Within minutes, I was fast asleep.

DAKOTA FOUND HER THIS way two hours later. What was she doing sleeping outside the lodge? He scooped her up and slipped inside, laying her on the pile of hides. She mumbled in her sleep as he made sure she was covered.

"Don't leave, Wind Dancer. I'm afraid."

Her eyes did not open, but her brow furrowed. She was dreaming.

"Please," she begged.

"I'm not going anywhere, I swear," he murmured. He was tired; it had been a long night. Taking another hide from beside his own pallet, he lay beside her. Blaze rolled over, the blankets rustling, and he spooned next to her, his arm over her body—a reassuring shield. She cuddled closer, comforted by his closeness and warmth.

Dakota flinched as his body reacted to her nearness, but Blaze shifted back, ensuring they remained connected. This was torturous, but he did not move away again. He needed sleep. This arrangement kept him awake, his body fully alert even as his brain begged for rest. When he heard her slow, steady breathing, he relaxed, assured she was asleep.

Had she been dreaming of him? He would not ask. He had enough to tell her, and for now, he would just enjoy being close to her.

───── ⚜ ──⟋

WHEN I WOKE, MY brain felt cloudy and my mouth was extra dry. I felt closed in and cramped. Re-closing my eyes, I shook the cobwebs from my foggy mind. Moving the hides that covered me revealed a larger hand draped over my waist. It could be no other person's but Dakota's.

But why was he sleeping next to me on my pallet—and so darned close?

I lay still, listening to him breathe in a heavy, deep sleep. My mind raced back to last night, or perhaps the wee hours of the morning. I wasn't sure.

What had happened? Yes—I remembered. My dreams had woken me. I went outside, took a short walk, and then what? Oh yeah, I'd huddled under the buffalo hide outside the tipi. I must have fallen asleep.

Had he carried me back to bed and taken that opportunity to slide in next to me? Of all the gall. Here I was, dead to the world—what happened?

Angry, I yanked back the hide and flipped his arm off me, rolling away from his warmth. He didn't wake up, which made me madder. I pulled off the buffalo hide, cleared my throat, and grunted, trying to wake him. I rolled my eyes, thinking I was incredibly foolish. I could've roused him by shaking him, but I preferred to avoid physical contact with him at the moment.

Now why am I afraid to touch him? I thought. *This is even stupider.*

"Dakota, wake up." I grasped his shoulder and gave him a shake. Still no response.

"Dakota!" This time I spoke louder and shook him with more force.

He stirred. "Mmm, yeah, yeah. I'm getting up. Just a few more minutes." He never opened his eyes as he rolled away, his back now facing me.

"Wake up." A surge of anger flared.

His eyes flicked open. "Why the devil are you mad?"

One hand tugged at the hide to ward off the morning chill, and with the other, he rubbed the sleep from his eyes.

"Blaze, it was a long night and promises to be a long day. I'll get up—but not until the sun has just crested over the stream, warming the waters. Now be quiet, please."

He rolled over, turning his face away from mine, refusing to argue.

Well, fine, I thought. *I'll not say another word.* I was so mad that once I got a word with him, I was going to let him have it—both barrels of the shotgun. What the heck? We shared one measly kiss, and he thought he might sleep in my bed without even asking.

Not to dawdle, I huffed out of the lodge and headed for the stream, muttering the words he'd verbalized: "When the sun crests over the stream, blah, blah, blah."

Looking up, I could still see a smattering of stars and the moon lingering in the new light. It was early, but I didn't care.

My dreams forgotten, I looked back at the village still sleeping. It was not as ominous in the light of day, but it had spooked me last night all the same. One or two dogs stretched and went about their morning constitutional; the horses grazed. This morning's silence was different from last night's—more peaceful—but last night's silence had been filled with my fears.

⁓ ⸎ ⁓

DAKOTA WOKE GROGGY, EVERY bone aching. Maybe he was getting old. Here in this day and time, forty was ancient, and he was far from forty. He crossed his arm over his eyes, shielding out the partial ray of sunlight intruding into his sight. He thought about it for a second. Was he aging? Here he was, well over one hundred years backward, which meant he was at a standstill and couldn't get older.

He wished he knew more about this phenomenon. His thoughts jumped to Blaze. She was gone, no longer lying next to him. It made him feel empty and sad. He knew she was still here, outside somewhere, most likely sulking and thinking things that weren't true. Although nothing had occurred, he secretly longed for a spark to ignite between them.

Dakota had wanted her last night—all of her. He had no clue when he'd started feeling this way about her, but he knew he had. Whatever spark she'd triggered hit hard and fast. This wasn't good. His feelings for her could blind him to the mission. For God's sake, what *was* this blessed mission, and what was he trying to accomplish?

He got up and shoved the hides aside with his feet, venting his frustration on the dead animal skins. Had he overlooked a sign, a phrase—something that would guide him? All these many months, he'd enjoyed being here, being part of these amazing people. He relished the action and interaction of these people—his people. Nothing could ever top this. This would be, forever, the most memorable experience of his life.

It sounded like someone telling a story about a vacation—nothing more. This was more, so much more, but he wished he knew what it meant. It was back to business.

Donning his boots, he left to wash up. He needed to tend to personal matters, clear his head, and then find her.

—— ᴟ ——

AFTER PUTTING MY FEET into the chilly water, I wriggled my toes, waited a short while, then took them out and put my moccasins back on. Standing, I walked the bank of the stream. My thoughts didn't flow; everything was tangled inside my head. When I turned back, the village was just a faint spot, and I realized how far I'd walked. I trekked back at a faster pace, mindful that I was alone, and a lot of *what ifs* popped into my head.

Chief Black Raven — same day, same hour

Chains clinking, alone in the stale tent, Black Raven closed his eyes and slowly deepened his breaths.

His mind entered a twilight state, and his body relaxed. One might think him dead if they stumbled upon him.

As he chanted the words repeatedly in his mind, he felt his spirit's pull tug at his physical body, yearning for release. He relaxed, commanding his worldly body to release his spirit to travel and soar. His chin fell to his chest as his head went limp. His spirit escaped with a soft swoosh, leaving a cool breeze in its wake, and began its journey back to his people.

He could see the treetops. Swooping lower, he could almost smell the fall leaves and feel the tickle of prairie grass. Black Raven traveled faster and farther in a shorter amount of time. He was growing stronger with each spiritual journey.

His spirit halted near the new village location. Despite his efforts, it would not move forward. A presence—something so strong—held him back. His physical mind urged his Indian spirit, but nothing happened. Black Raven was a patient man, but this was not the time to wait. At the edge of the last clearing beyond the trees, his spirit remained—not close enough to see and too far away to hear. Why would it not move forward?

The jolt was strong. It held him back, and for a moment he thought his physical body was calling him home, but no—he was still strong in spirit form. Then he saw her. She was walking and mumbling.

He knew this woman was strong, and once more Black Raven felt a kinship with her spirit. He was drawn to her the moment she brushed past. She pulled him. Had she been the reason his spirit stopped cold and would not continue?

This exhilarated him. She was powerful magic—stronger than any woman or man he had encountered, stronger than even his beloved daughter, Maka. This was good—so very good.

***

THE VILLAGE WAS UP ahead; I felt safer. The sun had risen, bringing a beautiful day to bloom, and although I was no longer as angry as I had been, I was still frustrated.

"It's a new day—that's true," I reasoned with myself. "Beginnings... they seem to happen even when you're not expecting it."

A chill ran through me, and the hair on my arms prickled and rose. Yet it wasn't cold—the sun was out. It was a warmer morning, even though fall colors had changed throughout the land.

BLACK RAVEN'S SPIRIT HOVERED. She spoke to no one, using the dragoons' language, not the Lakota tongue. Moving closer, he wanted to see if he could read her heart and soul. His spirit guided her to look forward—to observe her future world—and once she understood, she would find Wind Dancer.

My heart filled with Black Raven's presence, and I sensed his blessing, as though he understood my love for his daughter, Maka. As his unseen spirit backed away, my fears rose—then calmed. An involuntary shudder rippled through my body.

"Get a grip on yourself. You've been here long enough not to let this time-travel stuff get to you," I said aloud, fanning my hands in front of me, shooing away imaginary evil.

17

THE TREES RUSTLED AS a flock of crows scattered at a breeze, and the whinny of a few horses broke the silence. It felt eerie. I was alone yet felt some kind of presence, though nothing—or no one—was there. With the village in my hindsight, sitting at the far end of the stream, I stayed quiet, listening, wondering if my Aunt Meda might try to communicate with me somehow.

If I had traveled back hundreds of years, then anything was possible. I concentrated on my aunt, envisioning her face, her scent, her voice. Closing my eyes to see more clearly, I glimpsed far into my future world.

Aunt Meda relaxed in her old wooden rocker with a worn Indian blanket across her lap. An old, leather-bound book lay atop the blanket. Her eyes closed. Was she humming or chanting?

I relaxed my neck, letting my head lull from side to side, and yes, Aunt Meda was chanting softly. It was a pleasant vision. As the wind blew over my face, I did not open my eyes, even when the gust grew stronger, cooler than just minutes ago. My head down, still moving side to side, eyes closed, I heard the rush of water coming from a very calm, shallow stream.

I watched wrinkled, weathered hands take the book, turning pages as the older fingers traced each line. Her hands moved with care, and as her faded eyes followed the text, I could see understanding light her face. My aunt beamed as the truth of the words reached her.

Her hand went up, and I mirrored the gesture, touching the fine silver chain around my throat. As I lowered my hand, my aunt closed the book, and the vision vanished.

Reopening my eyes, I felt something brush against my neck, like fingers, then the sensation was gone. I looked down at the water in the stream. Not a single ripple. The trees were still. There was no wind. Something strange had just happened. Was I hallucinating? It had felt so real. I'd never used a narcotic in my life, so I wouldn't know an acid flashback if it hit me. Yet the fingers against my neck had felt undeniably real. Eerie.

I glanced around, just in case someone—or something—was there. No. Just me. Alone. Touching the chain, I felt the charm of two circles. Was my Aunt Meda giving me a clue—or a key to part of this mystery?

Perhaps one might call these visions, but each time, my charm had been central.

BLACK RAVEN WAS GROWING weaker, and his body called him back. He had brushed her neck, attempting to lift the chain and see its contents. She had felt him. If his spirit hadn't grown weak, he would have succeeded. He longed to see it, to confirm his hope—a circle within a circle. The definitive proof of her bloodline. But the sound of heavy iron chains rattling brought despair. It was time to return, and he was far from where he wanted to be—back in the clutches of filthy renegade deserters, men soon to be a threat to his people.

FULLY AWAKE, WITH MUCH on his mind, Dakota went in search of Blaze. A few children poked their heads out of lodges, and other tribal members began their day. Dogs whined for food, and women gathered wood and water for a morning meal. It was like any other normal day.

The air was brisker than the day before. Soon, the tribe would plan their move to winter lands. Dakota would miss them all. He needed to talk to her, to explain the next step. She would ask why, and he would admit he did not know. She might think he was lying, but he would never lie to her again. He was following gut instinct, nothing more. Lord, how he wished she held some insight, more like Aunt Meda—or like Maka. These older women had the gift of foresight—not fortune-tellers, but intuition that offered direction. He was just a warrior, brawn over brains.

It saddened him to be merely a guide. Unlike Blaze, this was not his tribal bloodline. All the Sioux tribes were connected, and each nation mattered—Sioux history was at stake. He was there for her, yes, but it had to be more; he too was Sioux. His heritage, his life, were affected. Dakota wasn't angry, just a little jealous. Had he been the focal point, he would have been sent to his exact ancestral tribe. He would have met his ancient ancestors. Blaze was lucky.

He spotted her farther down the stream, sitting alone. She looked neither sad nor happy, just thoughtful.

"Your thoughts look deep for so early in the morning," Dakota said, standing over her bent head. "I suppose there's a lot to think about. We need to talk." He took a seat beside her.

"Yes, we do. Dakota, about last night—I have no earthly idea—"

"No, not about last night. About here and now."

I gave him a sideways glance. "Fine, but we will not ignore last night and how we ended up on the same buffalo hide."

"Fair enough. We can discuss that later. We're leaving in a week."

"But what about—"

He held up a hand. "It's time to go. Make a mental list of questions; I have no pat answers. I only know it's time to leave." He folded his arms, staring across the stream.

"My mental list is getting pretty long," I grumbled. "Where are we headed? Do you at least know where?"

"As deep into the Black Hills as we can, and I'm not sure why. That's the place tugging at me. I even dreamed about it."

I rested my hand on his folded arms. "Tell me the truth, Dakota. How much stock do you put in dreams?"

He pondered. "In this era, shamans and visionaries see things unfold through dreams. It's a piece of a puzzle for them. In our time, a dream is the subconscious blowing anxiety or fear out of proportion. Sometimes we handle things better asleep than awake."

I stared. "What? I never knew you were so... Freudian. Wow, very intellectual."

"It's just my thought. You asked, I answered. Why?"

Shrugging, I touched his shoulder. "I had a dream—darkness, being alone, unnerving. When I woke, I was scared. I went to find you. That's why you found me asleep outside the lodge."

At least he now knew why I had been outside. I wanted to make sure he did not leave me. Nothing more. My heart sank; he had wanted me to need him—not out of fear.

"Dakota, there's more. Earlier, don't think I'm crazy, but right before you arrived, something happened. I might be imagining it, but here we are—hundreds of years ago—and it wasn't imagination."

He nudged me. "Is that all?"

"My eyes were closed, thinking of my aunt. The wind came out of nowhere, and the shallow stream sounded like a rushing rapid. I didn't open my eyes. I continued thinking of Aunt Meda back home in her old rocker."

I held up my hand like a Boy Scout. "This is the honest-to-goodness truth. I felt someone touch the back of my neck. Nothing—no wind, no ripple. What do you make of that? Am I bonkers?"

The hair on his neck stood on end. "No, you're not nuts. Tell me everything. For some odd reason, I feel this is significant. Perhaps it gives insight into why we're here."

I explained my visions, including the chains. I displayed the circle-within-a-circle charm.

Dakota reached out and touched it. Thick, yet fragile. A wave passed through him. He lifted it with two fingers, studying it, then returned it, careful not to invade my space.

"Tell me about this charm. You say your aunt has one matching this?"

"Yes. She said it would keep me safe as a child. I never believed it, but later she explained the past has a future, and the future has a past. One cannot exist without the other."

I gazed at the charm (I had never called it a necklace). The two circles, one inside the other, did not overlap. I grinned.

Dakota eyed my grin. "Does something amuse you?"

"I never noticed until now, but the circles barely touch. A slender line of silver connects them—so thin it's almost invisible."

"And this means what to you?"

"The past and future barely overlap. On my charm, they touch slightly. My aunt's charm is different."

"How so?"

"Her circles touch more. It's as if the past and future intersect—mine don't."

We sat in silence, pondering its meaning.

"This is just a coincidence—circle of life, past touching future, visions, charms, time travel—all nonsense, right?" I watched a leaf float downstream.

"Or maybe it's no coincidence we're here. Perhaps a spirit wanted you to take out this charm. That's why you felt fingers, or your thoughts willed Aunt Meda to reach you."

"If you're trying to scare me, stop." I punched his arm.

"This isn't a thriller. Something deeper, spiritual. Don't be afraid. I promise no harm will come while I'm alive."

Reassuring. As long as he didn't die or return to the future without me, I would be okay. Jiggling that thought from my mind, I focused on the present. I didn't need him every moment. But we still had to discuss why he'd been on my pile of hides without permission. That could wait.

* * *

OVER ONE HUNDRED AND forty years in the future:

Meda sat in her old wooden rocker. In one hand, she held the old diary, yellowed and worn with age. In the other, the charm of two circles, unclasped from around her neck. She paused, spooked, feeling as if she were not alone. Someone breathed on her neck, watching as she meditated over the silver charm. The feeling passed as quickly as it had come, but it had been there. Even with eyes open, she could see Blaze—her face, her features, her breath. It was vivid.

Closing her eyes, she shut out everything but Blaze's image. She heard the faint trickle of a stream and the quiet neighing of a horse. Her niece was not alone. Was Dakota the other presence? Meda felt comforted. She let go of the trance, and Blaze's image faded.

Meda opened her eyes and smiled. All would be well. She felt it in her heart, in the depths of her Sioux soul. Knowing the history of Paha Sapa and the battle for gold, Meda wondered what wrongs they were to make right. Perhaps to return Sioux land taken by the White man, or to save someone from certain death. Who would they save, and what task would they complete to return to their own time? She did not know. If wealth motivated this magic, it was not monetary.

"A life is worth more than a bag of gold," she recalled Gray Wolf saying. Blaze's father had been wise. Meda's thoughts turned, pondering if her people would suffer, their history altered, affecting the present. She shook the thought away.

With reverence and pride, the old Sioux woman walked to her back porch, surveying the distant hills. Squaring her shoulders, she spoke in Lakota:

"Colapi, Ai, mieyebo cha kikipapi, wayo-kapi, hecheto welo. Kiksuyapi, Lakota Oyate."

Translation: "*Friends, yes, I am without fear; it is the truth, and it is done. It is good; do not forget. Remember the Sioux nation.*"

18

AT THE STREAM, SITTING on their boulder, Dakota stood, offered her his hand, and helped her up. She no longer bothered dusting off, righting her hair, or worrying about what she looked like without makeup.

Dakota walked beside her, silently contemplating her.

He saw her as just Blaze, a natural beauty.

She did not view herself as a spirited, zealous woman. However, she was smart and adaptable and had come to terms with a life without future luxuries.

It delighted him, the way she'd embraced her life. She fit in when he knew she hadn't thought she would. Over time, she'd become impassioned about her people and her heritage. He'd felt her heart. How was that possible? Was time travel doing a number on him? How could he know her heart, and if he did, did it have room for him? Dakota had to stay focused and stop thinking about her in that way.

He watched as she walked ahead of him.

The sway of her hips. Just below the hemline of her buckskin dress, her shapely calves. From a head-on stare, she was a captivating woman, a rare beauty, inside and out.

In the silent space of his thoughts, Dakota mentally cataloged her attributes.

Deep brown hair, highlighted from all the sun exposure. She kept it in braids to keep it from becoming a ratted mess.

Her face was devoid of makeup. The color of her skin was a light caramel, and her cheeks had a delicate pink hue.

And her eyes. Lord. Her eyes were a stunning cobalt blue, so dark they were almost black, like the deepest ocean depths.

Dakota stopped himself short—not just his thoughts, but in his tracks.

What was he doing? Why was he sizing her up? Then it hit him. He had fallen—and fallen hard. It was as if someone had picked him up and thrown him facedown from one of the nearby cliffs. He had hit hard, hard, hard. He stood nailed to the prairie ground, not moving, not a twitch.

I thought he was right behind me, but when he didn't respond, I turned to see him stop dead in his tracks.

"You're scaring me a little. What's the matter now?" I half-stomped back to where he stood. "You look like you've just heard someone died." I poked him to wake him from his apparent daze.

Death—indeed. Dakota Kangee, the bachelor, had died. Now his ultimate fear was certain death if she never felt the same way.

"Uh, I'm fine," he lied. "I was just thinking about saying goodbye, and how much I'd, um, miss them, and this life," he stammered.

"Me too. It's sad, and I hate to say goodbye, but if we want to get whatever it is done, then we have to go, right?"

"Yup. So, let's get going." His heart skipped a beat, and then another, as he gazed at her. "By the way, I hate it when people poke me." He feigned anger.

"I'm learning about you little by little—the good and the bad. Although, I don't want to hear about the bad, unless you have a very shady past I should know about." She wiggled her eyebrows, trying to lighten the mood, which had become too serious.

As they walked together, Dakota was visibly shaken by the recent revelation. He found himself falling for this woman. The problem was, what was he going to do? In a few days, they would be leaving, and they would be alone. No tribal members—no chaperones—nothing to keep him preoccupied. How would he keep his feelings in check?

Could this be his mission—to see if he could tolerate being close to the woman who set his soul ablaze, captivated him completely, and for whom he would give everything?

How could Chief Black Raven know he'd fall for Blaze, and why travel through time for love? It was absurd. There had to be more to it than this.

He had a strong feeling this wasn't their objective, or his specific task. Blaze clearly didn't care about him at all. She hadn't brought the subject up, but she was still irritated by how closely he had lain next to her that night. How would he cope being alone—just them?

Dakota, just tell her, he thought. No, he argued with himself. He'd have to change his approach. Wind Dancer would transform into the stoic Indian warrior, a hunter seeking out foes, a man of few words and a rough exterior. The task at hand was not to woo this woman. There was a lot to lose—perhaps their lives—if he messed up. Dakota squared his shoulders and readied himself. He would accomplish this mission, not risking either of their lives for foolishness called love.

———※———

I WAS SMILING AS we approached Maka's tipi. The old woman smiled back with a big, toothy grin. "I see you two share mornings by the river. You eat?" Maka winked at Dakota, and I swear I thought I saw him blush when I cut my eyes at him. Then I looked back at the old woman.

"Uh, no, I—we—didn't eat. We were talking by the river, that's all."

"Come. I have extra corn mush and some dried buffalo meat. You eat. We talk after." Maka guided me into her tipi.

"Dakota, are you coming?" I called over my shoulder.

"No, you go ahead. I have, uh, some things to attend to."

"Then go, do what men do. You,"—Maka took me, pulling me all the way inside—"come eat."

Inside, I smelled the corn mush and vapors of dried buffalo meat, and I was famished. Maka smiled, watching me while I ate, pleased that I enjoyed a healthy appetite.

"Is good you eat. You need food. Seems like many moons have passed, but has been short time you are here. Swift Eagle and I talk. You are big mystery to us. You not full Sioux, but here—" She pointed to her heart. "—just like you are daughter to me. You and Wind Dancer must leave. I dreamed this."

A small smile perched on my lips. "Yes, we do," was all I said.

"I cannot stop future, but I know is true when I say you will live forever in my dreams and in my heart."

I tried to be strong, but the tears still came.

Maka wiped my tears with her fingers, then placed her wet fingertips to her heart.

"I keep you in my heart, with your sadness and fear; with that, I blend in the happiness stored here." She tapped her chest. "No one shall ever take you from here, from me. You live forever with me now, and in the spirit world, I find you amongst the many spirits now watching over us from many moons ago and many moons to be."

"As I shall carry you." I touched my heart.

That Sioux woman didn't realize she was my very distant aunt. I would forever keep Maka and this tribe stored deep in my heart. They had embraced me, a newcomer, and I was sure they had known about my mixed heritage from the beginning. However, that didn't matter to them. This tribe gave me a wonderful gift—the gift of my own Sioux heritage.

Armed with my newfound knowledge, if asked, I would gladly go without fear. I'm glad I got sent back without knowing, because I would've bolted if I had a say—far away from anything like this, or even the idea it was possible. Now I wouldn't change a thing. For if I'd run, I would've missed out on one of the most significant moments of my life. I, Blaze Clark, daughter of Gray Wolf, was now She Cougar, and no longer the coward I had once thought myself to be.

IN TWO DAYS, DAKOTA and I would be leaving for the end of this time-warp journey—or so I thought—to fulfill a destiny and travel back to our own time.

I had more than enough to think about.

What was my destiny?

What was the plan?

That question perplexed me. Maybe this was all to get me to embrace my Sioux ancestry, and nothing more. Shaking my head, I sighed heavily. This was a very elaborate way to do that. Knowing that no one could change the past or stop the future, what could I do to change it? None of this added up.

Love popped in and out of my thoughts many times. Yet again, this was a complicated measure to infuse love into my life. My thoughts turned to him—to Dakota. Lord, he was an enormous issue that weighed on my mind.

"Am I here for him? Could that be possible?" I thought, my heart skipping a single beat as a small smile curved my lips. New feelings had emerged, and I felt differently about this one man.

If that were the case, then why was I trying so hard to keep my distance? And why was he so withdrawn if this darn love thing was our purpose here?

Lately, Dakota was less talkative, his face etched with a simmering anger.

A feeling of déjà vu hit me. I'd traveled right back into the past once more, since I was right back at square one with him. We'd grown apart, but it was his choice, wasn't it? Or was I to blame?

Well, let the chips fall where they may concerning love, because that can't be why I am here. There has got to be a bigger reason, something of greater magnitude. I had to believe this. For if it wasn't happening, then I had to be lying in a coma somewhere in the future, having an in-living-color dream.

One thing was for sure: if it were a dream, I didn't want to wake up. Leaving this place, this era, saddened me to the point of despair. Without them—and him—I'd be alone again.

LAST NIGHT WAS THE worst night I'd had, albeit I'd experienced many. This night bothered me the most. As we were getting ready to end the day, I rolled over to talk to him.

"Dakota?" I whispered.

"Mffp," was his muffled response.

"Are you asleep, or do you have your face buried in the fur?"

"I'm trying to sleep," he grunted, emphasizing each syllable.

"Uh, I didn't want to wake you, but since you're not asleep yet, can we talk for a moment?"

"Fine," he groaned. "We can talk for a minute."

Dakota did not roll over to face me. He could not bear to look at her; his heart could not take it. Her languid, relaxed look after a full day—her hair spilling out, fanning her face. Seeing Blaze like this only fired him up and kept him from staying focused. Add in the fact that he didn't want to have dreams like he'd been having about her as of late.

"Well?"

"What?"

"Are you going to turn over and look at me when we talk, Dakota, or do I get to talk with the back of your head?"

"I'm comfortable, and I can hear you fine. I'm not trying to be rude, Blaze, but after today, my body is as tired as my mind is," he lied.

I thought for a minute. He had worked hard, and why did I need to see him to talk? Oh, crud—I knew all right. I wanted his face to be the last thing I saw before I closed my eyes and the first thing I'd see at the break of dawn. God help me, I had to stop this. This was more than idiotic; I had a mere schoolgirl crush on him, nothing more.

"This too shall pass," I murmured under my breath.

"What? I didn't catch that," he grumbled.

"Nothing. I'm just talking to myself."

"And here I thought you wanted to talk to me. Night—and I hope you have a nice, quiet conversation with yourself," he retorted.

"Dakota, please don't get all bent out of shape. It can wait till tomorrow," I pouted.

Dakota heard the heavy sigh and understood her frustration, though it wasn't the same kind he'd harbored. He didn't want to vent on her.

"Sorry, Blaze. I'm just tired. What do you want to tell me?"

"I'm sorry too. You should rest up and sleep."

As DAWN BROKE, I finally fell into a deep sleep. The wind rustled hard enough to move the tipi flap, and the swooshing sound woke me. I rolled over, stretching my arms in the air, and shuddered.

"Burr, it's getting colder these past few days," I half-muttered. "Are you awake yet?"

Oh yes, he was awake—had been since dawn. Every manly part of him was awake as he'd watched her sleep.

His eyes soaked in everything about her, memorizing every facial movement and the sounds of her breathing right before she woke. When he saw her stir, he rolled over again, turning his back to her.

Thoughts of Blaze crowded his head. Wishing he could find the power to turn back over, because he loved watching her wake—stretching like a fluid cat, eyes closed, mouth slightly open, lips so beautiful and kissable. If she shuddered, and if it were within his power, he would ensure she never woke cold another day in her life.

Dakota pretended to stretch, as if waking. He fiddled with the hides and faced her, calming his racing heart and steeling himself.

"Oh, morning," I yawned, covering my mouth. "Sleep well?"

"Not as well as I'd hoped," he admitted. "But I will survive. You ready for that talk?"

"Right now, I need a private minute, please. Meet me at the end of the stream."

"Of course. I need the same minute to myself, too."

I turned my head away, but he still caught a glimpse of my blushing cheeks as I fussed with the hides, straightening edges that didn't need straightening. Dakota wondered what had flustered me.

I'd have to control this as best I could—but could I? If I gave my feelings away and he found out, I'd be mortified. Fortunately, my hot cheeks cooled as I went about my morning business.

We met back up by the shallowest end of the stream. Walking side by side, we enjoyed the moment before Dakota broke the silence.

"So, what have you got on your mind, Blaze?"

"Let's walk to the bigger rock and sit," I suggested.

He half-nodded, half-shrugged. "Whatever you wish," he said, his tone flat, feeling as if he could walk the length of the stream ten times and not care.

After fifteen minutes, we found the larger rock downstream, past our boulder. I reached out for his hand as I climbed. With a tiny jerk of my head, I urged him to join me. He complied, and we sat with our legs crossed, looking straight ahead as the sun peeked over the tops of the mountains.

We sat there forever before I spoke.

"It was with me again."

"When?"

"For the past two days. I haven't mentioned it since you seem to have so much on your mind."

"Are you scared?"

"No. It consoles me. It is so very close to me—so close, Dakota. I swear I felt fingertips brush across my neck, almost human. It seems to offer me protection."

No one—not even a spirit—could offer her the same level of protection and love that he could.

Had he just admitted to himself that he loved this wonderful woman?

Yes, he had.

Dakota let it sink in for about ten seconds. Ten very long seconds. He stared straight ahead, jaw tight, wrestling with what he felt and what he could safely say.

"You are protected," he finally said. "By more than you think."

I turned to him slowly. "You sound very sure of that."

"I am." His voice was firm. "Whether it's a spirit, your ancestors, or something we don't yet understand, you're not alone in this."

I hugged my arms around myself—not from cold this time, but from the weight of everything pressing down on me.

"Sometimes I wonder if this place knows me better than I know myself."

"This land remembers," he said simply. "It remembers bloodlines, footsteps, promises. Maybe that's why it feels alive to you."

"What if I'm not strong enough for what's coming?"

"You are."

"You don't know that."

"I do." He paused. "I've seen it."

"Seen what?"

"You adapt. You endure. You feel deeply, even when it scares you." He shifted on the rock. "Those aren't weaknesses. They're strengths."

"I don't feel very strong most days."

"No one ever does when they're becoming something new."

We sat in silence again—not awkward, not strained. Just heavy with things neither of us dared say aloud.

After a while, I touched the charm at my throat.

"Dakota... can I ask you something?"

"You already did."

I huffed softly. "You know what I mean."

He nodded. "Ask."

"What happens if we don't finish whatever this is?"

"Then the balance stays broken."

"And if we do?"

"Then something is set right." He hesitated. "But something may also be lost."

"That's what scares me."

"It should. But fear doesn't mean stop. It means be aware."

"You sound like you've already accepted something will change."

"I have."

"What?"

"Us."

My heart skipped, then stumbled. "In what way?"

"That depends on choices we haven't made yet."

The wind shifted, carrying the faintest whisper—not words, not sound, but presence. I felt it press close, warm and familiar.

Dakota felt it too.

"You felt that?"

"Yes."

"It's stronger today."

"It's closer."

"Then we're running out of time."

"Yes," he agreed. "We are."

We rose from the rock together. As we walked back toward camp, I knew—deep in my bones—that whatever awaited us would demand more than courage.

It would demand truth.

And neither of us was ready for all of it yet.

19

One Hundred Thirty Years Forward

MEDA RUBBED HER WEARY eyes. She'd read and reread the last few pages until they were a blur, and the old scribbling looked like a mess of nothing. Leaning her head back with closed eyes, she relaxed her neck muscles, trying to release any tension her body felt. It was there. She knew it—right in front of her—but she could not see it.

Why was she missing it? What in the name of the tribal sun gods was she missing? She thought back to the first time-travel ritual, then to the ritual that sent Blaze back. She went over each step in her mind. Nothing leaped out. She concentrated on the visions each council member had, pondering hard on any significant point each person's vision made. Nothing came to her; her mind was a blank, pure nothing. Oh yes, she had morals, but she felt like cussing a blue streak.

It was time to stop and regroup, fix dinner, settle down for the night with some mindless television. Yes, she would not think about this any longer. She'd spent countless hours going over the old journal, along with everything else since the book was found, and nothing was happening, and she felt a twinge of failure.

"Stop it, old woman," she chided herself, clicking her tongue. "You act like you're defeated."

Stopping at an old mirror hanging in the hallway to her kitchen, she smiled at herself. Her old, crinkled laugh lines and her faded but still-black eyes mocked her, and she poked at her image. "You're one with the world. Don't you ever forget that, old woman."

Meda Clark had predicted things before they had happened and knew about the past. She would conquer this puzzle, this mystery—whatever it was—and she'd find the meaning, the reason, and see the outcome. Humming, she made corn mush and pulled out dried beef jerky, suddenly hungry for an Indian breakfast.

Puffs of vapor scattered the black skies of the night, and no one noticed the stars bursting out—shooting star after star— weaving in and out between the puffy clouds, flashing through- out the sky like a laser light show. The wind whipped in and out of trees, yet not a sound was heard as the limbs bent, touching the ground. Far away, a rumble from under the earth shook, but no one in the future felt it.

Overhead in the dark skies, the clouds faded and the stars dimmed, but a white, foggy substance hovered over the area. Many shapes formed and then whooshed about. Ancient In- dians chanted, and one could hear—if one listened and could separate the wind noise from the chanting voices.

Chief Black Raven watched this phenomenon. He had seen this vision many times in his dreams, but being here now, watch- ing it, was nothing like his dreams. The old chief was thankful for his captors; if not for them, he would have never perfected this out-of-body experience. It had forced him to keep trying, since they'd bound him with chains. Yes, he knew he had the gift, but it had only been in brief spurts—transporting his spirit from his own tipi to the center campfire in their village. Nothing more exciting, until now.

Never had he shared the gift he had with anyone in his tribe; he felt no one would have understood. This was a supreme accomplishment, the most significant in his life. Not only could he take his spirit out of his physical body and move it from place to place—farther and farther than he'd dreamed—he'd traveled well over one hundred years forward to hover now in spirit form. He hoped in time he'd find another who could share this experience, understand it, even have the gift or ability, and that it would pass from descendant to descendant and grow stronger.

The old chief watched as spirits from far back faded, as did the sounds of the Seven Sioux Nation tribes from many moons ago—chanting and whooping faint war cries. They swirled in tornado fashion as they ascended upward, and in the quick blink of an eye, they were no longer visible. The skies were dark yet clear, void of clouds, and just a smattering of stars shone.

He felt his strength wane. His time was up as he felt the pull of his world calling him back. This memory he would never forget—the feels, the sounds, the deep emotions. Knowing he might never have this chance again, he took in the area below him, committing it to memory. It was a peaceful area, and he wondered whose lands these were after all the years had passed. He did not recognize the area. He was sure it was not his old ancient lands, yet he felt something familiar.

A tug pulled from inside his gut, and he heard faint murmuring. Two soldiers entered the tent, talking and walking toward him. Black Raven's time was up, so he closed his eyes and relaxed from top to bottom, letting his spirit make the journey back to his body.

20

OUR PACK MULES WERE laden with furs, dried meats, clay pots, hides, various tools, extra weapons, and other miscellaneous items—all we'd need for our journey. Where this journey might lead, or how long it might be, were questions neither Blaze nor Dakota could answer.

Blaze sat cross-legged in front of the fire, looking about, trying to memorize each speck, each moment, freezing as much of the time in her mind as she could. In less than a few hours, they would head to who knew where, for who knew what, and most of all, for who knew how long. *Is this how the Jews felt in Biblical times,* she wondered, *not knowing they would be lost in the wilderness for forty years?* She sighed, hoping their ordeal didn't last forty years.

So many uncertainties ran through her mind—unclear about her future, uncertain why she was here. More pointedly, she was unsure what it would be like alone with Dakota. What would take place, and would it break her heart?

Wild animals, other enemy tribes, the elements—none of these scared her like the fact that she would be alone with a man who made her heart stop, flutter, and race, and made her weak in the knees. *Huh,* she thought. *I'm a coward after all.* Could he just let her stay here and go on with this life as if it were her real life? Dakota could do this alone; she was positive. The truth was, she was nothing but a hindrance to him. And he—well, he was a definite distraction to her heart.

"Are you ready to go, Blaze?"

"Uh, yes, I think so. Dakota?" she hedged.

"What?" he grumbled.

Dakota wondered if he should leave her here and face this mission alone as a single warrior. They had come to this place each on their own, sent back in time a year apart. Why would he assume they would get back to their realm together? If she got there first, it would make him sad, but he would find her when he returned to their world—to their time. He had to find her.

He waited for her to speak. She had left a question hanging in the air with his name preceding it, but she said nothing.

In that brief lag of silence, it took Blaze less than half a second to know what she wanted. She wanted Dakota—no matter the circumstances, no matter the year—whether it was for only a moment or the rest of her life. She wouldn't let him go without her.

He prompted her gently. "Blaze, what is it?"

"I'm emotional, that's all." Deciding to hide her feelings, she resolved to be as detached as possible. She already knew what it was like to be crushed by love in her future life; she could not let it happen here, now, in another lifetime. One lifetime of hurt was enough. She would keep this secret, and Dakota could never know. Even so, her heart ached for him.

"Blaze, I know your heart hurts."

Her head shot up. Had she said something aloud? Did he somehow know what she was thinking—how she felt?

"These—our people—were fine before we got here and will be fine after we leave."

His eyes swept the area, taking in the people and the way of life he loved. His expression revealed his own sadness about leaving.

Relief washed over Blaze, followed quickly by guilt for being selfish, for not considering the people and their feelings—only her own.

"I know, Dakota. I feel sad for many reasons." It wasn't a lie.

She uncrossed her legs and stood, looking around at the village, the people, and then him. "How much time before we leave?"

Dakota glanced upward, then toward the direction they had come from. "We need to leave soon. The weather's cooler, and I want to get as far as we can before nightfall. Winter will be setting in soon. It'll make travel harder."

"You've been here more than a year. Was the last winter bad?"

"Honey, it's always a hard winter in this time period for these people." He spoke casually, unaware he'd used an endearment.

Blaze's heart melted. She wanted to place her hand on his arm—just a small gesture—but stopped herself. He hadn't meant anything by it. Heaven help her if she was reading more into one simple word.

"We need to say our goodbyes if we're leaving." She turned toward the village, walking ahead of him. Dakota followed at a slower pace.

Saying goodbye to Maka would be emotional for Blaze. Dakota watched her approach the lodge, his heart aching for her.

He knew this farewell would be the hardest. He didn't want to be the arms she fell into afterward. This was a final goodbye to a woman who loved Blaze as more than just someone the tribe had taken in. Maka felt deep in her heart that she truly knew Blaze.

Maka had confided in Dakota. After getting to know Blaze, she believed they were of the same stars, the same blood flowing through their veins. She told him She Cougar was a distant spiritual manifestation of her great-great-grandmother's niece.

Long ago, she had an aunt with a daughter who looked exactly like Blaze.

Dakota had wondered if a White man had been involved in that union, if that explained Blaze's resemblance. Half Sioux, half White. The thought unsettled him—of a White man entering the tribe uninvited, with uninvited advances.

Maka had enlightened him on the night of the feast while Blaze slept alone in the tipi.

"Many, many moons ago," Maka said, "the tribe found a White man left for dead by his family. We nursed him back to health. In gratitude, he worked many years for the people who saved him, for he owed them his life. In time, the chief blessed him with a woman of his choosing, for he had served the tribe well and became part of the clan."

She explained that the White man favored the chief's niece, and she returned his affection. It was considered a blessed union.

As Maka continued, Dakota learned the couple had several children, though some died before one moon. Of all the births, three lived—her mother's mother, her great-aunt, and a great-uncle. Their only brother later died in a buffalo hunt, trampled by a raging herd. It had been a sad day, as the White father had wanted his son to carry on his lineage.

"The girl was more like the White man than Sioux," Maka said, "but no one was ashamed. He was an upstanding, brave man."

"There's more?" Dakota asked, fascinated.

"Yes. These daughters married Sioux men, and the White man's traits weakened with time. When he died, the tribe buried him as a Sioux warrior and never forgot him. Then I see She Cougar, and I remember those eyes—just like *I'sta-to. Blue eyes*, like dark coal stones. Passed down by spirits. Her face, same as my family line."

Maka studied Dakota with hooded, knowing eyes.

"White man face and eyes still in our family. Women marry only Sioux not mean White man eyes not return in babies. You think so, Dakota?"

"It's hard to say much about She Cougar," he replied. "No one knows where she's from. She was found alone on the prairie."

"Hmph. You know little," Maka said, not unkindly. "I know more—from my dreams, and from the past."

Dakota knew Maka was shrewd, insightful, and secretive. He wasn't even sure how much she told her husband, Chief Swift Eagle—only what she believed he needed to know.

Today, he hoped Maka would not share too much with Blaze, nor Blaze with her. These women were bound by past and future alike. Too much truth might alter what was yet to come.

Swift Eagle stood motionless, his expression thoughtful, as if pondering the secrets of life. Dakota stepped closer, standing beside the old chief, waiting for him to speak.

Dakota admired these patient men—leaders who thought deeply, without haste. Men in his own time rushed through life, armed with technology but lacking wisdom. No one pondered life anymore; things simply were.

Swift Eagle saw life as a gift, not something owed. Dakota had learned this by watching the people survive daily hardships, grateful simply to live.

The chief tilted his head. "You must go."

It wasn't a question. Dakota nodded.

"It is good you were here. One day, things will be made right. The gods heard our silent cries, and through you, they will answer."

Dakota was stunned. "You believe I was sent by the gods?"

"Maka dreamed of you before you came," Swift Eagle said calmly. "In her dreams, you save something. The meaning is not yet clear."

Dakota stood still, realizing they had expected him all along.

"You came from nowhere, divided from your people. You knew our ways. My wife is wise. She said no one must harm you." Swift Eagle smiled slightly. "Sometimes she believes she is the chief, not I."

Dakota smiled, knowing the truth of it.

The old Indian continued. "She told only me of a dream many moons ago. Maka dreamed the same dream each night, each one stronger. The day before you arrived, she dreamed of you again—dream so real, she says. Powerful spirits told her a strange warrior would appear, and we should not be frightened. So we welcomed you, not afraid. No other tribal member knew you were not who you said you were."

Swift Eagle and Maka had accepted Dakota, knowing he was not part of this time. He could have asked questions, but what would he have asked? *Hey, I'm here. What needs fixing?*

"You are Sioux, but not Sioux of this time. This is true," the old chief stated.

Dakota heard the statement and knew the old Indian already knew the answer.

"I am Sioux, proud of my heritage. I come from a long line of Sioux far from this time, but that makes me no less Sioux. I do not know why I am here, but there is a mission to complete—one I must figure out. In my future world, a journal with powerful magic was found buried on our lands. It was written by a powerful chief from your time, one who knew how to create the magic that sent me here."

Dakota watched the chief's reaction. Swift Eagle grew pensive, then nodded. The only words he spoke were, "Chief Black Raven."

Maka watched as Blaze approached, noting the uncanny resemblance to her long-ago ancestor. This young woman was part of her tribe, but from a place far, far away. Maka wondered if Blaze knew the truth—if she felt the kinship and connection they shared. She could not speak it aloud for fear the spirits would be angered and life would change for her people now, and her people yet to come.

Blaze and Maka walked toward each other until they stood face to face, and time seemed to stand still, their emotions hovering in the air. Unspoken words passed between them, each wanting to say what they knew, but fearful of disrupting the universe and upsetting the balance of life.

"In my heart—you will always be in my heart," Blaze declared.

Maka nodded. "And you in mine."

"I have learned so much from you, Maka. You are a wise and kind woman."

"She Cougar, you are not the same woman Wind Dancer found alone on the prairie. It is strange. You look Sioux, yet you did not know Lakota words—and soon you learned, like magic."

The old woman tested the gods, lifting her eyes to the sky as if waiting for lightning to strike on a clear day. Nothing happened. Blaze remained silent, leaving it to her.

"Wind Dancer came in my dreams, then appeared as man, in flesh. He knows Lakota. He knows our ways. Still, he is strange to me. I seek answers from past spirits, but even peyote juice no help my visions."

"I would like to—" Blaze began, but Maka raised her hand, stopping her.

"No. I do not question this magic. It is what the gods intend. If you speak of it, you upset the spirits, and something bad will happen. Just know this—you are Sioux. You are us and will always be one of my people."

Blaze's brow furrowed. This woman knew—she knew who Blaze was, but not why she was here. How Blaze longed to wrap her arms around Maka and tell her she was indeed of her blood, a future family member from far into the years ahead.

"I am Sioux, proud of my heritage, proud to know you, and blessed beyond what most deserve. There is much to say that cannot be said, for fear lives could change," Blaze told her.

Blaze feared the ripple effect of even the smallest change. If Maka ceased to exist, then Blaze herself might never exist. For fear of what that could unleash, neither of them said more.

Blaze glanced toward Dakota, knowing it was time. Without speaking, she and Maka walked to where Chief Swift Eagle and Wind Dancer stood. As the four faced one another, the air stilled. No sound came from any direction. In that suspended moment, only the four of them existed. All other people and noises vanished, as if two lifetimes passed between heartbeats before time moved again.

Then sound rushed back in—dogs barking, children laughing, soft winds swishing the flaps of tipis.

Blaze looked around at what she was leaving behind. This was real life—real struggles, real people. She envied them in ways she never expected. Her former needs for malls, Starbucks, pedicures, and future comforts had long faded. This time had given her a gift. Life was so much more than the shallow pleasures her future once offered.

FAR INTO THE FUTURE, at the same moment Blaze and Dakota prepared to leave the tribe, Meda Clark felt the ripple.

A strong gust of wind swept in, and her aging house shuddered as the ground trembled. It wasn't an earthquake—nothing the weatherman would explain. It was something deeper, something that struck her soul.

A shift. A new vibration of life.

Meda stood motionless, gazing out the back door at the open land behind her home, the distant mountains, the vast sky. Yes—something had happened. She couldn't name it, not exactly, but she knew.

It was Blaze.

A tug pulled her outside. Meda reached for the charm at her neck. The metal felt warm, though her skin was cool. She nodded to herself.

Their history was secure.

Whatever occurred, any sacrifice would be worth it—so the Sioux would never disappear from the history they all knew.

THE ENTIRE TRIBE WATCHED as Blaze and Dakota mounted their horses, leading two pack mules laden with supplies. A longing to dismount and stay—no matter the consequences—passed through them both, but they knew, as did Swift Eagle and Maka, this was not a possibility. All of them understood this unspoken truth.

Dark Cloud rode up. "I ride with you. Help if trouble comes, so people not worry."

"It is good you do this, my brother," Dakota said.

Dark Cloud answered, "I do not understand why you have to leave. It makes no sense, and I am not happy to lose my new warrior brother."

Dakota nodded, acknowledging Dark Cloud's concern, but did not answer it.

Blaze lifted her work-worn hand, not caring that her nails were brittle or calloused from labor as a true Indian maiden, and waved to the tribe watching their departure.

As if choreographed, the tribe waved back all at once—all but Maka, who crossed her right hand to her heart and patted it gently, as if to say, *my love goes with you, and my thoughts are never far from where you are.*

⚊ ⚜ ⚊

MAKA WATCHED AS THE horses began moving away from camp. She felt the spirit of her father, Chief Black Raven, shift into her heart, and she knew he would journey with them, guiding them from beyond the spirit world.

Shouts rang out in Sioux—farewells calling on the gods to watch over them—as children ran back and forth, shouting goodbye again and again. Once Blaze and Dakota were well beyond the camp, the children turned back toward home, followed by barking dogs.

The sound of hooves striking the earth and the jangle of items on the pack mules were the only noises as they rode in silence for several miles. Finally, Dark Cloud's voice broke the heavy hush.

"You know where you are headed, my brother?"

Dakota thought only a moment. "Paha Sapa. Winter coming. We stay hidden by the mountain forest."

Dark Cloud grunted his approval. "Yes. Better."

This brave warrior felt emotions he did not understand. He had never missed anyone before. Death and the spirit world he could face—but this was different. It was not death, yet he knew it was forever. Dark Cloud believed Wind Dancer had a higher purpose for his people, and though selfishly he wanted him to stay, he knew he had to let go.

One day, he hoped to meet his warrior brother in the skies, after the spirits called them both home.

What Dark Cloud and Dakota did not know was that this would not be the last time they would speak. Together—the three of them, including Blaze—they would save the Sioux Nation. This was the prophecy one powerful chief had dreamed, seeing visions of a future that might never exist had the three not met.

That powerful chief created magic so future Sioux could return to the past, so one man might live. That man—Dark Cloud—would become the turning point to preserve a Sioux legacy.

For the next hour, they rode in silence. The sun still rode high in the sky when Dark Cloud pulled the reins of his spotted pony and stopped.

"It is my time now to go back. I leave you only for a short time from this life of flesh. One day—not soon, but one day—we shall meet again and rejoice in the spirit world together."

Dakota nodded and reached out. They clasped forearms in a brotherhood grip, each nodding in respect.

"It will be. I'm sure of it," Dakota said.

Dark Cloud gave Blaze a slight nod, then a crooked grin—at least it was a grin for Dark Cloud, who rarely showed a softer side.

"She Cougar, you are right squaw for Wind Dancer."

Blaze nodded, knowing that being Dakota's squaw was far from the truth. There was no need to explain this to the fierce Lakota warrior. He could leave believing whatever he wished.

Dark Cloud turned his pony, struck out at a lope, and gave one final whoop before disappearing behind them.

The hooves of the horses and pack mules were the only sounds as Blaze and Dakota rode on. Occasionally, a crow cawed, or the wind stirred tall prairie grass into a soft swishing. Otherwise, the world was silent. Even the horses seemed unwilling to whinny.

As Blaze rode, her emotions surged, but she refused to cry. She was a strong woman. She knew her fate was not to remain in this time. The sadness etched her face at the thought of never seeing this place or these people again. A darker fear followed—what if another tribe, or white men, attacked them? If they were killed here, would they die forever, never returning to their own time?

Dakota watched her from the corner of his eye. Blaze was sinking into a dark place; her features drooped, her expression growing sullen. Neither of them would ever forget this experience. It had given him profound happiness—living, working, and hunting with the tribe—and pride in who he was. Yet the sorrow of leaving weighed heavily, returning to a world that did not accept the red man.

What had this journey done for her? Dakota knew it had revealed her roots and given her pride in being part Sioux. What he did not yet realize was that this journey had also awakened the woman she had locked away for many years.

As they rode, his thoughts turned to how his feelings for her had changed. He cared for her and wanted her safe and happy. Did he want a future with her? He had never felt this way before.

Get a grip, he told himself. She might not feel the same once they returned to their own time—if they returned. If they did not, they would still have each other, but that thought made him frown. He would never want her to choose him out of necessity. Dakota Kangee wanted her to choose him freely, above all others.

"You okay?" he asked.

"I'm going to be fine." Her voice cracked as she wiped tears she could no longer stop. "I must look a frightful mess."

Dakota looked at her. Though she had not sobbed, her tears had been many. The spark in her eyes was gone, replaced by sadness. Yet she was the most beautiful woman he had ever seen—because she cared deeply about her Sioux heritage and had shown him her heart.

"You look fine, She Cougar, and I think you're an amazing woman."

"Thank you, Wind Dancer." She sniffed, wiped her eyes one last time, squared her shoulders, and inhaled deeply before letting it out.

"Do you have any idea where we're headed, and what we're in for?"

The question revealed her inner strength. She was ready for the next step of the journey.

21

Army Camp in the Black Hills

COOPER WAS TIRED OF fighting Indians and White men. If anyone knew who he truly was, his life would be in danger, so he pretended to be just another part of the team. He watched the skinny, weasel-faced private disappear into a small cluster of tents. He despised most of the men in this camp. Matter of fact, he liked the Injun better than most of the White men. It was unfortunate he had to pretend to be Captain Ardenhert's friend—he loathed the man.

The lieutenant rapped on the tent post.

"Captain, may I come in?"

"Cooper, what can I do for you?" Ardenhert didn't rise. Instead, he leaned back from the maps spread across the table and lifted the cup of whiskey he'd poured, taking a long swig. "Seems I'm drinking more whiskey these days. Must be the stress of this particular—shall we call it—*maneuver*?" He grinned, teeth yellowed and decayed from neglect.

"Yep, Cap. I can see how this mess might make a lesser man take to drink." Cooper inclined his head toward the barrel.

"Sure, sure. By all means, Cooper, sit. You wanna drink too?"

With a wave of his hand, Cooper declined. This was not a social visit, and he had no intention of chatting like old friends.

"Thanks, but no. I want to discuss some things with you, sir."

"What's on your mind, Cooper?"

The lieutenant stared down at his boots for a moment, then looked back up.

"Gene, we've dragged a lot of young scallywag boys and lowlife men out here. Like us, they're deserters—marked for hanging if they don't keep running and looking over their shoulders until they're too old to run anymore. If they leave without the gold you promised, they could turn on you, and you might not live to see any riches yourself. I can take what's coming to me, Gene—but the Injun..." He raised his hand to stop an interruption. "I don't care if the rest of them are at war with the redskins—we're deserters, not soldiers at war with the Injun. His death is not one I want on my conscience. Listen. The Injun's a war chief. I'm sure his tribe thinks he's dead, but he ain't. I'm not saying I believe all the hogwash about him being some powerful shaman, but yeah—I'm a bit spooked."

"Lieutenant—Tom—you worry too much. I ain't gonna kill the old chief. But we need leverage in case we run into a band of Injuns. We can use him to keep from getting skinned."

"Ha. After we turn him over, do you think the tribe won't hunt us down once he tells his story?"

Cooper knew how this would end if left to Ardenhert. Black Raven's death was certain. He would not allow that to happen. He changed the subject before Ardenhert could accuse him of being an Injun lover. If Ardenhert discovered he was a government agent, Cooper was certain the captain would arrange an "accident," and that would be the end of him.

BACK IN HIS TENT, Cooper stretched out on his army cot. He was trapped between priorities—getting the chief back to his people and returning to civilization. Sleep eluded him. Even with his eyes closed, the weight of the past year pressed heavily on his mind.

When the end came—whatever end it was, whether the mission or his life—he would face it with honor and without many regrets. Cooper had no family and would leave no one behind. It should have saddened him, but instead, he felt at peace.

If he left this world for another, that would be fine with him. Perhaps he had spent too much time with the old chief. His ability to speak Lakota meant he and Black Raven could have conversed freely, but Cooper had stayed silent, never revealing his understanding of the language.

Still, the chief spoke—of other worlds far beyond this realm. Cooper never understood why the old Indian spoke only when he was nearby and fell silent when others were present. When others were around, Cooper feigned disdain for the Sioux chief, because Lieutenant T. H. Cooper had to appear tough.

The old Indian saw through Cooper's charade. He knew the real man, and he knew the lieutenant's destiny.

Black Raven closed his eyes and focused on the future. He saw them—the new tribe forming, prosperous and many. This future would exist only if the band of men reached the Black Hills. They needed to get him there. After that, the men were expendable.

He did not need to open his eyes. The visions were clear.

Maka. Swift Eagle. Then Meda. Then Gray Wolf.

And finally—Blaze and Wind Dancer.

They were the future of his people.

His lips curled into a faint smile as warmth spread through him. Black Raven was seeing more than one hundred years ahead—something no chief or medicine man had ever done in this realm of life.

⚶

MEDA RESTED THE JOURNAL on her lap as it opened to a random page. So many years had passed. It was far back in time, yet so near she could almost smell the camp—the dirt, blood, sweat, and unwashed bodies.

She closed her eyes.

The wind whispered. A twig snapped beneath a worn boot. A horse snorted, then whinnied. It was real—too real.

Opening her eyes, she set the journal aside, overcome by the need to go outside. At the back of the house, she pushed open the screen door and froze, lifting her gaze to the sky.

She saw him.

A shadow in the dark—but unmistakable. The chief stood there, holding the journal in his hands. As his image faded into the night, a cool chill passed through her.

⚶

FAR BEYOND THIS WORLD, the chief chanted.

Cooper could hear him.

Meda could feel him.

The spirits could see him.

The snow fell.

22

"THERE." DAKOTA POINTED.

I followed his finger to a mountain range on the far horizon.

"Do you have any clue what mountain range it is?"

"Is it the Paha Sapa?"

"Yes, and this is where I believe our final destination will be."

"Our final destination? Now that sounds scary," I said. The word *final* felt heart-wrenching, dismal.

"Yes, but it is only our final destination in this world, not our future world."

"Maybe." I replied, the single word heavy with doubt. "How much further till we get there?" My eyes never left the mountains.

"We can go for another few hours and then we'll stop and make camp."

Stop and make camp? Those words were scarier than final destination.

A shiver ran through me at the thought of being alone with him, in the dark, with no tribe nearby—just the two of us. Could I be strong? Could I manage this? My only fear was absolute—of him. I could handle wolves, coyotes, perhaps even snakes, but alone at night with Dakota, the handsome Sioux warrior, Wind Dancer, who held my heart captive... I couldn't handle this.

My heart pounded as I realized I was living an Old West love novel—no, not just a novel—I was living it. Except they weren't savages; they were people. My people. My fear subsided, replaced by memory: Maka, the chief, Dark Cloud, and the children in the camp. Even the women who had been mean had grown to respect me. I thought of the thunderclap of understanding, when suddenly, by magic, I comprehended the language. And then Dakota told me the truth. Everything I'd endured... and yet one man could scare the wits out of me? Nothing else frightened me anymore. Except this fear—because I was in love with him.

"You have grown silent, She Cougar. Are you alright?" Dakota asked, using my Sioux name as he gave me a sideways glance.

WHAT WAS SHE THINKING, that so many expressions crossed her face at once? Surprise, fear, pure panic. What could scare her now? He promised to keep his distance. Was she afraid he would attack her in the night, shower her with kisses, caress her? His middle burned when he was near her, and his mind was on high alert for her safety. In his arms, letting him hold her, kiss her fears away, and love her—here was where she would feel safe, if she'd let him protect her.

"Are you okay, Blaze?" he asked for the second time.

I swallowed my panic. I couldn't tell him I was afraid to be alone with him at night. He might read it the wrong way. Oh Lord, if he only would. I shook that thought from my head and said the first thing that came to mind.

"Umm, oh, nothing. I was just remembering the last few months with the tribe."

It wasn't a complete lie; I did think of them and was sad to leave. There was no way I would ever tell him I secretly hoped for one night in his arms before this ended—before I woke up or died. Again, I wondered if I was already dead or, worse, caught in some elaborate dream loop I'd never escape.

What would he do if I became the seductress, the siren? I held back a snicker. The lamb devouring the lion—would that work? Or would the lion snap my neck for trying?

"What's so funny?" he asked, and I jerked, caught off guard. Was he watching my every move?

"Uh, I was just remembering the day I passed out when they gutted that small buffalo," I lied.

"Why is that funny?" He raised an eyebrow, skeptical.

"Oh, I don't know. I'm sure it was comical. I mean, you dragging me by one foot out of the way. They must have thought it hilarious. Poor little half-breed, sick at the sight of blood and guts," I rambled.

He smiled. She was nervous; she rambled when scared. He knew she worried about what could happen when darkness fell.

Minutes passed—or a lifetime. The sun set, the air cooled. It was time to settle in.

"We can camp over there," Dakota said, nodding to a cluster of trees. "Use them for a windbreak and cover. No rain yet, but it's going to get cold, I imagine."

He looked at me sideways. "We have enough blankets, for us. Do you think?" He leered slightly.

My eyes widened. "Uh, y-y-yes, I'm sure we both have plenty, each." I emphasized *each* as if that mattered.

"Then let's get the horses settled and gather wood for a fire. Small fire only."

"Small? Why small?"

His brow furrowed. "To avoid being noticed."

Ducking my head, I let out a hearty belly laugh. "Out here? You think someone's watching us?" Oh lord, I needed this comic relief, but when I looked at him, he was dead serious, and my laughter died instantly.

"The fact is, I'm not sure what to think. Wild animals, sure, but it's the unknown that worries me. How we got here, why we're here... what else could happen? We could wake in the middle of an Egyptian dig, a mummy's tomb, a dinosaur cave, or inventing the wheel."

I blinked. Where had that come from? Why was he rambling?

"Dakota, are you okay?" My hand brushed his arm.

"Yes. Tie up your mare and the packhorses. I'll ride out a half-mile radius to scout. You'll be alone for an hour—will you be okay?"

I gaped at him. Why the sudden sternness?

"Of course. I'll be fine," I half-lied. "I'll gather wood and start a tiny fire." Emphasizing *tiny* mockingly.

He left, and I muttered, "Together." No matter what, we'd face this together.

From the pack mules, I pulled dried buffalo meat and crushed corn. Mixed with wild herbs and water, it would make a decent broth. I arranged the buffalo hides to sit upon, buffalo bone cutlery nearby. Dinner in the wilderness, Wild West style. I laughed. This was not a seduction scene—yet.

The yellow-orange sun dipped behind the western ridge. Soon, firelight and a trillion stars would fill the sky. I hugged myself. "If only," I whispered.

Kneeling, I stirred the corn broth, more pasty than intended. Standing, I turned—and froze. Dakota stood there, breathing quietly. My heart caught.

"How long have you been standing there?"

"Long enough to wonder what you meant by 'if only.' If only what, Blaze?" Dakota stoked the small fire, poking at the flames.

"Oh, you know. If only we were home—steak, potatoes, fresh salad, apple pie." My tone was flippant.

"Hmm. I think this will hit the spot. Filling, but not too much." He inhaled the aroma of the cooking corn and herbs. "Besides, if we were back in our own time, we might not be sharing this meal together. That's the best part, don't you agree?"

My hands shook, spilling a bit of broth over the leaves I'd used for a bowl.

"I'll be back in a minute. I, um, I need to... you know." I stumbled toward the trees for privacy.

———— ෴ ————

Dakota saw my hands shaking as I hurried off. I was nervous. Could I be more nervous than he was? The way I had touched him a moment ago, it was like fire to him, but he had held still as it scorched him.

He lay back, propping himself up on his elbows, pretending to survey the area as if keeping watch. He had scouted the area; there was no danger for us tonight—not from wolves or coyotes. The real danger was each other tonight, and that was scary enough.

*

I sat at the base of a tree, knowing I couldn't hide there long. He would come looking for me, so I had to get it together and remember that one day soon, I'd wake from this nightmare.

I couldn't stop the grin from spreading across my face; what a wonderful nightmare I was having. I'd be safer with wolves. Who was I kidding? I felt like the wolf, wanting to pounce on him—my fear was his rejection. I was a woman who'd been broken before, and with all I'd endured, I thought I could handle it. Or could I?

*

Dakota thought he could handle it. He watched for her to reappear from the trees. If she didn't want him, it wouldn't be the first time he'd experienced rejection. He hadn't played any trump cards with a woman in a long time. Was this the right moment to see if he was still as charming as he thought? He knew he didn't want to just take what he could get—he wanted a relationship with a woman brave enough, worthy enough for the best. Was he that man? Could he be the best for her?

I returned, sitting beside him and handing him the bowl. My fingers grazed his, sending a jolt through him. He knew he needed me; he didn't just want me—he needed me.

I handed him dried meat, suggesting he dip it in the broth. He nodded approval, and I mirrored his actions, tasting the meat and savoring the moment.

～ ⚜ ～

SOMEWHERE ON THE OTHER side of the Paha Sapa foothills, a camp of unkempt soldiers slept. An old chief sat in a dank, smelly tent, shackled to a heavy wooden stake, and he closed his eyes, smiling. He could sleep tonight; his soul and mind were at peace. The future was unfolding as it should.

～ ⚜ ～

"MORE WOOD ON THE fire, we need it bigger." Dakota added larger logs.

"I thought you wanted the fire smaller?"

"Yes, but we need it big enough to die down slowly. No tipi tonight. Less to break down, we can leave sooner. It will keep us warm as it dies down."

"You're right. Get warm first. I have extra hides." I carried more hides and laid mine next to his.

"You don't mind if I sleep closer, do you? I'll feel less afraid knowing you're near." I smiled, teasing.

"Okay, we can pull this together like one bed," he said, testing me.

DARN HIM. I WAS caught off guard. I'd been thinking about so many things—what I wanted, what I feared. I wanted real. And now I was here, facing it. I mumbled to myself, working through my feelings.

"So, I'm going to sleep while you take the first watch."

"What? The first watch?" I snapped my head up.

He laughed. "Yeah. I thought I'd take the late watch. Early start tomorrow. Weather can change, we need better cover fast."

I was dumbstruck. Our sleep schedules didn't overlap, but he knew. Now I was fuming. Darn it, I'd been outplayed. But I had to stay composed.

"Fine, I'll take the first watch, keep the fire going, and the coyotes away." I moved a buffalo hide and wrapped a blanket around me.

"Any instructions?"

"No, but wake me if anything happens."

"I won't be a crybaby," I said, crossing my arms.

His breathing deepened as he slept, and I sighed. I had time to think. Dakota had offered me everything but himself. What would it have been like if we'd met after college, before being displaced here? My heart felt heavy. If he never noticed the real me...

A distant coyote howled, and I shivered, pulling the hides tighter.

Just as I drifted off, night sounds jolted me awake. I added sticks to the fire, glanced at Dakota—still asleep, peaceful, undisturbed. I watched him, wondering about his life before all this, fighting to keep my eyes open.

23

FUNNY, IT WASN'T COLD yet, just a tad windy. Winter hovered at the edge of each day, and indifference had settled into my heart. I'd become almost robotic, resisting any closeness to Dakota. We talked only when necessary and rode in silence. Any instruction he gave, I followed wordlessly. When he said stop, I stopped. Whenever he directed me, I rode, slept, and ate. I nodded, shrugged, or shook my head—no longer caring.

Five days—what happened to reaching our destination in three to five days? That was three days ago, and now it was day six, no closer to the mountains. Dakota mumbled complaints, but I didn't speak. Oh Lord, this nightmare wouldn't end. Dakota was friendly, yet standoffish—not interested in me—and I was no seductress. If he wanted me, he'd make a move. After that first night, I'd waited, hoped—but nothing. Disappointment flooded my heart. Not talking to him was the safest choice.

Blaze had stopped speaking, so he had too. They only spoke when necessary. He tried small, friendly conversation, but she stonewalled every attempt. Dakota grew frustrated with the extra days added to the journey; silence gnawed at him. It wasn't normal. Women had to talk. They acted like robots, and he was sick of the routine. Each night, when they stopped, he gathered twigs and brush for the fire. They would eat, she would excuse herself to wash and relieve herself.

Sometimes, I took longer because I needed to cry—but never in front of him. I tried to stifle it, but tears still stained my face. Not once did he comment, and I assumed he simply didn't care.

Each time she returned, Dakota knew she'd been crying but couldn't understand why. She had no interest in him—or so he thought. Maybe fear kept her silent, but that was ridiculous. Blaze had completely closed herself off, and he wasn't sure how to break through.

The first white flake fell unnoticed. Then, as the wind picked up and small flurries swirled, I murmured, "Snow... there's snow."

Dakota called my name, but I was lost in thought. "Blaze! Blaze!"

Stopping my pony, I turned back. He'd dismounted. Reluctantly, I rode toward him.

"Did you not hear me, woman?" he asked, offering his hand. I ignored it, sliding off the horse. The wind whipped my braids across my face, fringe flapping in the gusts. I waited for him to say something—but it didn't matter. I had no choices—not in this life, not in this realm—and I'd accepted my fate.

Dakota surveyed the area, eyes landing on a small thicket. Inclining his head, he led his mount and the packhorses there. I followed, glancing at the gray sky. Was the weather changing?

Inside the thicket, there was enough cleared space for camp, and tonight it would be cold enough for a small tipi. He untied straps and began setting it up while I watched.

"Why a tipi tonight?" I finally spoke, voice quivering.

He didn't look up. "It'll be colder tonight."

Was I worried I'd have to share such close quarters with a man I pretended to despise? His job was to keep me safe—at least until he could understand what the future might hold.

We ate, and I huddled close to the fire, thankful for the trees blocking the wind. Proximity to him wasn't necessary for warmth—I reminded myself of that. I sat with my knees drawn up, rocking slightly, thinking of a song from the future. A Beatles song, "Let It Be." Just let it alone. Accept what comes. What one wanted and what one got were never the same.

For crying out loud, I was more than a hundred years from my real life—was this what I wanted? I frowned, staring into the dying flames.

"Are you ever going to talk to me again?" Dakota snapped a twig into the fire.

I shrugged, keeping my face impassive. Crying wasn't an option tonight; it was too cold. He walked to the tipi, pulling back the flap.

"We need rest and to start before daybreak. Winter is coming; we need to move faster."

His irate tone didn't surprise me. I complied like an obedient soldier, ducking into the tiny tipi, claiming the edge of the bed. I would not let our bodies touch. I would tune out his breathing and lay still. Stiff, I stretched out straight.

Dakota lay on his side, back to mine. Too close. When he rolled onto his back, I froze. Only when I knew he was asleep did I move again, rolling onto my right side. I looked at him—tired, peaceful, long lashes framing his closed eyes. His full lips parted with each breath. Raven-colored hair pulled back in a ponytail. I touched my own head, knowing my hair needed washing and brushing. Dakota didn't smile in his sleep—but he didn't need to. I knew his smile and what it did to my heart.

One teardrop escaped. Then another. As I reached to wipe them away, his hand caught mine. His dark brown eyes opened, meeting mine.

"My Iye Igmu'watogla, my cantkiya... please don't cry." His hand brushed my tears. Rolling onto his left side, he faced me, nose-to-nose.

"Please... talk to me. Let me in." His right hand pressed over my heart, eyes never leaving mine.

I stammered, "I—I, uh, I—"

Dakota didn't care if he startled me. It was time. His left arm slid under me, right arm around me, pulling me close. He trailed kisses up my throat, to my chin, and finally to my lips. I exhaled, my body relaxing.

He broke the kiss briefly, holding me tight.

"No, please," I half-whimpered, "don't stop."

"Oh, my cantkiya, we aren't stopping. We're just getting started."

He lay me flat, rising over me, eyes locked on mine. I untied the top of my beaded dress, revealing skin for him to kiss. He removed his shirt. We were soon skin-to-skin. I arched my neck, giving him access from my breasts to my throat to my lips.

Fingers entwined around his neck, I drew him close. He swung us, me ending up on top. Blankets tossed aside, our bodies sparked heat of their own.

Half-dressed, I tried to pull away, but he held me. "No, you aren't getting away."

I giggled. "No, silly... my dress. I want it off."

He relented, letting me slip out of it. Dakota paused, taking in my full form, desire growing—not just for my body, but for me.

"It's my turn, Wind Dancer," I called, grinning as he disrobed. Laying me down, we faced each other. Slow, sensual movements—a dance of fire. Our joining was complete combustion, the prairie wind rivaling our own howls.

Satisfied, spent, he lay atop me. I welcomed his weight, his protection. Dakota moved over, pulling me into a spooning embrace under a blanket. We slept for hours, passion waking us again.

⁓

THE OLD INDIAN CHIEF smiled, leaning against his pole, shackled but elated. The future—of him, his people, his tribe—was secured.

Blaze had overcome her fears. She would now know what she had to do. When the time came, her woman's heart would guide her.

24

THE NEXT FEW DAYS we traveled during the day. Winter slowed our progress, but we didn't care. More time together was a gift. Our nights were filled with fire and passion, each one better than the last, and in this realm, nothing would ever be the same.

I was sure this was Heaven, and nothing could taint the feelings we shared—surreal, wonderful, and intense. I sensed Dakota's protectiveness, and I felt his worry. He didn't have to say it; I knew he feared what might be waiting for us. And it was my concern too, what the future held for us, what we were meant to accomplish or correct.

Too bad there wasn't a how-to manual on time travel. Danger was inevitable. No matter what, he promised to keep me safe, and silently, I vowed I'd never blame him. I understood this was out of his control.

"Let's rest the horses here," Dakota said, dismounting.

I pulled my horse to a stop, shivering as the wind whipped my hair across my face.

"How much further, do you think?"

"Less than sixty miles," he replied.

I quickly calculated: a few more days, and we'd arrive. Would our time together then be limited?

After making camp and eating just enough to satisfy us, another desire pressed closer—more intimate, more personal. Hand in hand, we ducked into the tipi. I sat beside him on the buffalo hides. He put his arm around me, letting me lean against him, my head on his shoulder.

"Would we ever have gotten to this point back in our own time, do you think?" I asked.

"You know... I don't know. But if this were the future, I would love you."

Love. Did he just say it? I stiffened—not at the word, but at its weight. He had declared he loved me.

His arm tightened around me.

"Blaze, I didn't want to scare you," he said, his voice rough but soothing.

I turned my face to him. "No matter what the future holds, I'm not worried about my feelings... or even yours." I paused.

"But—" he started.

"No. There are no other issues other than that we don't know what each second brings, or how this will end. If it ends... well, maybe things won't be the same in our real time. I don't want declarations or promises," I finished.

He understood. Right here, right now, he had me, and he would do whatever it took to keep me. His lips touched mine lightly, warm and tender. With every second, the kiss held, soft and lingering.

Facing him fully, I let him cover me with his body. Our kiss deepened—not just physical, but mental, intimate in ways neither of us had experienced. I traced his face with my fingers, kissed his lips, his ear, his cheek, his neck. His hands slid through my braid, loosening it, as he nuzzled my neck. Dakota buried his face and heart into me.

Satisfied, without pushing to the full extent, we rested, me in his arms, covered by hides. The moon shone bright, and hours later, naked, touching, loving, passion ignited between us like a fire ready to consume. Somewhere along this trek, I had become adept at loving him, knowing him in a short time.

I teased him seductively until he could no longer resist. His body pressed mine with unbridled passion. We slept, spent, and at dawn, we were ready to face the next day. Strange how little sleep we'd taken, yet our energy doubled. More than ever, we felt a purpose—a tangible purpose for each other—and that was enough.

The days and nights repeated, each ritual blissful, each day a gift. Time passed. Finally, we reached what we deemed our destination: the foothills of the Paha Sapa. Beyond them loomed the dark, foreboding mountains, filled with the uncertainty of our future.

Back Home, Far Away

"Sam, we don't have much time," Meda said, beckoning him forward. He took a chair backward, facing the others.

"Because of the white men long ago, we lost most of our land, our fortune, our honor, and pride. What is happening now won't change our lives—it will ensure our history," Sam said. "Many lives were lost. Many warriors fought to keep the Sioux Nation from vanishing. Now, we must make sure history stays unchanged."

Meda listened intently, grasping the circle-within-the-circle amulet in her hands. "I know strange things are happening with Blaze and Dakota. It is with them that our legacy will remain, not end in history books. Without them, history would fade."

Blackie leaned over to the window. "I haven't seen a thunderbolt that means a thing, but there's been rain lately."

"Maybe it's a peyote aftereffect," Pete said, sheepishly. "We acted like teenagers, doing that stuff. But seeing what we saw... it feels important, doesn't it?"

"No," Meda said. "We've been given a chance unlike any other—to make sure our ancestors live on in history. It's time," she said, reaching for her amulet. "We do what we must and see what happens."

Sam raised an eyebrow. "You mean old magic, Meda?"

"Yes. The power is in our amulets, but they must be joined to release their force."

Sam placed his amulet next to hers and looked at Pete. "Do you have the one father left you?"

Pete took his sun amulet from his key ring and placed it on the table.

"Blackie?" Meda asked.

He removed a thin braided leather rope, revealing the arrowhead marked with Chief Black Raven's sign.

The four artifacts—circle-within-a-circle, golden feather, sun amulet, and arrowhead—lay together for the second time in history. Centuries ago, these Sioux amulets had been joined to unleash a power shaking the Paha Sapa. Once more, they would unite.

Meda pressed the four together. The circle-within-a-circle at the center, others touching three sides. She chanted.

Sam nodded and chanted, followed by Blackie and Pete.

The glow started dim, then brightened. The arrowhead revealed a warrior's face, the feather gleamed gold, the sun sparkled red. Together, they formed one powerful piece.

"Powerful magic," Meda said, cradling it.

"How in the—what?" Pete faltered.

Blackie leaned in, wide-eyed.

"This ritual is in the journal," Meda said, smiling. "It shows how to bring them back. I just didn't connect it before."

She opened the journal to the last pages, reading the pictures and translations aloud:

"Our people, our nation, with these two we rise again—to have what could be lost, to keep our honor, our pride, and our people's history. To save our history, one from our future must come back; if not, the Sioux nations' history will be lost, and our lives changed forever. Two shall be joined, creating a life to restore our people to greatness. If one should die before that time, history itself will change."

Then, a thunderbolt struck, long and loud, shaking Meda's house. It was magic—more powerful than they had ever imagined—and it unfolded before their eyes.

25

WE'D REACHED THE BASE of the Black Hills. Then everything that'd happened—every moment we'd shared—flashed through my mind. Would everything we'd grown, every sweet moment, end right here?

I grimaced at the thought.

"Keep alert," he said as he dismounted.

I did as he did and climbed off my horse. It was close to sunset, but there was still enough light for us to get our bearings. There wasn't much to explore—just mountains, hills, and trees. So, we rested just below where our future Mount Rushmore Monument would one day stand, albeit far into the future.

"Do you remember your history lessons, Dakota?" I asked as I piled kindling on top of the large logs he'd gathered.

"What lessons? Be more specific, would ya?"

"I guess all the stories about General Custer, the Black Hills, the gold, and the Sioux. I'm not sure what day it is, and we aren't sure of the year, so all these what-ifs keep popping into my head." Squatting, I struck the flint to get a fire going.

He paused mid-motion while arranging the stakes for the tipi. Several minutes passed before he spoke—or even moved. "Blaze, I think you asked the right question."

"I did? What question is that?" Sitting on top of the hide, I wrapped myself in a blanket as the wind turned chillier with the coming night.

"Well, here we are, right smack in the middle of where all that craziness happened. I know the two of us aren't conquering any army, saving Custer, or hauling gold back to the Sioux. But what if this time-travel stuff means we're here to keep history from changing?" Dakota stopped and looked at me.

I shook my head slowly. "I didn't care at all about Sioux history. I hated it. Dad went on and on about it, and now I wish I'd listened. He'd be happy to know I've learned to love this part of me—to embrace who I am. But what if we make a mistake? What if we change history and then we never exist?" My eyes filled with worry. If I didn't exist—and this was the past—how could I even be here right now? It was all too crazy.

~ ⚌ ~

DAKOTA WAS CONTEMPLATIVE BEFORE he spoke. He was amazed by her intuitive insight; it was something he hadn't considered. "I never thought about us being here to trip up one occurrence—to make sure something happens a certain way to safeguard our Sioux legacy."

"One thing's for certain—we're going to do *something*. Otherwise, why would we be here?" she said. "Lord only knows why I'm here. You I understand, but me? That's still a mystery. I disassociated myself from the Sioux and that part of me years ago."

She looked both saddened and angered, as if miffed at her future self for being so callous about who she was and where she came from in the long line of Sioux people.

Dakota studied her face, wishing he'd known her better in their future. "How do you feel now that you've seen this side of Sioux life?"

"Being here now, I'm not just honored to be Sioux—I'm proud to be Sioux. Seeing how hard their lives were, yet how they thrived on family and unity... I can't imagine them not fighting for life and for what's theirs. This is their land, and the government shoved them off it. Over the years, they've lost everything—not just wealth, but lives. Even when they tried to be peaceful, someone was always there to blame the Indian." A tear slipped down her cheek. "It doesn't seem fair now."

It warmed his heart to know she felt such a strong connection to her Sioux side. Not that it changed how he felt—if anything, it only reinforced it. Dakota wasn't afraid of losing anything but her.

"Darlin', you're here now. And who knows—you and I could be changing things. The futures we have years from now may be different." He slid next to her and wrapped his arms around her. "Let's go inside the tipi and warm up."

They crawled inside, warmth enveloping him—and not just from the fire. He didn't have to be a soothsayer to see where this night might lead once they slid beneath the horse blankets.

———— ⚓ ————

NOT FAR AWAY, SOLDIERS huddled around several small fires burning north of Blaze and Dakota's campsite. Chief Black Raven sat on a threadbare blanket, shielding himself from the chilly night air. Chains bound his ankles, his hands secured with leather straps—the shackles removed. Captain Ardenhert had decided the old chief was too frail to escape; even if he tried, he wouldn't make it a hundred yards before collapsing.

If only he knew the truth. The old Indian had traveled years through time and space without ever leaving camp.

T. H. Cooper sat beside the captain, watching the chief as he drank whiskey to ward off the cold. "What's the plan?"

Captain Ardenhert groaned. "Guess we try to mine or blast for gold. We can't stay long if we blast—not sure where the rest of the outfit is or how much time we've got."

He scanned the camp. If he had a second chance, he would've chosen smarter, stronger men.

Cooper watched the disgust flicker across the captain's face, knowing Ardenhert despised the men under his command—men just like Cooper: greedy.

The chief sat only a few feet away, his dark, knowing eyes following their interaction. As the two white men talked, Black Raven felt safe enough to travel once more. With closed eyes, he chanted silently, willing his spirit free. Once unbound, he floated southeast toward the hills—and there he saw it: a tiny fire.

He was with them. He felt what they shared, the heat radiating between them. Patiently, Black Raven waited.

"WILL IT ALWAYS BE like this with us?" I exhaled, placing my palm against his chest, my fingers splayed over his heart. I smiled at the rapid beat, knowing I'd caused it.

He didn't answer—not with his usual smart-ass reply. Instead, his expression shifted.

"Blaze, get dressed. We need to go outside."

He was already pulling on his breeches and shirt, panic jolting through me. I dressed quickly, trusting his instincts.

Outside the tipi, we stood side by side. The world was unnaturally silent—not even an insect stirred.

I started to speak, but he pressed a finger to his lips. Taking my hand, he led me to the horses.

"We have to leave now," he whispered, throwing a blanket over his horse and slipping on the bridle. He mounted, then pulled me up behind him.

"What are we doing—leaving everything? My horse too?" I breathed.

"I can't explain it. Something's telling me we have to go. Now."

He nudged the horse forward.

Black Raven followed, his spirit merging with Wind Dancer's mind, guiding him.

At first, Dakota didn't see it. The trees were thicker here, but as he rounded the base of the Black Hills, he spotted a tiny light—a campfire. He placed a hand on my leg and leaned back to whisper.

"Not a peep."

He dismounted, then helped me down, motioning for me to stay still. Fear tightened my lips when I saw the fire.

Dakota tied the horse quietly among the brambles. Hand in hand, we moved through the darkness, moonlight our only guide.

Above us, Black Raven urged us forward.

⁕

PRIVATE GRUBER SNICKERED, TOSSING a stick of dynamite from hand to hand. "This little beauty could make us rich."

"I don't think so—not till the captain says," his companion hissed. "You wanna blow us up in the dark?"

Gruber sneered, pulling out matchsticks. "I don't mind blowin' you up too."

The fuse hissed.

The blast was small—too small. Both men emerged shaken but unharmed.

"Must've got wet," Gruber muttered.

They slunk back toward camp, unaware of who watched.

"WHY ARE WE OUT here?" I whispered.

"I felt something," Dakota said. "Something telling me the time's come."

The ground trembled. I squeezed his hand.

"Is this the end?" I wondered aloud.

"It's not nature," he said. "It's man."

"White man?"

He grinned in the darkness.

Go, go back.

The words trickle through Dakota's head.

"We need to get back to camp." He pulled her from where she stood. "I swear I feel like I'm hearing voices. Something just told me in Lakota to leave."

She yanked at his hand. "Uh, I may be just as crazy as you, Dakota. Did it say go, go back?"

"You heard it too?"

"Yeah, but I'm not scared. This entire situation and the craziness we've experienced—" She trailed off, not finishing.

He understood what she meant.

Dakota screwed his face up. "But why now? Why are we both hearing voices?"

Chief Black Raven's spirit held his head up higher in a majestic, chiefly way: *Because I so wished it.*

26

As it had grown darker, the men in the camp were shaken by the small blast, aware that someone had just marked their location.

"What the hell!" Captain Ardenhert jerked open the tent flap and rushed outside.

Cooper was just coming from the back of the camp, gun cocked and aimed at... well, he wasn't sure at what.

"What in God's name, Gene? Someone already setting off dynamite?" Cooper un-cocked his gun, easing the hammer back into place.

"I'm going to kick someone's ass," Gene snarled, looking around to see who wasn't in the camp. "Everyone, get out here on the double!" he screamed. His face turned red with pure anger—so livid the vein in his forehead seemed ready to pop.

Men ran from all directions, scrambling to get front and center, not wanting to incur the captain's wrath. They had all suffered it before.

"I'll check on the prisoner," Cooper said, leaving Ardenhert waiting for his bedraggled unit to muster.

Cooper reached the tent, his Colt revolver cocked and ready. With caution, he pulled the flap open, sticking the barrel in first. "I'm coming in, and I'm ready to shoot to kill if anyone makes a wrong move." He entered, gun in hand, prepared to act at a moment's notice.

Reddons was standing watch over the chief, who looked as though he'd just awoken.

"What the tarnation is happening? I heard a blast, and now you're announcing you're gonna shoot if anyone moves?" he squeaked.

"Where is the other private?" Cooper noted it was only Reddons and a sleeping Injun.

"Went to relieve hisself," Reddons replied.

"You go assemble with the other men."

Reddons was more than happy to oblige. He was sick of watching that old Injun sleep.

Cooper sat on an old crate and stared at the sleeping chief. How in the world had he slept through the blast and all the yelling?

Black Raven's inner spirit was traveling back, in a hurry. He knew the blast would alert the camp, and he did not want anyone coming into the tent who might be smarter than the idiot men who had been guarding him. They assumed he was sleeping; fools were easy to fool. These idiots might even assume he was dead. A man without his spirit was just a flesh-and-bone body, devoid of his life's essence. If they thought him dead, they might try to bury him, as White men did their own dead.

Cooper continued to stare, wondering if the old Indian had died in his sleep. He didn't appear dead, but he didn't seem to be breathing either. The old war chief might be better off dead. Then again, he hoped like heck he wasn't.

"Hey, what's going on? Where's Reddons?"

The private who'd drawn watch with Reddons walked in, and Cooper leveled his Colt at him.

"What the... hey, what the hell, Lieutenant? Aim that Colt anywhere but my face, would ya?" the private gasped, holding up his hands.

"Get out there with the captain and the others. Someone set off a blast, and the captain is hopping mad. He'll think it was you since you aren't out there with the rest of the men," Cooper barked.

The unkempt private backed out. Cooper's glare was not one he wanted to turn his back on.

Cooper needed to think fast. He needed supplies and horses before he took off. First, he wanted to see what Ardenhert was up to, then plan his next move.

⚊⚊ ⚌ ⚊⚊

BLACK RAVEN'S SPIRIT RETURNED to his body and stirred. Opening his eyes, they adjusted to the darkness of the tent. Alone, no guards—this was good. The blast had caused the men to gather; he was sure their White chief was on a White man's warpath now.

The blast in the hills had ruined everything, and time was of the essence. What to do, what to do... he had to act fast. Ardenhert stopped pacing, turning back to the men, knowing there was only one thing he could do. He pointed to six of them.

"You guys go get the pack mules ready, and gather the dynamite, guns, and ammo." He paused for half a beat. "And be damn careful with the explosives. Now get to it."

They scrambled. He ordered the next group to break down camp and snuff out fires. Others were to get the tools needed for the caves, and all the kerosene lanterns filled and ready. The camp became a beehive of activity—rushed activity—as the captain's last words rang out: "Get it done, and without a lot of noise, boys."

—✣—

THE CHIEF LISTENED. HE could feel the activity in the camp but did not hear it. His eyes now focused in the darkness. It would not be long, and he knew they would be there to take him. He did not have time to float his spirit out again; he would have to trust the people in the future.

The captain had the men running in all directions, giving Cooper the advantage of no eyes watching him. Gathering his knapsack, he began filling it with dried beef jerky, ammo, and another Colt revolver. He grabbed his shotgun and four metal canteens—full of water to avoid an extra trip to the shallow river nearby. Time was running out, for him and for the chief, so he hurried.

Slipping on his threadbare coat and grabbing his shotgun, Cooper thought. Taking up his army knapsack, he packed a dry shirt, socks, a chaw of tobacco, a worn army blanket, and flopped it over the flap. Slipping on both straps, he hoisted it onto his back. Amid the feet and mumbling around him, no one noticed him slip away. As long as Ardenhert didn't see him, he would get out with no questions asked.

Grabbing two more shotguns, Cooper packed another empty knapsack with more supplies, slipped it over his arms, and ducked out of the tent to fetch the old chief.

Everyone was busy following the captain's orders, scrambling to get shovels and pickaxes to dig, and dynamite to blast holes inside the cave to find gold faster. No one bothered to check on the old Indian chief. Perfect. This worked out well.

Cooper squatted, his face inches from the Indian's. Dark black eyes met blue eyes. They held the stare for a quick minute, then he nodded. The chief nodded back. In that moment, the chief realized freedom waited beyond this army campsite.

Lieutenant Cooper helped him up, ensuring the man was strong enough to make the getaway. Black Raven stood tall, no wobble in his step. Chained up all these months, he had assumed the old chief would be feeble. Cooper raised an eyebrow, surprised at his strength.

"Still strong for an old man," the chief said in Lakota.

"So I see," Cooper responded in Lakota.

The chief's brows rose in wonder. Tilting his head sideways, he nodded with a slight grin. He had not known Cooper spoke Lakota. This revelation was a pleasant surprise. Cooper was always more than he seemed, and now Black Raven was certain of it.

⁜

WE BEGAN GATHERING ONLY what we needed for survival. While Dakota packed a few hides atop one of the horses, he stopped when he saw me standing still. My arms rose, and my hands covered my face as I tried to hide the tears.

Dropping the hides, he ran to me. I turned, wrapping my arms around his neck and laying my head on his shoulder as I cried.

"It will be okay, my Iye Igmu'watogla. Please don't cry. Believe me, I won't let anything happen to you." He held me close, whispering the words.

"I'm not worried about getting hurt. I'm worried you will disappear, and we will be lost from—from each other," I stuttered through tears. "What if this ends, and it's like it never happened? Dakota, I love you and never could have dreamed I would love again. I never want this dream to end—any of it." Sniffling, I turned my head to see his face.

"I assure you, us, we will never end. My love for you is just the beginning. Right now, though, we need to focus on what needs doing and get moving. I feel the climax of why we were sent here is happening, and we must be ready." He squeezed my arm.

I agreed. The pinnacle was occurring, and I would have to be strong to face whatever might come next.

We stashed our supplies in a small cave, covering the opening with brush and limbs. If nothing happened, these supplies would be for the future. *Future*—what an underrated word; one should live in whatever present they were in, because this was the true glory of the moment.

"No matter what happens, no matter where we end up, Blaze, I want you to know I have never wanted a woman more, never loved a woman deeper than I have you, and I promise to do whatever it takes to make a future for us together. And somehow, I think this was a backward trip to get you to your roots, and me to you. We, you and I, here, together... and I can't see what we can do to change the future or what we need to do to make it right. So—" He stopped, his arms snaking up to hold me tight, kissing me with such pure passion it shook me to my toes.

THE CHIEF AND COOPER were on horses, heading away from the camp. Another commotion resembled an ant farm—ragtag soldiers scrambling to avoid the captain's anger or the line of fire.

Cooper and the chief rode in silence through the wooded area toward the east, back toward Sioux lands, away from the lunatics, the gold digging, and exploding dynamite. They couldn't run the horses yet, so they crept quietly, using the treed areas for cover.

It amazed Cooper; the captain thought he could hurry and find his riches. They had been mining and digging without dynamite for weeks, with nothing to show for it but a few insignificant nuggets of gold. Now the men, exhausted from labor, were itching to blast.

It was time to blow up a mountain to get what he came for when Ardenhert remembered he had the chief—his ace in the hole. Where was Cooper?

He looked but saw no sign of the lieutenant.

"Don't start blasting yet. Wait until I get back." Ardenhert ordered, walking to the tent where they held the chief. Untucking the flap, he ducked in—and found it empty. He raced out, face red, yelling for Cooper at the top of his lungs, charging toward Cooper's tent.

The lieutenant was gone too. That bastard had taken the chief with him. They couldn't have gone far. In a running stomp, he got back to his horse, ordering four men he trusted to go after Cooper and the chief and bring them back.

"And don't kill 'em. I want Cooper's head, and we need the old chief alive too."

They took off while Ardenhert and the rest of his weary men headed toward the caves of the Black Hills on the northern side.

DAKOTA GOT ON HIS horse, then pulled me up so we could ride double, heading northward and up the hills. It would be harder, but this ensured we wouldn't be separated if trouble arose. We left the other horses loosely secured; if commotion occurred, they could break away. If it got that bad, survival would far outweigh concern for extra horses.

The ragtag dragoon misfits headed north. Cooper and Black Raven headed east, while Major Bellamus, chasing the AWOL dragoons, had his camp just south of the Black Hills. Far into the future, Meda, Sam, Pete, and Blackie stood outside on Meda's back porch. All but the Major, Cooper, and the chief faced the North Star.

I could feel so much going on; it was beyond explanation. An impending feeling sent a shiver up my spine and tightened my arms around Dakota's waist.

Dakota felt my grip tighten and his jaw muscles flex. He wished he could ride away, taking me to safety, but they had to keep moving. They needed to get this done—whatever *this* was.

Years into the future:

Meda began her chant. As her chant rose to a crescendo, Sam joined, then Pete, and finally Blackie. It was a chant of the Lakota Sacred Spirit.

"Ly-O Lay Ale Loya," Meda chanted with expression, and Blackie followed with fervor. Sam started the Ghost Dance, and Pete followed suit.

As the clouds rolled in, the sky grew darker, and although it was well past sundown, the night deepened in an odd way. The chanting and dancing reached a peak, and a starburst lit the sky.

***

I SAW THE SHOOTING stars—several, more like a light show. Dakota halted our horse, looking up.

The sky blazed as if Halley's Comet had tripled and come at rapid speed, so bright one had to shield their eyes.

"Whatever is going on, I feel Aunt Meda's presence," I whispered.

Dakota nodded wordlessly. Whatever was happening was surreal.

"We need to speed up and get closer to the camp by the caves we saw earlier." Feeling time slip away, he kicked the horse, and we continued at a faster pace, jolted from my star-gazing trance.

⁓ ⚶ ⁓

THE SMALL GROUP OF Sioux elders from the future stared at the amulet and heard a thunderclap. They watched as the new amulet turned red like the sun, then black like night before glowing brightly again. It was happening. It was imminent.

⁓ ⚶ ⁓

COOPER AND BLACK RAVEN traveled at a faster pace, attempting to distance themselves from the motley deserters filling the caves in search of fortune. Black Raven spotted the bursts in the sky a second before Cooper and stopped his steed abruptly, looking up into the heavens.

To the unknowing eye, it might have looked like large shooting stars, but Black Raven knew it was far more. The old chief saw the souls of the past as they shot upward, scattering in a hundred directions.

Cooper nearly fell from his horse as he stopped short, almost running into Black Raven's steed. He berated the old Indian in his native tongue for stopping without warning but glanced up when he saw the chief staring into the sky.

What in the devil—the sky was filled with shooting stars... or spirits?

The lieutenant rubbed his eyes and looked again. Yep, it was something, but no ghosts. Perhaps thin twirls of clouds or a high updraft.

"Wasichu kawapi Wangi," Black Raven said.

"White man is chased by spirits," Cooper repeated in English, looking first at the chief, then back up into the sky.

If he hadn't already believed in Indians and their magic, this was certain proof. He wasn't a man who indulged in mumbo jumbo, but this surpassed his imagination.

"Let's go," Cooper said, swatting the hind end of the chief's horse.

The Indian lurched as the horse took off, grabbing the reins. "It is time to get back to my people," he announced, smiling.

Cooper followed, still in awe of what he'd witnessed.

The frazzled soldiers outside the caves saw the shooting stars—nothing unusual for night—but they ignored them, continuing to dig and pick for treasure.

Less than a mile away, dragoon troops led by Major Bellamus discussed the amazing display of stars bursting in the sky. The major was livid about this new assignment; he had more pressing matters. When he reached the renegade soldiers, a lesson awaited them.

"Humph, soldiers, my great, fat fanny," he spat out his chaw of tobacco. Rinsing his mouth with creek water and a swig of whiskey, he set off to impose order.

27

"I FEEL WE'RE HEADED to the end of our journey," Dakota commented as we rounded a bend, spying the small cave we'd seen earlier.

"You believe that, don't you? Why?" I frowned. I wasn't ready for this to end—not now, never.

"Because I have a terrible feeling," he paused, "and a feeling of elation, too."

I understood, even though I didn't want it to be true. We'd been together every day since I'd been shot back to this time by magic, and in my heart, I felt I was here for only one thing: to fall in love with this magnificent man, a man I'd never have dreamed would love me back. Yet, here I was, in a vortex of times gone by, with a man I'd lay my life down to save. In my heart, I knew two people did not need time travel to fall in love. There was more, but I needed to find out what it was, and why.

Something stirred inside me then. It was more than a feeling—it was a premonition of my future. At peace, I steeled myself for what was to come. I knew my purpose, and although I couldn't explain it, I understood that a life hung in the balance. Whose life, I wasn't sure, but it was a life that must be saved at all costs—a life that, if lost, would mean the Sioux legacy would cease to exist.

"Blaze," Dakota asked, "are you ready?"

"I'm ready, no matter what. We can't stop what's going to happen. Just know that I never thought I would feel this way about you, and I want you to know, regardless of the outcome, I'll never stop loving you."

Walking to me, he took my hands and bent his head to kiss me. It wasn't a passionate kiss, but a kiss that held our future. He didn't have to say the words—my heart knew he felt the same way.

Tethering the horse to a small bramble of bushes at the outer part of the hill, next to the cave mouth, we entered and huddled together, waiting. The cave wasn't large enough to stand in, just enough room to sit with our backs against the cold, hard wall. Hand in hand, we waited until it was time.

<hr />

COOPER AND BLACK RAVEN covered over three miles, stopping to rest the horses. Black Raven felt it. His people were near, and he felt joy. The old Indian was happy to see Maka and Swift Eagle, to see the looks on their faces when they realized he was alive. He grunted a half-laugh, and Cooper glanced at him, wondering what he found funny in this situation.

"Mis amapsa," Cooper asked in Lakota. (You laugh.)

"Mieyebo `at wowahwa," Black Raven replied. (I am at peace.)

Away from the men who fed him gruel and kept him chained, he was truly at peace. Cooper knew there was more to this peace, but he wasn't ready for a full conversation with the chief—his Lakota wasn't fluent enough yet.

Black Raven knew that in the years to come, Cooper would become fluent; he would become one of them. His life would change, and his future had been set the moment he released Black Raven from his chains.

⸺ ❦ ⸺

THE MOUNTAIN WAS ALIVE with men digging. Dawn had broken, and Ardenhert was frustrated that not a single man had hollered, "I've found a vein of gold."

Wiping his forehead with a dirty kerchief, he walked to the water barrel, dipped the cloth in, and wiped his face again—just as Gruber approached.

"Uh, sir, we have the dynamite packs ready to set off, iffin' you give the order."

Ardenhert produced a flask, un-popped the top, and took a drink of rotgut whiskey. Cooper, damn the man; here he was, fixin' to blow up this side of the mountain, taking all the heat of the search party with no telling what else. What if the gold was only a myth and all he did was blow up a mountain? Cooper second-guessed his own plan. He had to grow some balls, get it done, then grab what he could and hightail it out.

Looking at the flask, then at Gruber, he drained it and tossed it next to the water barrel.

"Get the men out of the caves, then we'll set off the blasts. Afterward, have the men ready with picks and shovels—we gotta work fast, hear me?"

Gruber nodded, spat on the ground, and sneered, leaving a disheartened captain with no whiskey left. Ardenhert had no idea what was bearing down on him. Soon, the mountain he planned to blow up would collapse, ending his pitiful, greedy life. It was too late to change, and nothing could stop it.

Riding ahead of the chief, Cooper sensed Black Raven had stopped. He trotted back. Now, why was the old chief halting?

"We need to keep going," Cooper said in Lakota.

Black Raven, atop his stilled mount, lifted his head as if peering over a mountain. Cooper asked again, in Lakota, why he had stopped.

The chief grunted, "My people—they are near."

Cooper looked back, scanning the horizon. Nothing. He shook his head at the crazy old chief and aimed his horse east, beckoning him to follow.

The chief moved, but only at a walking pace. Cooper shrugged and slowed.

Over the next rise, the moon provided clear vision. Cooper stopped, mouth agape. Less than three dozen Sioux Indians came over the rise at a fast pace—no whooping or hollering, just riding as he'd never seen before.

The leader saw them and let out an Indian cry a dead man could have heard.

"Dark Cloud!" Black Raven exclaimed, whooping back as he charged. They bounded off their horses and, in one fell swoop, embraced in a manly hug. Cooper kicked his mare into high gear, heading straight for them, needing to show he was a friend.

Seeing the White man charging, a few braves called out, but Black Raven stopped them, explaining in Lakota that Cooper was an ally. The chief recounted a few events, promising more later, but now was not the time. It was time to return to Paha Sapa—the Black Hills.

Cooper couldn't believe his ears. The chief said they were going back from where they'd just fled. Not his choice—but with a small Indian army at his back, he felt secure.

IT WAS TIME TO go. We left the cave on foot, heading around the base of the mountain to the northern side. The trek was tough, and only a few hours remained before dawn.

We came upon a group of ragtag soldiers spreading out to take cover from the blasts. We ducked back, but one turned at the snap of a twig and caught sight of us just as we dove into a small cluster of young spruce trees.

Gruber only saw two Indians, and this worried him. Where there were two, there might be two hundred. He backed away, pretending to head another direction.

I froze, heart racing. Had he seen us? Whipping my head toward Dakota, I saw him shake his head and put a finger to his lips. He veered in another direction, moving obscured but not directly toward us. Once out of sight, I exhaled. Dakota took my hand, ready to lead us forward—but as I stepped, he didn't follow.

Turning, I found him nudging Dakota in the back. Closing his eyes, Dakota cursed under his breath in Lakota.

"How did he sneak up on us?"

"Well, lookie here... now whadwe'e got? A brave and his squaw?" The man smirked, yellow teeth chomping smelly chewing tobacco.

I looked to Dakota for direction. He shook his head, and I stayed silent. The soldier didn't understand Lakota, which was in our favor. Dakota explained calmly that he would disarm the man, and I needed to run—fast.

"Where do I run?" I asked in Lakota.

"Back to the cave. Hurry. Take the packs off the horses, untether them, and give them a hard whack. Let them run off, then drag the packs into the cave. Cover the opening with brush," he instructed, eyes never leaving the soldier.

"Why? Won't it take too long? We need the horses. You want me to just scare them off? I don't understand."

"No. Go straight down, not like we came up. Once you're on flatter land, run—and don't stop. We want them to think we're on the horses with our supplies, headed away."

Afraid but trusting my instincts, I obeyed.

In one quick motion, Dakota flattened the soldier and took his rifle. I ran as if for my life, every heaving breath a prayer that Dakota was behind me.

Rounding a corner, I slipped, scraping my hands and crashing one knee against a boulder. Winded, I cried but willed myself upright, catching my side. Painful as it was, I had to keep going. Dakota depended on me.

As I ran, a single gunshot rang out. I froze, heart pounding. Who was hit? Dakota? My mind raced. I considered going back, but hesitated—if he was hurt, I might run into the soldier. My cries caught in my throat. I mustn't make noise.

Tears streamed down my face. Surrounded by trees, bushes, rocks, and cold snow at the mountain base—home to wild animals—I felt doomed, but eventually, I ran again, back to where Dakota had said he'd be waiting.

—⚊ ❦ ⚊—

THE SOLDIER HAD RECOVERED enough to take advantage of the brush. Raising his left leg, he shoved his foot into Dakota's knee, making him stumble. Dakota regained balance, but the man rolled upward, grasping the rifle by the barrel.

Yanking the stock sent Dakota off balance, but he compensated, using the White man to pull himself upright. They wrestled, the rifle awkwardly positioned, pointing half up, half sideways. The soldier held the barrel tight, trying to pull himself upright. Dakota swung his left leg to trip him, missing. The stranger lunged at Dakota, hoping to knock him flat. Dakota sidestepped, placed his finger on the trigger, and pulled.

The .45 hit the soldier's knee squarely, blowing a medium-sized hole straight through the kneecap. He went down instantly. Dakota knew the blast would alert others, and he needed to move fast.

Blood gushed from both entry and exit wounds. Dakota grabbed the rifle, checked the soldier's pockets for bullets, then began running to catch up with Blaze. Not two hundred yards out, he heard others searching for the injured soldier. He had to stay ahead. Darting upward into heavy brush on the mountainside, he clawed his way to higher ground. Hands bleeding, ice biting, he kept moving.

BLACK RAVEN, COOPER, AND the braves made excellent time. Almost back at the base of the smaller hills, the Indians, knowing the land, took shortcuts AWOL dragoons would never have found.

Cooper marveled at their horseback skill, maneuvering through treacherous terrain in near silence. Out of the ravine known as the Ravine of the Dead, they galloped southwest of the Black Hills. Cooper grinned, watching Black Raven in the lead, head held high. Dark Cloud had given him a spear adorned with magnificent feathers. The old chief lofted it like a charging warrior.

Black Raven, warrior chief of the Lakota Sioux, was in his element. Cooper was glad to be on their side.

The braves carried Winchester rifles, bows, arrows, and spears, ready if the ragtag soldiers attacked. Cooper thought of the old chief—the soothsayer, the magic. Could it be true? Could the chief have known his people were this close? He wouldn't dispute the surreal magic at work. Cooper also knew Major Bellamus was headed this way, chasing the turncoat soldiers. Were they riding into war, or merely death and destruction caused by greed?

It wasn't the gold these Indians sought—it was their land, their livelihood, their game and buffalo. White men and their greed threatened it all. Cooper frowned; he didn't want to die today—or any day soon.

28

TIME BUILT UP INTO a ball, wound tightly into a powerful sphere, filled with the past, the present, and the future. Souls far into the future waited, worried, and prayed that the two people they loved would come back safe and unharmed.

Those two individuals, jettisoned by magic from the future into a faraway past—a past that was their heritage—moved forward by instinct, neither understanding why nor what they needed to do. They could not have known the passion and love that would crescendo once fate had thrown them together.

Here, in their present—which was the past—Indians were on their way to protect what was theirs, brave and ready to die for their people. A wise chief led the tribe, wielding his magic and knowledge of what the future held. Soldiers, honorable and dishonorable, cared little for the Red Man or his land. All of this rolled into a force so powerful that even Black Raven could not have guessed the magnitude of what would happen when this power was unleashed.

Meda felt it. The ground shook, and Pete, Sam, and Blackie turned to look at her. She nodded; the time was near, very near. The four of them went back into her house. Meda took the journal from the shelf, collected the amulets—now joined as one—and pulled the circle-inside-a-circle pendant away from the others. The inner circle spun.

I WAS OUT OF breath by the time I ducked into the small cave. Dragging the largest piece of brush I could find, I covered the opening. What if Dakota didn't see it? What if he missed it and couldn't find me? I cried for a short two minutes before calm overtook me. Inhaling deeply, I sat back as far as I could and, in the darkness, pulled my knees to my chest.

I heard footsteps, many footsteps, and voices. I shut my eyes tightly. The soldiers were hunting Dakota, which meant he was alive. Twigs snapped, leaves rustled, rocks slid, and voices faded, but I didn't move, leaving nothing to chance in case one remained behind to ambush Dakota.

The bush wiggled as a hand pulled it away. I kept my eyes closed, holding my breath, praying my life wouldn't end this way. I felt hot breath on my face, so close, yet I did not breathe nor open my eyes. When his lips touched mine, every ounce of me went limp. I expelled all the air in my lungs, wrapped my arms around his neck, pulling him closer, and opened my eyes, still fearful.

"Did they follow you? Did someone die? I heard a gunshot."

"No. I wounded him. The soldiers are gone, but not far enough yet. We'll sit here for a while."

All this time together, we'd never had to fear for our lives. Now everything had changed, and I was terrified.

THE CAMP APPEARED EMPTY when Black Raven, his warriors, and Cooper rode in. Ardenhert had apparently decided one minor explosion was enough to sound the alarm, leaving the men in the caves, working like mad. A major dig was in progress, and when the charges were set, blasting would be his only choice to get gold, if he got any at all.

The light from the sunrise played against the winter skies, and Black Raven halted his warriors. Cooper heard him instruct them to encircle the camp on the outer perimeter and stay put. They obeyed. The chief and Dark Cloud, still on horseback, stood side by side near the primary fire of the camp, its embers smoldering.

Cooper rode up, and Black Raven nodded. Dark Cloud did not look as inviting. In Lakota, Cooper warned him that the soldiers were in the hills mining and would soon begin blasting in the caves. He suspected another group of soldiers was nearby, hunting those who'd held the chief captive.

"The dragoons who held you captive should be concerned with the men hunting them, not the Sioux," he said. "Once the new regiment arrives, all hell will break loose. White men will fight White men. They are not concerned with the Sioux. We should leave."

"You speak Lakota," said Dark Cloud. "Impressive."

"It is not easy to impress Dark Cloud," said Black Raven.

Cooper didn't care about impressing the warrior. He only wanted everyone safe. "What is your decision? Do we stay or leave?"

The army lieutenant watched Black Raven mull his words. He saw astonishment fill Dark Cloud's eyes. The younger warrior would never have suspected a White man could speak his language, and in addition, warn the chief where all the White men had gone. No White man had ever worried for the Sioux's safety.

The three sat on horseback in silence, waiting. Black Raven stared trance-like at the mountain terrain to the east, then dismounted, motioning for them to stay.

"Cooper, you good man. I'm pleased you fear for our safety, but we are not cowards. This—these Hills—are our land. We must not run; we must make it known we will fight if necessary. Soldiers will return, and we must be here. You and Dark Cloud stay and watch for soldiers. Kill them—in silence, no guns yet. Dark Cloud, you lead the war party if they are many and I am not back in time."

Dark Cloud grunted his acknowledgment. Cooper looked at the chief about his duties.

"You, my friend, are now part of my tribe, part Sioux in spirit, as you are the one who freed me. Stay with Dark Cloud and fight by his side. If life is your reward, you will share it with my tribe." It was not a question—it was a statement. Black Raven made it known the White man was now one of them.

T.H. Cooper was speechless, staring at the great chief and warrior, a man of magic. Black Raven was welcoming him into his tribe. In an instant, Cooper understood his future. He had no family, wouldn't return to the dragoons, nor serve as an Indian agent. He didn't feel AWOL or like a traitor; this was his new beginning. He was ready.

Cooper thanked the chief in Lakota, stating this fight was his as well. Black Raven gave an insignificant affirmative head jerk and turned to walk back to the tent where he had been held captive. Cooper wondered what the chief was doing, but he trusted the old man. The wise Sioux chief ducked into the tent, walked to the pole where he had been bound, and leaned back, laying his feathered, adorned spear on the ground.

He gathered the loose bindings in his hands. Closing his eyes, he took slow, deep breaths, letting his spirit rest. His head lolled from side to side, then in circular motions as thoughts of spirits filled his mind, and he heard the chanting of those who had gone before him. Black Raven felt lighter. Soon his spirit hovered over his flesh once again, ready to wander.

⟶ ⟵

THE CAVE WAS DARK and cramped. No noise. No snapping twigs. It had been quiet for a while, and I squirmed, cramped from sitting too long. Dakota shifted to a knee.

"They've gone. We can move."

There was no space to stand, so we faced each other, knowing in each other's eyes that we had a million questions and not one answer.

⟶ ⟵

THE CHIEF SOARED, HIS spirit moving faster than before. Time was of the essence; he needed to find them. Major Bellamus was closing in on his renegade men, and as chief, he needed to save his people. Letting his heart guide him, Black Raven sought Blaze, and his spirit swooped low to the footpath and bramble, finding her undisturbed. He felt her presence—and the one she called Dakota.

As I felt Black Raven's spirit near, something urged me to sit down. I pulled Dakota down next to me.

"It isn't time yet. We must wait," I whispered.

"Not time yet for what? No one's out there. Blaze, we need to go back," he paused, "well, I don't know what we need to get back to."

"Dakota, you must trust me," I said.

_____ ❧ _____

FAR INTO THE FUTURE, Meda, Sam, Pete, and Blackie watched the inner circle spin, picking up speed. Seconds later, the outer circle spun in the polar opposite direction, making it appear as if one circle ran over the other without touching. The spinning increased rapidly until the circles looked like one giant, solid silver ball, spinning out of control.

_____ ❧ _____

THE AMULET I WORE grew hot. I pulled it up and slipped it off. Holding the chain, I watched the tiny circle inside the larger circle revolve. Dakota shook his head, closing and reopening his eyes as if to confirm what he saw. I could have sworn Black Raven's spirit entered the cave. The magic was almost overwhelming. Looking over at the opening, I could have sworn someone passed through—but the brush was still in place, not a leaf rustled.

The chief's spirit hovered, touching both Blaze and Dakota. They felt it simultaneously, as if a shiver ran through them. An impending feeling—not doom, but sadness—filled the cave. In an instant, the presence withdrew, returning to its physical body.

We watched as the spinning charm slowed to a steady, visible rotation. Our eyes darted between the cave opening and the amulet, observing the change in motion.

"What does this mean?" Dakota asked.

I answered with conviction. "It means it's time to do what we were sent to do... then go home."

29

BLACK RAVEN RAISED HIS head once his spirit rejoined his body and smiled in a knowing way. The mission was not yet complete, though, so he stood and took up his spear, taking his leave for the last time from the place where he'd been held captive—the place that had helped him create his powerful magic.

Cooper and Dark Cloud moved toward the chief with the ponies.

"So, what's next?" Cooper asked, waiting for an answer.

Black Raven, still in awe of the man's knowledge of his language, grunted and then waved for Dark Cloud to bring him his mount. Once atop, he surveyed the area. He knew Sioux warriors were over the ridge, waiting for his signal. Soldiers were readying the insides of many caverns to blast with sticks of dynamite, and more soldiers were chasing them, only a few miles away. Wind Dancer and She Cougar were in the cave, and the magic from the past and the present had been set into motion. He hoped this magic—his magic—would be as strong as the spirits of the past had promised.

"We wait, there," Black Raven said, pointing to the trees at the back of the camp. "When they come, we watch. White man coming not looking for Sioux—they search for other White

man. Dark Cloud, you go tell others: no one make move until I
say."

Dark Cloud acknowledged with a nod and a gruff grunt.
Cooper watched him leave to carry out the chief's orders, then
turned his gaze back to Black Raven.

"What the—" he stammered in English, then reverted to
Lakota. "What type of conquering the enemy is this? You know
soldiers are on the way, and these hills—the majestic Paha Sapa,
your people's land—are in danger of being destroyed, and your
lands invaded by White men, and we're just going to watch? We
have the advantage of surprise."

The frown on Cooper's brow deepened, but Black Raven
stopped him from saying more.

"You only know what you see with your eyes. I know what I
see here," Black Raven said, pointing to his heart and then his
head, "and here. There is much you do not understand, Cooper.
Now go, stand with Dark Cloud, and wait." The chief's words
were final.

Cooper knew a battle was about to break loose, and he didn't
mind keeping his distance. However, the old chief was a lu-
natic if he thought they would just watch. All kinds of hell and
fire would descend on this mountain—and they were simply
going to observe? They were in danger, and the soldiers were
outnumbered. Major Bellamus and Captain Gene Ardenhert
would combine forces to slay the Sioux if necessary. Cooper
wasn't sure Black Raven had considered this.

The old chief walked his pony through the encampment
and back again. Cooper watched as he dismounted, held his
spear aloft, and danced around the spot where once a fire
had glowed—now nothing remained but warm black soot and
burned tree limbs. Glancing around, Cooper watched for signs
of oncoming riders. From his vantage point, he had a front-row
seat to watch the chaos unfold. There was no way out except

into the mountains. Cooper wasn't sure if Major Bellamus would lead the men in, but he knew somewhere the major had hanging ropes ready for any deserters he'd capture. What would he do with the Sioux? Would he view them as hostile and kill them, or let them go? Once again, Indian Agent Lieutenant T. H. Cooper pondered death. Again, he wasn't ready to die—not today, not when his new life had yet to begin.

He watched as the old chief mounted his pony but did not urge it to move. Cooper wasn't sure what to make of him—the man, this chief, this warrior—but his life was in the balance, and he felt safer here with the Sioux than with his own people.

Sure, he had the papers proving he was a governmental agent for Indian Affairs, and yes, that would get him back home with Major Bellamus and his regiment. But Cooper's heart was not there. He had no family or home, and he felt his place was now with the Indians of the Sioux Nation. Cooper felt at peace.

ARDENHERT WAITED FOR THE men to finish setting the charges, ready to blast and get out of the area, but time had run out. He knew what was breathing down his neck, and he also knew there would be no gold, no riches—nothing. If it were possible, he would try to get out of the area and return later. Next time, with stronger, braver men, all he needed were a few. That would mean more gold for each of them.

Gene Ardenhert's anger flared. Damn Private Gruber. That one stick of dynamite had turned this mission on its ear. The captain had risked it all and was going to walk away empty-handed.

Cooper, the coward, had run off, and Ardenhert was sure he'd been the one to let the Injun go. His ragtag men would be no match for the well-fed and rested troops headed to hang the lot of them. They might not hang him, but they'd make sure he paid for this desertion for a long time. Well, that wasn't going to happen either. They would never take him alive, and if he had to, he would blow them all to kingdom come. After that, he'd have to face the Devil for all the bad he had done or created in his life—he was ready, no matter what.

30

MEDA SAT CENTURIES APART from Blaze; the spinning amulet clutched in her hand. Blackie, Pete, and Sam watched her, staring at the charm, displaying no fear.

The old woman reached out to stop the amulet from spinning, and time stood still—for all of them—the past and the present—for what felt like an eternity.

With Dakota looking on, I stared at the hypnotic silver charm. I felt no fear. An unseen power took control, and I reached out to stop the spinning amulet. Everything stopped.

I thought about how much my life had changed, from when I thought I was done for on the prairie to my first time making love with Dakota. Fear and fantasy chased one another, mixed with excitement and desire. The surreal time travel experience, along with past reflections and the reality of the future, had to be nothing more than a fleeting dream.

In my other world, time stilled— my eyes closed. I could read my aunt's thoughts, feel her heart. She thought back to her past, her life story, and her time as a young Sioux maiden. I lived it all with her—a life lived centuries ago. Everything she felt through the ages, I felt with her. She suffered through pain and hardship, a time when being Native American was a struggle.

My own suffering as a kid felt insignificant, a mere trickle of tears compared to the storms she had weathered.

Then I saw her full face, looking at me in my dreams. A shared vision of the future brought smiles. Her heart spoke to me—it said all was saved. The Sioux world would be righted, and our legacy was safe.

⁘

CAPTAIN ARDENHERT FELT THE breath of horses and the cold press of metal rifles at the nape of his neck bearing down—he would wait no longer. There were three plungers within running distance of each other. All he had to do was hit them, and the mountain would go up. He hoped the men he'd assigned to set the charges knew what they were doing. If they didn't, he'd be blown up with the mountain. It was too late now—he had no other choice.

A clump of trees hid forty soldiers. A few dismounted, moving on foot to search beyond large, snow-covered boulders as fresh flurries swirled around them.

The fall of footsteps and the sound of horses' hooves on rocky, snow-covered ground sent Ardenhert into action. He sprinted to the closest plunger, leaned in, and with both hands shoved it down. Somewhere to his left, he heard the boom. Without a minute to lose, he charged the next plunger fifty yards away and engaged the next set of charges with a forceful shove.

The years had passed for Ardenhert, but fear had him moving like a man of twenty, adrenaline pumping through his veins. He reached the next plunger, and the second boom's rumble shook the ground beneath him.

Surrender was not an option. Since the riches were no longer there for the taking, he'd blow it all to smithereens. Only one more to detonate, then he'd escape during the pandemonium. Gold could rot in hell, along with his men. Survival was his only concern.

The blasts rattled everyone. Horses went stir-crazy, bucking and pitching their riders. Men appeared from nowhere, bedraggled and screaming—some trapped in rockslides triggered by the explosions, one after another after another. Snow flew upward, along with trees, smaller rocks, and dirt, scattering across the sky before floating back down to the ground.

FAR INTO THE FUTURE, Meda, Sam, Pete, and Blackie felt the earth tremble as the lights flickered for seconds. It was as though two separate time periods, divided by years, converged—one moment stretched toward the other, meeting for a fraction of a second.

ALL THE NOISE SNAPPED Dakota and me out of our trance. We ran out of the cave, down the hill, stumbling and sliding.

Smoke filled the air as the caves exploded, and rockslides began. Men scrambled from nowhere, desperate to reach safety. As boulders of all sizes fell—slow at first, then faster—Dakota looked back and saw them rolling straight toward us.

"Come on, hurry!" Dakota shouted above the crashing sounds. "Take my hand—we have to get out now!"

I grabbed his hand, and we slid downward until he jumped, taking me with him. We rolled and landed near a small niche. He pulled me beneath him, ducking as the rockslide thundered

over our heads. As soon as it subsided enough, he yanked my
hand, pulled me up, and we ran toward the soldiers' camp.

Dark Cloud and the other braves hid on the outer edge of
the camp, keeping their eyes on the chief as he urged his pony
toward the caves. Dark Cloud waited for the signal.

Ardenhert hadn't been so lucky. When he dove for the last
plunger, he failed to consider the falling rocks from the second
blast. A large stone hit him in the head, rendering him unconscious. His army scattered to escape the explosions. The unlucky
ones were buried beneath rock and dirt—and if they weren't
dead, they soon would be.

Cooper felt time slow. He was in disbelief. He saw Major
Bellamus and his dragoons crest a nearby ridge, rifles, and sabers
drawn. There were too many of them. Chief Black Raven, Dark
Cloud, and three dozen braves would not fight them and win.

Cooper believed Ardenhert and his vile crew had earned their
fate. These Indians didn't need to die—nor did they deserve to.
His body reacted as his mind raced. He spurred his horse and
went down the ridge toward the camp.

Cooper watched the chaos unfold as his pony reached the base
of the camp. He saw the old chief move toward the explosion
and wondered why Black Raven was driven to return to that
chaos.

We reached the base of the camp scratched, battered, and
out of breath—yet invigorated by the rush of events. Dakota
spotted Dark Cloud and shouted to him in Lakota. Whipping
his head around, Dark Cloud—rarely one to smile—beamed at
the sight of his friend Wind Dancer. He lifted his spear and let
out a screech.

Cooper halted his pony when he heard Dark Cloud hollering and saw an Indian couple join the fray—two unexpected figures amid the disorder. Who were they, and where had Black Raven gone? Cooper scanned the area and, with a sinking feeling, saw the chief riding toward the cavern, swallowed by the dense trees on the mountain. Where was he headed, and why?

Dark Cloud motioned for his braves to follow the chief, then turned his pony toward Dakota and Blaze. His mind raced—three people could not ride one horse.

Cooper heard them before he saw them. He shouted in Lakota, warning Dark Cloud that soldiers were riding in fast. Mass confusion erupted as everyone scrambled to hide or prepared to fight.

I was completely composed. Letting go of Dakota's hand, I knew I wouldn't go with them. Dakota had to leave with Dark Cloud—there was no other choice.

Dark Cloud reached us. He offered his hand; I refused and looked at Dakota.

"Dakota, you must go with Dark Cloud. I'll run. It'll be okay—I promise."

My Lakota was flawless; there was no misunderstanding. I wasn't leaving with Dark Cloud.

Dakota's gut clenched at the thought of leaving me, but deep down it felt right. He understood his duty. Though he believed I'd be safe, his heart urged him to remain. Dark Cloud pressed again, so Dakota grabbed his arm and hoisted himself onto the back of the pony.

Dark Cloud looked puzzled. His face scrunched up, as I struck the horse on the flank, sending it galloping away. He looked back at me as I ran in the opposite direction. The brave probably thought I was cuckoo—but happy to have his friend back. Dark Cloud took off in the direction the chief had ridden. The other braves followed, disappearing into the thick trees along the mountainside. Within minutes, they were gone.

Only one soldier remained, sitting motionless on his horse, watching as it all unfolded.

When the gunshots rang out, I understood my purpose. Dark Cloud's life had been in imminent danger. I was there to save him, as I knew his death would change everything. Relief washed over me as I watched them ride away.

Gunfire, shouting, snorting horses, and scrambling men filled the camp. The commotion felt like a scene from a movie—except the bullets were real, the blood was real, and now I was in danger.

Major Bellamus and his men captured a few renegade soldiers trying to flee, but his focus was on the crusty, alcoholic, greedy captain. He wanted Ardenhert's head. If Ardenhert hadn't deserted, taking an entire unit, this unfortunate situation wouldn't have occurred. And what in the Sam Hill were these Indians doing out here? Bellamus had no time for an Indian war. He wanted deserters rounded up and the mess finished—cleanly.

Bellamus hated complications, but now he had one: the Sioux.

They were on their land, and he commanded the army. If necessary, he was ready for battle. He ordered his men to arms, prepared to fight—but only if necessary. That was all it took. One shot rang out, then another, and horses charged into the camp.

Cooper sprang into motion the instant he heard approaching hooves. He didn't know who this woman was, but he knew she wasn't ready to die—or face something worse. He rode to where she stood and studied her. Time slowed again. Her blue eyes told him she wasn't full-blooded Sioux—but who was she? It didn't matter. She needed help.

Their eyes met, and something familiar stirred in his soul. She lifted her hand. He took it and pulled her up behind him.

"Hunta yea," she said in Lakota—warning him to get out of the way. Something was coming.

He didn't question her. Soldiers were closing in. Kicking his horse, he took off at full speed.

Unsure whether to follow the chief, Cooper chose to be the diversion. His only fear was that if he were caught, the woman would suffer. Deciding both their lives were worth saving, he veered off, urging the mare into a full gallop.

Bellamus and his men rode into the camp, passing Cooper and his female Indian companion.

"Want me to send men after them?" a young sergeant asked.

"Nah. They won't get far," Bellamus replied. "One horse carrying two—she'll give out soon. I want Ardenhert. Find him."

At that moment, Bellamus couldn't have known the tumbling rocks had already sealed Ardenhert's fate.

31

DARK CLOUD, DAKOTA, AND the others caught up with Chief Black Raven in no time. Deeper into the mountains, they climbed until they reached a small, level butte.

Dakota got off the pony, then Dark Cloud followed. He greeted Dakota by grabbing her forearms. Black Raven, too, dismounted and walked over to him.

A frown deepened on Dark Cloud's face. "She Cougar in the spirit world?"

"Alive and safe. I know this, here." Dakota pointed to his heart.

Dark Cloud wasn't sure. He'd seen her, still on foot, as the soldiers had ridden into the camp. He was saddened. His woman was gone, but he knew other maidens would want him in the future.

The chief eyed Dakota before speaking.

"You know the spirit world, young Wind Dancer? Are you prepared to go into the holiest of places?" The chief stood, holding his spear like a scepter.

Dakota nodded. "I know my future, deep down, and She Cougar will be waiting for me, no matter how long it takes."

The chief nodded and grunted. "You save Dark Cloud."

This was news to Dark Cloud, who thought he'd been the one who had saved him.

Dakota replied, "No, She Cougar saved him."

Dark Cloud was indignant. A woman did not save him. He opened his mouth to speak, his eyes full of growing fury. The chief held up his hand to silence him before he could spit out a load of Lakota words and instructed him to be thankful.

"Ai, le mita pila," Dark Cloud said.

Dakota nodded. "She Cougar is pleased."

Dark Cloud didn't believe what he was hearing. He hadn't been saved; he had saved Dakota, but now wasn't the time to argue. They were both here and both still very much alive, no matter who saved whom. The chief watched as the other braves joined them on top of the butte.

"Wind Dancer, you stay here. Dark Cloud and the others will head for the holy dance grounds to wait. We follow later, and together again we'll go back to our people."

It was an order, but Dark Cloud looked at him, then at Dakota, in question.

"We will be close behind, but I must see," said Black Raven.

"See what?" Dakota and Dark Cloud questioned simultaneously.

"I just go see." The chief stood firm.

"Dark Cloud, your brother will be leaving—this time forever. He lives here." The chief pointed to his heart. "And here." The chief then pointed to Dark Cloud's heart. "And here." The chief made a large, swooping gesture through the air.

It meant Wind Dancer would forever be with them—if not in body, then always in spirit. Dark Cloud mounted his pony. Looking down at Wind Dancer, he grabbed his hand. "You will be my warrior brother always."

Dakota, too emotional to speak, nodded. His time here was ending. He watched Dark Cloud and the others ride off. They were his link to this time, and this link would last forever, regardless of the fact he wasn't born from this tribe. Sioux brothers of different nations would always be Sioux brothers. As they disappeared, he focused again on the chief.

When they were out of sight, Black Raven told Dakota to sit and wait, that he would return in a while. Dakota wanted to question him, but something stopped him. He nodded, finding a place to wait. He watched the old chief walk to a clump of trees, and then he disappeared.

Black Raven found a spot and sat against a tree, relaxing his entire being. He had to go see if Cooper had taken Blaze to safety. They didn't know he'd let his spirit float among the trees, and he would see. The chief wouldn't share this secret with them—not now.

Closing his eyes, he began the chant, freeing his spirit from his body to search for She Cougar.

Dakota waited for less than fifteen minutes. Then he got up to go find the old chief. Creeping into the shrubs, he found him leaning against the base of a tree, his eyes closed. What was he doing—taking a nap? Dakota wanted to go shake him, but a force held his feet in place, and he didn't move.

His instincts told him the old man wasn't asleep, nor was he dead. It was a peculiar feeling. After observing the old man, he sensed powerful magic and retreated.

Black Raven soared high above the treetops—looking for her. He smiled when he saw her with the man called Cooper. She was alive. He could return and lead his people again, knowing now that the unborn heroes of his time would live and the new heroes of the future would rise.

Just as he'd disappeared, the old tribal chief reappeared out of the trees, standing in front of Wind Dancer. "It is time, my son. We go now."

Dakota eyed the chief. "Before we ride back, you said I will leave this time forever. What wisdom do you hold?"

Black Raven's eyes fixated past Dakota for a fraction of a second before he spoke.

"Come, Wind Dancer, we sit and reflect."

Dakota sat with the chief beside him and waited. His thoughts were heavy on what had happened to Blaze and where she was.

Without asking aloud, the chief answered. "She lives."

Then he told him how he knew. Dakota listened as the chief told him about defying his worldly body and letting his spirit wander so he could watch over his people. He never doubted this strange phenomenon. How could he? He'd traveled over a hundred years to be right here, right now.

SOMEWHERE, FAR AWAY FROM the chaos, I rode behind a strange soldier. We rode the horse until it was exhausted.

"We have to stop; the horse has to rest," the man hollered through the wind.

Looking for a secluded place to hide, he maneuvered into a small area of brush, hoping for ample cover.

I slid off, grabbing a handful of snow, and licked it. The horse would not be so easy to please. The man eyed me, taking blankets and a flint rock from his saddlebag.

In Lakota, he said, "Get some small sticks so I can make a fire."

"Fire will alert them," I countered.

"I don't think we're being followed—not just yet. They're more interested in the soldiers, so we're safe for now."

With a nod, I agreed but said nothing. I didn't know him or his reason for being there, and he looked like the soldiers. Even though he could speak and understand Lakota, I wasn't necessarily safe. I'd seen him with an unknown Sioux man, but still I proceeded with caution.

"You know my people. You ride with my people?"

"Yes, on both accounts. Well, no, I just know Chief Black Raven."

I almost swallowed my tongue. Black Raven was alive. Oh my—this would make Maka so happy. Her father was alive. I became pensive, as I wouldn't see her when her father returned. Sadness filled my heart. A sense of foreboding settled in my gut as I knew my time here was running out. I wished I could have more time to see Maka again—hear her voice one more time.

This man, who spoke Lakota better than most Whites—had he once lived amongst the Sioux? My thoughts went back to the White man of long ago who'd lived with the Sioux, the one Maka told Dakota about.

"Who are you? Why do you speak our language so well?" I questioned.

The soldier smiled. "You're half-White?"

"Yes." This time I answered in English.

"My name is Cooper—Thomas H.—I'm a governmental Indian agent. I was sent to help Black Raven, although I didn't know how I was going to do it until now. And for the life of me, I don't know how it is going to end, since I'm here with you and not him. Who are you? And what the devil are you doing out here—and a woman to boot?"

I tried to ignore the sting of that last statement. A woman indeed. He didn't know who he was dealing with. If he did, it might scare the life out of him—but would he believe my story? Should I exercise caution and keep the truth to myself? Telling him everything—could this upset the continuum of our history?

I stared at him, deep into his dark eyes, trying to read him. Aunt Meda's voice came blasting into my head. *Do it, Blaze, trust.*

Looking at our surroundings, we needed to get to a place more hidden because it would take time to tell him my story. Telling this man, Cooper, an unbelievable story while worrying that soldiers were searching for us wouldn't work for me. Besides, this man might think I was looney and hand me over to them. No—we needed to move to a more treed area and higher up. In any scenario, I knew I would survive, with or without Cooper.

We rode up higher, and I saw the place, and it felt familiar.

"There"—I pointed—"up by the hanging rock and the stand of yellowish pine trees—higher up gives us the vantage point of seeing anyone coming. And the denser stand of trees will keep out the cold winds. The heavier, non-sticking snow would hide our tracks."

Cooper nodded. "Smart idea. I suppose I shouldn't discount you because you are a woman."

In less than fifteen minutes, we'd gathered brush to drag behind the horse to wipe away any tracks the snow had yet to cover and gathered more brush, piling it like a wall around two close-set pines. Staying concealed was vital.

I sat, and Cooper pulled out two smaller blankets from his saddlebags and handed me one. With the blanket wrapped around me, I pulled my feet up to my chin and huddled. Cooper wrapped the blanket around his larger frame, eyeballing me.

"I don't know how much time we have. But whenever you're ready, I'm listening. Who are you, and why are you here?"

I began giving him an account of my story.

Somewhere higher on a smaller butte, twenty miles away, Black Raven and Dakota sat. Black Raven nodded. It was now Dakota's turn to tell his story.

What he spun sounded like an unbelievable yarn—telling the old chief of the magic found in an old ancient journal that he, Chief Black Raven, had created. How this magic sent him and She Cougar in a spiral back in time. Only this was not fantasy to the old Chief, for he knew the truth.

<hr>

COOPER DID NOT BELIEVE his ears. He sat entranced, slack-jawed, eyes wide, and leaned forward to hear every word. This was an incredulous story—more folklore, a sort of tale he never would have heard. I'd left out the intimate details between Dakota and me; there was no need to share those.

The soldier noted a faint blush on her cheeks, figuring there had been some things she was not telling him. He smiled, but he wouldn't embarrass her. It was her tale of magic and drama, which intrigued him the most. He was not a man who believed in fairy tales. But this—somehow—he believed, as crazy as it sounded to him.

"And now, here we are. What's next?"—I held my palms up with a slight shrug—"I don't know."

Cooper sat, lost in thought, his eyes fixed on some distant point. He shook his head. I could tell he wasn't convinced, but how could I convince him?

My charm of two circles. Yes, this was the answer!

I let the blanket fall from my shoulders, then I undid the elk-skin winter wrap and retrieved a lengthy chain from beneath my dress. I flipped the amulet and pointed out the wider side to Cooper.

"See this inscription?"

Cooper leaned in, looking at where my finger pointed.

*For Blaze, on your 16th birthday, this is your connection to me.
Love, Aunt Meda, February 1996.*

Cooper looked at me, his face skeptical.

"Uh, I'm going to ask you something a man never asks a woman. How old are you?"

"Twenty-six, I think. I'm not sure how this time thing works and if I've aged—or does time stand still for time travelers?"

Cooper's eyes went wide. "This is impossible. What's going on here? Am I going mad?"

"Cooper, I know this all seems bizarre, but I assure you, I'm not in my own time zone, and I don't know how to convince you. I wish I could. But all of this is real—just as real as the danger we're in."

"There is something I can't quite put my finger on," he mused, "but it feels real, no matter how crazy it sounds." He paused. Then: "You yelled at the tall brave you were riding with. You told him he had to go with Dark Cloud. Why?"

"I'm not sure. Something urged me to make sure they both got out of the area. You know, Mr.—what's your first name, by the way?"

"Cooper. Just call me Cooper."

"Well, Cooper,"—I shivered—"I felt my aunt telling me to make sure Dark Cloud got out of harm's way."

"Who is Dark Cloud to you?"

"A brave from the tribe Dakota and I lived with. He's a friend."

Cooper sat back to think. If I was telling him the truth, what was next?

"I am not sure what to do next," I admitted, as if reading his thoughts.

"And I do?" he said, then: "I need to get back to Chief Black Raven and—" He stopped. Why did he need to go back? This woman was making him crazy. He was certain the chief was safe now. Black Raven had invited him into the tribe, so why did he have to go back? Then he recalled the letter in his pocket—his orders—hand couriered from his commander.

Cooper assumed it was a real order. The letter had been marked Urgent. He'd received it around the same time Blaze thought she had arrived on the prairie early last spring. He still had the letter. His instructions were to show the letter to any superior officer who might hold him captive—that would have been General Bellamus. Signed by his commanding officer, a new man by the name of—he couldn't remember.

Should he keep this information to himself because it might not include her? No. There wasn't any reason he could think of—she'd been straight with him.

From under his blanket and coat, Cooper revealed a long, tattered envelope. He pulled open the orders, the paper rustling softly as he read them in silence.

The envelope fluttered from his fingers, and before it blew away with a quick puff of wind, I snatched it. It was an automatic reaction. I didn't read the outside of the envelope; I continued to watch Cooper's face as he reread his orders.

He scrunched up his brow as he read. It all seemed normal and his face registered nothing shocking. He'd never believe me, but I needed him to accept the truth. As I pondered this I glanced down at the tatty envelope, turning it over—there it was—the proof I needed.

"Cooper," I said, then louder, "Cooper!"

His head snapped up. When our eyes met, I looked down and so did he. He saw my forefinger rubbed over it—the seal on the flap was still there. The wax, still thick and intact, formed a very distinctive shape. I was thrilled. Cooper stared unblinking, mouth agape. It was a seal of two circles, one within the other, matching the design of my amulet.

He stood and handed me the orders he'd just reread. "Look at the signature on my orders."

Thrusting the paper at me, I quickly read the orders down to the signature. It was signed, *Commander WD Dakota*. I smiled.

Cooper sat back down, a bit rattled. "What did you say Dakota's Indian name is?"

I smiled even bigger. "Wind Dancer."

Cooper muttered, "Could the WD in WD Dakota stand for Wind Dancer, the same person you referred to as Dakota? How is this possible?"

"You aren't dreaming, and we're running out of time." I stood and brushed the recent snowfall from my shoulders. Cooper looked up, his eyes confused and lost.

"All right, what's next, Miss Lady from the far—and I mean far—future? I have nothing to say that even makes sense right now." He scratched at the scruffy beard on his chin.

It had to be easier for me to believe than it was for Cooper. At least I'd been in the future before I'd been in the past. I knew the movies, pretend-magic, and make-believe time travel, but I'd never dreamed I'd live it in real life.

Cooper had no movies or TV to compare this to—only fables, ghost stories, and storybooks, if he read them. This had to be unfathomable for him.

"I have to find Dakota."

Something inside of me tugged. I felt tied to the end of a rope and someone was pulling it. I shoved my way out of the temporary break and immediately headed to the horse tied up a short distance away, without waiting for him.

Cooper followed, mounted his horse, and pulled me up behind him.

"Well, I guess we go back to the battlefield." He slapped the rump of the horse. We headed back to the place we'd left in such a hurried manner only hours before.

My grip tightened, my heart hammering against my ribs, aware of the dwindling seconds, hoping my time wasn't lost in bringing Cooper up to speed on my unbelievable tale. I also hoped he believed me and wasn't sure what part he played—but I'd ended up with this man for a reason. Whatever happened was supposed to happen.

Taking my right hand from his waist and holding tight with my left, I reached in and felt for my amulet. Grasping it between my thumb and forefinger, I felt a warming sensation, then a slight tingle.

I shuddered, but not because of the cold. Yes, it was time.

Cooper understood the urgency, and with a silent command, he spurred the mare, feeling her muscles tense as he urged her to move faster.

~ ⚶ ~

DAKOTA FINISHED RECOUNTING HIS tale. The chief nodded, his face without emotion. He waited, aware that pressing the old chief was futile.

Time was running out, yet he had no choice but to wait.

Unbelievable as it sounded—Dakota hoped the beliefs of this shaman would let him open his mind to whatever possibilities the future might hold. With such a wild story, he might think him evil or demon-possessed. Dakota sat, his thoughts spinning as he waited.

The chief didn't doubt his tale; he knew it to be true, as he himself had had the visions this was to happen.

Finally, he spoke: "She Cougar is with the White man, Cooper, and will be safe."

"Why isn't she here with us? I am confused. We both must go back to our world, our future selves. Why were we beckoned by your old magic?"

Black Raven pursed his lips, nodding. "You and She Cougar have met your ancestral past, and the spirits are pleased. The journey she took was to save Dark Cloud's life. You could have done that alone, Wind Dancer. Why do you think she was sent?"

Dakota shook his head. "I wasn't aware of my purpose, how could I know hers? Maybe it was because"—he cleared his throat—"I'm not sure. Was it for her to learn about her heritage and become more prideful of being Sioux? Or so we could..." He trailed off, keeping something private.

Black Raven snorted. "You're a wise man, Wind Dancer. You shall figure it out. One day, you both will understand."

He stood, stretching his frame and looking down at Dakota. "We must go."

"Go? Where?" Dakota questioned, falling behind the chief, walking toward the tied-up ponies.

"Back to my people. And try to send you home—to your world."

Dakota stopped short. "Try? What do you mean, try? Can't you send me back?"

The chief did not stop. "Come, Wind Dancer. She Cougar will be back in your world. She waits for you."

Black Raven hauled himself up on the larger of the two ponies. "You've done what you needed. Dark Cloud is safe. He is headed back to our people, and a new birth will arise."

The chief didn't leave any time for Dakota to waste nor ask questions.

As the chief told it, Dark Cloud was their mission. But why and what had he done? He'd only ridden out with Dark Cloud on his pony. Dakota's mind didn't comprehend this was what saved his life.

Hell, Dark Cloud could have ridden away without stopping to grab Dakota. Perhaps he had saved Dakota's life. Neither he nor Blaze would've known that if she hadn't shouted for him to go with him. Dark Cloud would have stayed, facing any soldiers, dying in his effort. Yes, they saved him, but they would never truly understand the path not taken, the potential destiny they had altered. It wouldn't be until they returned to their own century that they'd learn the truth.

The old chief put his heels into his pony's flanks and galloped away; Dakota not far behind, a million and one questions filling his head.

⚶

YEARS AND YEARS AWAY, the four sat—Meda, Sam, Pete, and Blackie. It was calm, and each was satisfied. Meda rocked and hummed.

The birth that almost didn't happen now was set in stone. A new birth, as foretold, delivered in the new world. Thus, guaranteeing the Sioux legacy would continue for many years to come. The past hadn't changed, the future now secured. It would continue as it should.

32

THE TROOPS WERE GONE, and a spattering of weak and injured soldiers were left behind—considered traitors to their own. Captain Ardenhert now lay dead. The rockslide had been enough to bring him down, and someone had put a bullet in his chest.

"Poor bastard," the young private hissed, taking stock of the area and the dead.

"He's better off, I'd say," remarked the skinny corporal, staring at the dead captain.

"Why do you say that? The man's dead. I reckon it makes him a poor bastard in my eyes." The private's eyes fixed on the captain. With the toe of his boot, the corporal nudged the dead captain's leg and then kicked him, taking the other man by surprise. "He ain't gotta hang now for desertion."

"Why'd ya do that?"

"'Causin' he got off easy, that's why. He weren't nothin' but a greedy bastard," the scrawny corporal grunted.

"Why are you here then, if you weren't the same as him? I mean, we all wanted the gold, right?" The boy did not understand. He believed they were on the same side.

The corporal smiled. "Boy, I'm here 'cause I was told to find the likes of you and bring ya back to stand trial for desertion."

The younger soldier turned from the dead captain's body to look at the man speaking. Pistol drawn. He was part of Bellamus' troop. There were many men he didn't know, and he'd stayed silent and out of everyone's way. All he'd wanted was to go home. He never wanted gold.

"I should 'a saved you the misery too and just shoot you." He cocked the hammer of his pistol.

The young soldier stood petrified. His life did not flash before his eyes, because he was too young to have had a life yet.

Hooves treading on small twigs, cracking and snapping, caused both men to turn and see Cooper and Blaze coming toward them.

"Hold it right there." The corporal turned, aiming his gun at them.

"Who are you, and why've you got a filthy Injun squaw with you?" His gun was trained on Cooper's face.

Cooper whispered to Blaze in Lakota. "Use your feet and keep the horse moving." She pressed on his back with her forearm, acknowledging his order.

The man with the gun snarled. "I said stop and get off your horse."

The horse kept moving forward, and Cooper let go of the reins.

"Look, Corporal, I'm not here to fight. I was assigned to this unit as an Indian agent for the U.S. government. My name is Lieutenant Cooper. Just who the hell are you to draw a weapon on me?"

"Well, I was assigned to bring in deserters. I was, er, er, I was just gonna take this here soldier in for desertion," he stuttered.

"Looks to me like you were fixing to shoot him, not take him in." Cooper's eyes never left the corporal's face.

"Tain't none of your'n business; you need to speak to Major Bellamus. I'm telling ya ta git outta my way, afore I shoot you and the Injun woman, I'm'a warnin' ya." He rattled the gun at him.

Cooper, tired of the smart-mouthing, leaned in, grabbed the reins, and gave the horse a swift kick, causing the horse to lurch. Blaze lost her balance, tumbling off and hitting the ground with a thud. Cooper's horse knocked over the corporal, who lost his balance and sent the gun flying from his hand.

Since he'd cocked the hammer on the gun, it went off, sending a bullet flying in no apparent direction. The skinny corporal was knocked to the ground, and Cooper sneered, "Don't move, jackass."

Cooper, leaping from his horse, snatched the reins and a rope, tossing them to the terrified young soldier who'd been threatened at gunpoint.

"Take 'em, hold her. And tie him up. Now!" Cooper shouted.

The boy came out of his trance and did what Cooper ordered.

Turning, Cooper went to where Blaze lay, thinking she'd gotten the wind knocked out of her when she fell.

"Blaze," Cooper said, rolling her over onto her back. "Are you—" He was about to ask if she was okay when he saw the blood oozing and spreading over her deerskin cover-up. The bullet had ricocheted, hitting her.

"Over here!" he yelled at the young private. "Is anyone else still here?"

"I don't know. I mean, I can't say. Seems we all scattered when the shooting started. Then I was hiding until this here fella found me." The boy's hands were shaking.

Cooper wanted to ask why he was hiding, but it wasn't the right time.

He yanked the deerskin off Blaze's shoulder to look at the wound. The bullet had gone through her left shoulder. It didn't seem so bad. But she was losing a lot of blood, and it didn't look good. When he moved her head a little, Cooper saw a purplish knot on her temple. She'd smacked it on a rock and was out cold.

"Give me your belt," Cooper barked, scaring the boy. The young man, fumbling, removed his belt and gave it to Cooper. "Dig in my saddlebags and get me the extra shirts," he ordered. Cooper took the shirts and covered the bloody area.

"Put as much pressure as you can on these shirts. I'm going to raise her up to get the belt under her. What's your name, soldier?"

The young man shifted from foot to foot. "Frank."

"Get down and hold these shirts like I told you."

Cooper got the belt beneath the deerskin cover she wore over her dress.

"How old are you, boy?"

Before the boy could answer, he stood, taking one end and looping it through the buckle, pulling it tight, forming a tourniquet with the shirts flattened against her wound, hoping to keep her bleeding under control.

"Uh, seventeen on my birthday in two months."

Cooper scoffed. "Lord, son. Why join the Dragoons? You've got a heap of life to live, kid." He looked at the young man.

The boy pulled up, stretching his skinny frame as tall as he could. "Well, I ain't afraid, if that's what you're thinking," he spouted with semi-courageousness.

Cooper let out a deep, robust belly laugh. "So that's why you were hiding, huh? You ain't afraid?"

The boy shuffled his feet. "Well, I didn't have no weapon, and when it all went crazy, I ran. I figured if I stayed hidden and stayed put, I'd be safer and then I'd join up with my unit later, after... I mean."

"What's your last name, kid? Frank who?"

Before the boy could answer, Blaze cried out, "Dakota, Dakota, please help me."

"Get me that canteen, Frank." Cooper ordered, lifting her head. Frank handed him the canteen, uncapped.

"Drink." Cooper pressed the canteen rim to her lips, tipping it up so she could drink. She sipped the tepid water and choked, and he pulled the canteen away but kept her head cupped in his hand. "You were hit by that stray bullet. Does it hurt when you take a deep breath?"

"No, it doesn't. I got the wind knocked out of me when I fell off the horse." I touched the side of my head and winced.

"You hit your head. Thank God it wasn't hard enough to kill you, but it knocked you out for a minute. You could have a concussion," he said, sitting me upright. Looking up at the boy, he inclined his head at the tied corporal again.

"Get his jacket off so she can lay her head on it."

Cooper kept me steady while he waited for Frank to comply. After the boy handed him the ragged jacket, he laid my head down, using it as a pillow.

"Well," he said, looking around the area, "we can't stay here. No telling who might still be around and looking for a fight. Blaze, we're going to have to move. You think you're up to it?"

I didn't need to think long. I was ready to get the hell out of here. What I really meant was this era, this time—I was ready to go home. Plus, I wanted to find Dakota. I knew in my heart he was with his people and was okay.

Cooper helped me stand and checked my wound. We were both glad I'd stopped bleeding. The bullet went right through, passing no vital organs. I'd been lucky if you call a gunshot lucky.

"I'm worried about your wound getting infected. We need to get somewhere safe and get a fire going so we can cauterize it," Cooper said.

The possibility of infection hadn't crossed my overworked brain. "Cooper?" My voice was weak.

"Yeah, I'm here."

I pointed. "We should go up the mountain, over there."

"Any reason you think that?" I heard the worry in his tone.

"Because I feel this is where Dakota and Chief Black Raven have gone."

He didn't question my Indian woman's intuition; he had to trust it.

"Okay, let's get moving then."

Leaning against him for support, he got me over to the mare.

"Ya can't leave me here tied up, Lieutenant," the corporal yelled.

"You bet I can. You sit there and watch me do it. Someone will find ya. You can count on it," Cooper snarled. He was a dirtbag, just like the others, deserters or not.

"Hey, what about me?" the young boy-private whined.

Fed up with all these stupid boy-man soldiers, he said, "You got yourself in this man's army, Frank, so I suggest you get yourself out. I will not be your nursemaid."

Cooper bypassed the main camp area on purpose. Blaze had seen more than she needed to see already. He picked a path around the deserted army camp and took a shortcut up the mountain through the trees.

As the ride jostled her, Blaze winced, slouched, leaning into Cooper.

"You need me to stop for a bit?"

"No, we need to keep going. I don't feel there is much time."

Her voice was weak, and she slumped further with each stride.

Cooper masked his worry. "I don't think you're going to die, not yet. Getting shot hurts, but it isn't fatal. You'll live to tell another tale."

"No, not me dying. We need to get to Dakota. I feel our time in your era is ending; I didn't get here with him, but I need to be with him again before it ends." She urged him to hurry.

Cooper forged on at her demand, hoping he too would wake up from this—was it a nightmare, a dream, or Hell?

BLACK RAVEN WAS IN the lead, Dakota following, his mind on Blaze, wishing she were here with him. He hoped that whatever was supposed to happen in the last days had occurred, and she was back in their time, safe and sound. He closed his eyes, hoping to see her again.

"She isn't far from you, my young warrior," Black Raven spoke. Dakota came up alongside him and the trail widened.

"She is here," he pointed to his heart. "You will live a long life with her." His words reassuring.

"Chief, are you a prophet? Do you see my future?"

The old chief chuckled. "I am many things, young Wind Dancer, many things." He fell silent.

Dakota planned to research the Sioux line and Black Raven's history thoroughly if he returned to his time. There was more to know about Black Raven; more he could learn, yet time was short. It would take another lifetime to know the old chief. It was clear that this incredible chief was connected to Blaze.

BLACK RAVEN RODE, A glimmer of a smile touching his lips. He knew Wind Dancer and his lineage was a powerful line of well-known Sioux. He was a breed of powerful chiefs and had earned his feathers with this trip back in time.

They moved as the mountain dropped to a flatter field and the trees became less dense.

Dakota's eyes scanned every inch of the area ahead. He hoped for a sign of her. His pony descended the hill. He wanted to rush, kicking the pony into high gear, but the situation demanded patience.

Since it was just him and the old chief, they needed to exercise caution. Dakota couldn't be certain how many soldiers were still around, either roaming or ready to attack. What if they had her? What if Blaze was in trouble? He blinked to erase the picture in his mind. He couldn't think like that.

After his pony reached the level ground, he waited for the chief. He had come this far; parting was not an option, given the stakes.

33

BLAZE WAS WEAK. COOPER needed to stop and did so, despite her protests.

"Listen," he said, helping her down. "You're no good to anyone if you're too weak to travel. Rest, drink some water, and then we'll get going again."

Cooper was no caregiver, but he'd treated many men with gunshot wounds. Her injury was clean, through-and-through, but she'd lost a lot of blood, and he needed time to cauterize it.

He got a small fire going and laid his knife on the embers. Wishing he had something to dull her pain, he mentally smacked himself. Then he remembered the rotgut whiskey in his saddlebag. During the rush of everything that had happened, he'd forgotten he had it.

Kneeling beside Blaze, he watched her blink, trying to shake the cobwebs from her bleared vision. She'd drifted off, then closed her eyes again. Cooper touched her forehead, checking for fever. Her eyes flew open.

"I'm—oh my, I'm so sorry! I must have fallen asleep for a second, I-, please." The words stumbled out.

Cooper grinned, shaking his head. "Don't apologize. You've been shot and lost a lot of blood—that would sap anyone. Here."

He offered the flask, but she shook her head.

"No, no whiskey. I have to stay sharp."

"You'll need it to combat the pain when I put a hot knife to your skin to stop the bleeding."

She didn't argue and took two large gulps. "I hope I don't get sick and throw up."

Carefully, Cooper removed the belt and wadded-up shirts. Untying the ties, he slipped it off her shoulder and cleaned the wound with water and his neckerchief. Assessing the damage was impossible; once the wadding was removed, it bled again. He needed to get it closed.

He grabbed the knife from the fire. Blaze inhaled and stopped him.

"Wait. Let me have another drink of whiskey and something to bite down on. If I scream, it might cause problems."

Nodding, Cooper held the flask. She wiped her mouth and bit down on the small totem carving he had been working on. He pressed the hot knife to her skin to seal the wound, first on the front, then angled to reach the back. The pain was excruciating, yet she never lost consciousness. When finished, she removed the carving, surprised her teeth hadn't chipped the wood. Her bleeding stopped, though she felt weak.

Cooper marveled at her endurance. Stronger men had fainted from less. She trembled slightly under his gaze, and he kept her covered against the cold.

"We... we have to go," she murmured, then went limp. Cooper checked her pulse. It was weak. Shaking his head, he whispered, "You ain't going anywhere, little lady, not for a while. Here, drink some more whiskey to help you sleep."

She obeyed, too weak to protest. He tucked the three blankets around her and went to his horse, unsaddling it. Swatting the mare, he nodded. "Yep, everyone needs a rest."

After one last check, Cooper huddled closer to her in the remaining blanket. Off the beaten path, hidden in brush, he estimated they were a little over a mile from the army encampment. Closing his eyes, he tried to shut down his thoughts. He needed rest if he was to be any use.

Eight miles away, Dakota and the chief retraced the others' path back to the tribe, moving through lands Black Raven knew well, less traveled by White men. Dakota worried over Blaze's whereabouts, telling himself she was where she should be.

Thicker brush slowed them. The chief reined in.

"We must rest our ponies, Wind Dancer." Sliding off, he led his roan to a thicket and tied it.

Dakota, still on his pony, shook his head. The chief gestured sternly.

"If you have no pony, what shall you do, young spirit?"

Reluctantly, Dakota slipped off and tethered his pony next to the chief's. Watching him walk down the incline, Dakota wondered where he was going.

"Doe key ya lay hey?" (Where are you going?)

"Ableza wichahpi." (Look for water.) Without another word, the chief disappeared among the trees.

Dakota smiled. He would miss this old man once he returned to his future—if he still had one.

Blaze lay covered as best Cooper could manage. He considered adding a few fir limbs for warmth. When she awoke, he'd warm her with the whiskey he had left. He took a swig himself, easing the jitters.

The thicket was sparse, but it would do. They were headed northwest, mostly uphill. The powdery snow would get icier higher up. Winter had just begun. He had been cautious not to leave Blaze alone, which meant he hadn't scouted the area fully. Soon they'd need water or a larger fire to melt snow, though he had extinguished the small fire used to heat his knife.

He didn't want to advertise their position. Eyeing the hillside, he saw that traveling certain directions would be futile—too steep with two bodies on one horse. He wouldn't risk their lives unless necessary.

Watching her sleep, he considered this fearless half-Sioux, half-White woman. Her story seemed incredible, told with such conviction. But could it be true? He'd never heard the name WD Dakota, and his battalion was large, many unknown to him. The odds of her story matching his orders were astronomical. It had to be real, didn't it?

As he thought, he nodded off, then stood and stretched. Bending, he ensured Blaze was covered and still breathing; her foggy breath made her nose ice cold.

He tucked her face with a thin scarf, leaving room to breathe. Adding fir limbs for warmth and camouflage, he surveyed the area. A twig snapped behind him. He whirled, pistol raised. A rabbit froze, then scurried away.

"Hmmm," he whispered. "Rabbit, now that would be tasty." His stomach gurgled.

He scouted the area, noting the easiest route back to camp. If soldiers were looking for them, they would have found them by now. One last check confirmed Blaze wasn't stirring. No one would know she was there.

My DREAMS WERE VIVID, filled with the tribe and Dakota. They were whimsical, like watching a colorful Indian musical revue without music or singing. I was a main character, living a life of hardship and happiness so real I could almost touch it. My visions turned fitful, and I grimaced, brows knitting with fear, as I cowered in a deep, dark cavern, unwilling to see what unfolded. I was alone. No one came to save me.

"Aunt Meda, Dakota, where are you? Please, please answer." My dream-self cried into the darkness. Silence answered.

My body twitched, and I moaned—not from pain, but heartache. A single tear fell. My mind wandered from the start of my life to the day I realized my true feelings for the warrior called Wind Dancer.

A smile flitted across my sleeping face as I envisioned life with him by my side. Then, as if time had stopped and rewound, it all fell away, like colored sand in an hourglass now plain and still.

My life reversed into darkness. I wept, afraid, a withered hand stroking my head. Gone were those who had raised me. In my nightmare, I opened teary eyes, recalling the day my parents were laid to rest, leaving me alone. "You'll never be alone, my Iye Igmu'watogla, my She Cougar," whispered a strong, older voice.

I dreamt on, moving through my life to the day I lay beside a cold, dilapidated woodshed in North Dakota, watching two strangers perform a strange ritual.

My heart screamed, *No, don't dream this way. It will erase your memories.* But my mind pressed forward. Each figment repeated, adding details without changing the storyline, like reading a book with missing pages only to find new ones added, richer, more vivid, driving toward a finale. It was a bottomless cycle, repeating endlessly, time folding in on itself. I never woke, trapped in a vortex with no release.

The final dream was more vivid, completing the story. Cold had seeped into my bones. I tried to wake but remained in the dream state. My mind stretched my body; toes flexed, fingers twitched, feeling frozen in ice and thawing unevenly. A shiver ran from ears to feet, loosening the numbness. Yet my eyes stayed shut. Was I dead or sleeping? Déjà vu washed over me—had I felt this before, without the cold?

I began moving slowly, testing life. Eyes wouldn't open. Saliva was warm; my mouth dry. Something prickly covered my face. My tongue touched it—it was fuzzy, not tape. Relief.

Wiggling toes and feeling thick socks, I cracked my neck, realizing I was layered in clothing. Panic rose. Where was I? How many years forward or backward? Could one die twice in a lifetime?

Desperate, my mind raced. I wanted arms to hold me again, a mouth to kiss me, making me less afraid. Whose? Who had appeared in my dreams?

"I must be crazy," I said aloud, the words echoing.

Opening my eyes, I confirmed I was back in my time. Cold and furious, I realized how long I'd lain there, passed out, possibly risking hypothermia or frostbite. Where were the two strangers from the woodshed ritual?

Rolling away from the shed, I rose on my knees, crunching icy snow. Alone. I stretched, wiggling hands, feet, fingers, toes, even my nose—testing function. Pulling scarves from my face, I began the trek to my vehicle, thoughts alive with memories of the vivid hallucinations.

Unlocking the doors, I paused to look back. Desolate, abandoned, yet strangely full, the scene lingered. Images and faces flashed in my mind. Warmth spread from toes to head, a fire igniting in my belly. One face stood out—an Indian warrior, tall, lean, beautiful. I slipped into the car, preparing for the journey home.

"If only," I muttered, breath fogging. Sliding the key in, I waited for the car to warm before touching heat or drive, wary of mishaps. Surviving passed-out in such cold was beyond comprehension.

The Suburban warmed. I aimed heat toward my face, removing gloves. Warm air soothed my freezing nose. I turned the blower to my feet, revved the engine, and prepared to drive.

Civilization—such a funny word—made me sad, yet I craved its comfort.

Removing my hat, I shook out my hair, shedding layers to settle for the drive. A hot bath at the hotel was my new mission. Lifting my arm to shrug out of the fleece jacket, pain shot through me. My body ached as if I were ancient, crouched too long. Jacket off, layer by layer, I massaged a sore shoulder, bruised to the bone. The thick sweater prevented inspection.

"I'll see what I've done to myself at the hotel," I whispered.

Turning to leave, I scanned the area in moonlight. Nothing unusual. Trees, snow, mountains. Hoping something would click, I blinked. Nothing.

Feeling an odd sadness leaving, I exhaled, closed my eyes, then drove out, thoughts filled with something strange, something unforgettable.

Dakota knew pain—but never like this. In all his lifetimes, past or future, he had never felt a heart so laden. Memories surged, yet it never felt enough. It seemed like two lifetimes had passed since he'd seen, felt, or heard her, yet so little time had gone by.

Why was he still here? How long before the gods of time-travel magic returned him to his future to be with her? Chief Black Raven's assurance did little to calm his frustration.

"You, my young warrior, need patience. Sit by the fire with Swift Eagle and me," the chief said, motioning.

Dakota obeyed, grateful to have returned to the tribe intact, yet frustrated to remain in the time warp. Something was off. Time felt backward; he was stuck, unable to move forward. How had Blaze returned while he had not? Discouraged and weary, he longed for his own time and the woman he loved. Had their mission already concluded? If she was gone, yes. Otherwise, she was still here.

Maka smiled, aware of his discontent but uncertain how to help. Dakota returned the smile. Her older version reminded him of Blaze, yet it stirred his heart. If there was more to do, he would see it through. Dakota's resolve was ironclad—he would wait lifetimes if needed to return to her; he had no other choice.

34

WEEKS AFTER I RETURNED to my own time, my dreams were no longer dreams, but nightmares. Aunt Meda tiptoed around, watching me with concern, saying nothing.

"Okay, I can't take it any longer." I stood in the doorway of my aunt's sitting room. Seeing all of my aunt's Sioux artifacts and décor, I breathed it in, as it gave me a sense of comfort.

"What can't you take?" Aunt Meda rocked in the chair, her hands clasping an old black book, faded and weathered by time.

"I don't know, but I can't take it any longer. You're too quiet and, well, it's just that something is off balance."

Walking into the room, I stood next to her and looked down into her lap. Eyeing the old, faded journal, my aunt Meda's hands fell away, giving me room to pick up the ancient leather book. As I did, something inside of me jumped, and a lump formed in my throat. These feelings were so powerful they shook me to the core.

With very gentle hands, I turned the book over, examining it, treating it as if it were a foreign object. An incredible feeling stirred within me, a passion I'd never felt—or one I had felt and was remembering. It was an odd sensation.

"Blaze, you okay?" Meda saw my physical reaction. Her eyes grew wide. "I can see the pulse in your neck jump. Your face is pale!"

"Auntie, what is that book?" My eyes never left it.

"It is something I've wanted to show you, but I've been apprehensive to do so, due to, well..." Aunt Meda trailed off, not finishing her thought.

I moved over to the divan to sit, and my hands shook as I opened the old journal. The outside leather was cracked and thin, and the pages were made of a substance I had never seen before. It was soft and tougher than normal paper, as if someone had taken leather and stretched it to the point of almost transparency, yet it was still viable. My eyes scanned the first page. It had odd writings and drawings. I turned to the next page, then the next, and saw the same. It seemed familiar.

"Auntie, does this have anything to do with, well, my dreams?"

Meda rocked, nodding. "It might, if you will tell me what you dreamed about." She hoped this would open the chasm that had formed between what her niece thought was reality and dreams. Meda knew her niece's dreams would reveal the truth.

I was about to learn that I needed only to speak about my dreams, as the old journal foretold. Only then would the past and the future meld together, righting not only my world but also his. I needed to trust and let my fears go. *Tell your story,* a voice cried within—a voice I'd heard long ago. It was the voice of a woman back in time, acknowledged as Mother Earth, the wise woman I knew as Maka in my dreams.

After contemplating her request, I knew I had to tell my aunt. It was an odd, unbelievable story, but as it spilled out, I saw that Aunt Meda believed every word I said—as I did, too.

———— ❦ ————

DAKOTA SAT ON HIS pony at the very spot he'd found her. His longing was as disquieting as his anguish was deep. The wind picked up, and the prairie grass swayed. He looked up at the sky, wishing she would fall from it into his arms.

Why was he torturing himself with thoughts of her, this place, and his memories?

Maka told him it would be the right place to go—the place he'd found her—to relive his memories. Swift Eagle agreed. Dakota couldn't see how it would help, but Chief Black Raven agreed with them. He needed to search his soul and connect his past.

Chief Black Raven was a mystery to him, as were his words. *Search his soul and connect his past*—what did that mean, and how would it help?

Dakota grimaced. His life was still in the past, and he couldn't get out of it. Even though he loved his ancestors and his heritage, and at one time during this ordeal he would've been glad to stay here and live his life, now he loved something far more—he loved Blaze. He would've stayed here forever if she had still been by his side.

Dark Cloud tried to cheer him up—of all people, Dark Cloud was not the cheerful type. He was a pure warrior, all business, the Sioux kind of man.

Dakota dismounted his pony, leading him to a nearby tree, then sat with his back propped against the trunk.

The sky was clear except for a spattering of clouds, the wind warm, and it was early spring—just like the day he'd found her, alone and scared out of her wits. He smiled, recalling the look on her face as an Indian had approached her. Over time, he'd learned how smart she was and how she'd fit into the tribe when he had doubted it so much. Somehow, Dakota felt she was a stronger Sioux than he was.

Leaning his head back against the tree, he shut his eyes. He saw her face, felt her breath on his neck, and could smell the sweet scent of her skin. It was inconceivable that these were just ghost memories—they felt real. He could hear her saying his name during the time he'd made love to her, and he could feel her hands, mighty and strong, pulling him closer than he'd ever been to any woman. It had all been so real, and now it was lost—forever, it seemed.

Dakota stood, surveying the area, and wondered aloud, "Blaze, can you feel me and my heart? Do you know I'm here and I wait for you? If I am here, I wish for you to return to me. If not, may the gods of time and the wind transport me to you, wherever you are."

His words carried on the wind in Lakota. He bowed his head, hoping the all-powerful gods in the sky heard his plea.

Mounting his pony, the Sioux warrior called Wind Dancer rode back toward the tribe, his heart just as heavy as it had been when he arrived at this place. The wind blew harder as he rode, and the clouds grew darker and thicker in the sky.

A storm, he thought. *A spring storm is coming.*

———

I FINISHED TELLING MY aunt the story, which I felt had been only a dream.

"Read Chief Black Raven's ancient diary, my She Cougar, and then you will know," Aunt Meda spoke in Lakota.

I understood her.

How was this possible?

I had fantasized that I knew the language—but it was real. I understood what she'd said, and I answered her back in Lakota.

"Will it tell me what happened to me and what has happened to Wind Dancer, the man I dream about?"

This time Meda smiled. "You spoke Lakota. This is proof. She Cougar, now you know all of this is real. You are awake, not dreaming. Your mind is awake, and now so is your heart."

I took the old journal, hoping to understand what this archaic diary had to say. Day in and day out, the book sat in front of me as I tried to find answers to the questions burning in my heart. How would I get my love back? Who was Dark Cloud, and why had I traveled so far back in time to make sure he lived—and, along the way, fallen in love with Wind Dancer?

As Dakota rode, the wind blew harder and the rain pelted him, but his heart somehow lifted as he entered camp. He smiled at Maka and Swift Eagle and went in search of Chief Black Raven.

"He won't be here with us much longer. She searches for him." Maka placed her hand on Swift Eagle's arm.

The old man nodded. "Yes, old woman, I know. It has been good, and now he must return to his own people—to his woman."

Maka smiled and patted her husband's arm. He was romantic at heart; he just never admitted it, wishing to be seen as a powerful warrior, not soft-hearted.

Time stood still in both worlds, as one waited to begin a new life while another tried to return to an old one.

The book revealed little. I read and reread, studied and searched, but nothing made any difference. For days, I picked my aunt's brain about Sioux history and burned up the internet looking for answers of any kind. Nothing changed. No magical revelation appeared, awake or asleep.

Months later, as we cooked dinner, I sat despondent, watching Meda hum as she crushed corn in a bowl and added other ingredients for her famous cornbread.

I sighed. "Auntie, I've read and researched, but there's nothing to explain anything—and I've seen no great change, either."

"That isn't so. You've changed. You glow, even in sadness."

"Me? You think I've changed? How—how do you think I've changed?"

"You're more Sioux now. You've embraced our heritage. You interact with the people. You've become involved in Indian politics. Blaze, you never knew who your neighbors were before, and you didn't care about our village or its people. I see you now. You speak Lakota to others, and you've given them hope that our past isn't dwindling away—not forgotten, never forgotten. You are our future."

"What a speech. I sound amazing," I kidded. "Maybe I should try for a place on the tribal council. You can be my campaign manager."

"Well, you know—" Aunt Meda began.

"No."

It was one word, but Meda wasn't deterred. She knew things changed—especially minds.

"Did you know there's an older woman who lives on the outskirts of Standing Rock Reservation? Only a few miles from town. She's an exceptional historian of the Sioux people."

My face knotted. "And you tell me this—why?"

"For weeks I've watched you search, and yet you haven't found what you're looking for. But you haven't given up. I've seen your strength grow each day. You may not see it, Blaze, but we do."

"We? Who is *we*?"

"The council. Blackie, Pete, Sam, and me. Those who knew you when you were the girl called half-breed—a child born to Gray Wolf, who never cared about the line of distinguished chiefs she came from."

"They called me half-breed? Our people?" I hadn't realized how far removed I'd become.

Meda laughed. "That's beside the point. Knowing you now, no one would ever say that again. The time has come for you to find your answers. Go to the old woman. Ask her."

"Why didn't you tell me this sooner?"

Meda took my hands and looked into my heart before speaking.

"It takes time for the heart to be pure. Sometimes what we fear most is what we want. Blaze, now you are ready."

I touched my shoulder, where the scar remained—real, tangible.

"Go to Silver Moon," Meda said softly. "She will tell you."

Taking a deep breath, I knew what I had to do.

I would find the old woman called Silver Moon.

35

DAKOTA SAT ALONE ON the rock by the stream where he had once sat beside Blaze, remembering her and how life for them had been an eternity ago. That life had faded and slipped away from him.

A light breeze blew, and the leaves rustled; some fell, landing in the stream, floating as if in a dream. A soft peacefulness permeated the air. All he could hear was the soft whooshing of air, and somewhere far away, a horse neighed.

Black Raven and Cooper sat atop a hill in the far-off distance, but they could see Dakota.

The chief turned as he spoke. "He'll be gone by morning."

Cooper was still in awe of what had happened. It had been a shock when he returned to the snowy hillside where he'd left a camouflaged Blaze, injured and sleeping, to find she had gone. In her physical state, she couldn't have gotten far, yet he couldn't find her anywhere. The search had been futile. She was nowhere, and he had been bewildered. Without her here, there was no reason to stay, so he had gathered his things and begun his trek up the mountain.

He had no plan; he just had to go. Cooper figured he'd travel up the mountain and scout out the area to see what lay ahead. He had to keep himself out of harm's way—one man against many—not his idea of how he had envisioned his future, not that day.

Four hours later, he crossed paths with Chief Black Raven and the man Blaze had called Wind Dancer. The woman had been right—Dakota and Chief Black Raven were exactly where she'd thought them to be. It was then the stories, unbelievable as they still seemed, poured out. The warrior, Wind Dancer, and the woman, Blaze, shared the same story—how could he not believe in the truth of it all?

"You now believe, Cooper?" the chief questioned, breaking into the man's thoughts.

"Yes, but I don't understand it. It makes me wonder about the dreams I have sometimes."

The chief nodded, his brow pensive, deep in thought.

"Cooper, you like here, with our people, you stay long time?" the chief asked, turning his attention back to the man next to him.

"Yes, Chief. Yes, I think I'll stay, if that suits you and the tribe. I'd like that a lot." Cooper didn't want to go; he had nothing waiting for him anywhere.

"Huh, is good. You find a woman, have children, and grow old with Sioux. I have dreamed it—you happy; you live a full life with us." Black Raven began turning his pony, then looked back at the man, Wind Dancer, as did Cooper.

"Your dreams tell you he'll be happy here too?" Cooper asked, turning his pony to follow.

"No, he must travel far, very far. He'll be gone before I dream again. Come, Cooper, we sit by my home fires." The chief tapped his heels into the flank of his pony and took off. Cooper followed.

Dreams—yes, Black Raven knew dreams, but he didn't always share them; there might be danger in that, even with his new friend and the newest member of his tribe, he'd decided.

Two unlikely men—the chief and Cooper—now joined, not by accident but because it was their fate, headed off to a life they'd live together as brothers.

At the bottom of the hill, as the water trickled in the stream and the breeze whispered through the trees, a lone warrior sat, his head down, his eyes shut.

Somewhere over a hundred thirty years in the future, there was a story a woman told that would start his slow, yet peaceful journey back home. Home—to a time he knew, to a place he was from, and back to the arms of the woman he had grown to respect and love for the fighter she was, for the beauty she emitted. For the soul of a true Sioux warrior, Wind Dancer headed back to Blaze, his Sioux Woman, She Cougar.

EPILOGUE

I SAT WITH THE old Sioux woman they called Silver Moon every day and listened to the stories she told. Silver Moon recalled stories of the life that had been lived by the Sioux Indian for many years before—before her great-grandfather was born, and even further back than that. She held me in a trance as she spoke these fantastic stories, speaking her native tongue.

There was so much that wasn't in the history books, so much vivid color in her stories, that even though I'd already been there through strange magic, Silver Moon's words transported me back to that time. It was as if I were reliving it through her stories all over again. None of the stories the old woman told gave me a clue why Dakota and I had been transported back in time. The time we lived in that era had not been written about, as it was so far into the past that time never recorded it. It was as if it had never happened. How could that be?

What the old woman *could* tell me was about the lineage of the Sioux, so she began, and I listened intently, looking for a reason I would have been transported through time.

"The lines of our tribe go back from many great warriors. Dakota's birthright was born from the line of Sitting Bull. A brave named Dark Cloud would have a daughter. And she would beget Jumping Bull."

Silver Moon stopped in the middle of her lineage story. She looked at me with sudden recognition, as if a light had shone above her head.

"You're the maiden who made sure Dark Cloud lived."

Silver Moon patted my hand, smiled, and continued.

"If it were not for you, She Cougar, our Sioux history would have been changed more than you could ever know. You told Wind Dancer to go with Dark Cloud."

"But there was nothing happening—no one was fighting, and the soldiers were not there." I had not forgotten a single detail. There was no insignificant moment in my mind that I could not see from my idyllic dream. I saw every color, knew every face, and even smelled the smells.

"Ah, but you rode out with a man called Cooper, and had you not told Wind Dancer to ride with Dark Cloud, the army soldiers would have shot him, as well as you, Dakota, and the man called Cooper."

Silver Moon folded her arms, her feet moving the rocking chair forward and back in a steady motion.

"It would have all been different if you had not uttered the words *go with Dark Cloud*. There were more soldiers coming, and more Sioux would have died, and Sitting Bull would never have been born."

It had taken many days to get to this story, and once there, Silver Moon shared documentation of the family history of Sitting Bull—records not written in history books. These documents bore a seal of authenticity that was undeniable, and they were the proof I needed to see. Sitting Bull was a prominent figure in Sioux history. What would have happened if he had never been born? Would history have changed so drastically that the Sioux Indian would have ceased to exist?

Understanding *why* I was there was still a mystery to me. Dakota could have saved Sioux history and the lineage of Sitting Bull without me, so why had I been there at all?

Silver Moon, Aunt Meda, and the other council members assured me it had been necessary for me to travel backward in time—to create my future and the future of our people, to save the Red Man's history. I had a purpose, and one day I would understand the reasons, as the truth would reveal itself through an old soul, a soul very close to me.

Dakota was home in his time, where he belonged, and he felt more at peace with who he was and with his future. Once he had lived a lifetime in the past, and now it was time to find me. He did not wait, nor did he have to search long. I wasn't surprised when he appeared—unexpected, yet so expected. Time no longer mattered to either of us; what mattered was that we were finally together.

It had been nearly ten years since we'd reunited from the past into our future, and life had been more than we could ever have dreamed. Dakota and I watched her. She was the light of our lives, full of so much life.

Raven Maka Clark Kangee, daughter of Dakota Wind Dancer Kangee and me, Blaze She Cougar Clark.

The roan pony walked up to our daughter without fear, and as she stroked its soft muzzle, the pony whinnied.

Raven, a girl with dark hair and sharp eyes, carried an old spirit in a young girl's body. Silver Moon and Aunt Meda called young Raven an old soul in a youthful body from the moment she spoke her first words.

Remembering the words of the council, I now understood the reason for my transport into the faraway past. That reason was not only to save Dark Cloud, but to bring an old soul back into my future—unconventionally.

Both Dakota and I were impressed with our daughter's uncanny ability with the Lakota language and her way with animals. Raven had a gift with dreams and the ability to foreshadow events. It was something we understood, because we knew we had conceived our daughter one hundred thirty years ago, bringing her into this world to be born in the future.

Raven was the destiny of two unlikely people—Dakota Kangee and me. We had been sent back in time to keep Sioux history unchanged and to create a child who would forge a new frontier for the future Sioux and for the Red Man throughout history. Our daughter had a purpose of her own. A destiny awaited Raven Maka Clark Kangee, one that would be of great significance to many American Indians.

All three of our lives were shaped by time—past, present, and future.

Time was an odd thing for Dakota and me. We had lived two lifetimes spanning centuries—from hundreds of years ago to the present. It was strange to think that we had one lifetime long ago and another we had shared for nearly a decade. And now, with our daughter, it felt as though our lives had only just begun.

The End

NOTE FROM THE AUTHOR

Word-of-mouth is crucial for any author to succeed. If you enjoyed *Saving a Sioux Legacy*, please leave a review online—anywhere you are able. Even if it's just a sentence or two, it would make all the difference and I would appreciated it!

Thanks!

Deanna

ABOUT THE AUTHOR

Saving a Sioux Legacy is the first young adult fantasy novel by author Deanna King. Deanna lives in Bedford, Texas, with her husband Travis.

Website- DeannaKingWriting.com

Facebook- Deanna King Writing Twitter- @dkingnovelist

Linked-In- Deanna King Instagram- Deanna.king777

ACKNOWLEDGEMENTS:
  To my beta readers Christy Williams and Thomas Faught, thank you for your valuable input. To Travis thank you for all your support and encouragement. Last, I must thank Google and Wikipedia for making my research much easier.

WANT MORE?

Protector of Legends

Raven's Story

Prolouge

I go by the name of Raven. My full name is Raven Maka
Clark Kangee, the daughter of Dakota Kangee and Blaze Clark,
known as Wind Dancer and She Cougar. My father is a
full-blooded Sioux and my mother is half Sioux, half White.
What does this make me? Proud. I'm proud of both my her-
itages.

My mom recounted the tale of how I came into existence.
A fairytale I loved—hearing about her trip back in time to a
place where people lived off the land, hunted buffalo, and life
was hard. My father told me about our famous Sioux ancestors
and the strength they passed down to me. My dad was pleased
I was one with the animals and with the acreage. I had a gift.
Mom got dreamy-eyed recalling how they made me in the Paha
Sapa during a winter storm. Paha Sapa is the Lakota word for
Black Hills, which are in parts of North and South Dakota.
Our Council sent her on a journey through time to guarantee
a legacy for the Sioux Nation. She'd saved the life of a Sioux
Warrior named Dark Cloud. If he had died, the famous Chief,
Sitting Bull, would've never been born and part of the Sioux
history would've changed.

"There was a battle between some Dragoons who'd run away from the Army to look for gold in the Black Hills, and a general was chasing them."

"Dragoons. Can they breathe fire?"

My momma hugged me giggling. "No, Baby Bird, they're Army men from the olden days."

Baby Bird was her pet name for me. Her story awed me how they'd lived in a teepee, traveling a long way on horses, and how scared she was when the Army men were fighting. Other times I would ask her to share the tale of how she went to sleep in the snow and woke up on the prairie to meet my dad.

Make-believe stories, fairytales, and infantile fables. I loved to hear them. To the same degree I doubted their truth, although what a lovely way to share the story of my Mom and Dad's love for one another and my creation—*until the day I discovered the books, yes, books, four to be exact. Books not on our bookshelves, books I'd never seen before, books that fascinated me and, in the end, would enlighten me.*

The first book was *The Diary of Blaze Clark Kangee.* My hands trembled as I browsed accounts written in my mother's hand, the same bedtime tales I'd heard as child, dated from before I was born. Just how could she have known these stories beforehand? Once more, I repeated the word in my head: *stories.*

After reading some of her diary, I took the next old book, its yellowed rough pages bound with tiny strips of thin leather, and covered with tanned animal hide. My heart raced, and with caution, I turned the brittle pages. Crude drawings which intrigued me and the words written in Lakota, words not foreign to me since I had long since embraced the language and I could read, write, and speak the language of my people. My heart stopped. This book talked of a supernatural journey to other worlds and times, how a favored one must travel to save people who would cease to exist. Chronicles of a chosen woman sent to save one man and the legacy of her people. I read pages and pages written by an old chief known as Black Raven and how he envisioned this type of enchanted transportation. Stories of how he'd learned to leave his physical body and watch over his people when held captive by Army men in tattered clothing. My hands trembled as I closed this book, my pulse hammered in my neck. I'd just read the true tale, proof I was the flesh and blood of what I had always deemed a fairytale.

I sat this book on top of my mother's diary and opened the next book. The pages also yellowed but not as brittle. Tied together by leather and fastened shut with the same thin leather straps. Words written in snaky cursive as the writer's hands shook while penning the words, *Book of Dreams—Meda Clark*. My great Aunt Meda Clark, my grandfather Gray Wolf's sister. These were her dreams, dreams with important meanings, visions which had occurred or would occur, no reasonable order, no dates. One might consider her past visions had happened already, but that wasn't how this worked. While I read, I noted early on she spoke of magnificent black birds, a male and a female, both large ravens. Fascinating since I'd heard the stories of Chief Black Raven from the 1800s and my name was Raven. Aunt Meda's reveries and her complex interpretations of what they meant, but dreams to me were like tarot cards. I wasn't a believer. If I had known then how to decipher the meanings, I would've understood her power. Whilst I flipped through her book of scribbles, the question of why we had her book popped in my head—why didn't *she* have it? I set it aside and grabbed the last leather-bound book, undoing the straps, turning to page one. The only thing written on the page was "Undocumented History—Hunkpapa Sioux, 1799," and underneath, "As told by Silver Moon."

Silver Moon, our own Siouan legend. An older woman with whom I had strong ties as did Auntie Meda and my mother. Her handwriting in the beginning was strong, dark, and bold. Over the decades, it grew fragile, and not so heavy-handed. The words she'd written shifted from cursive to printing, so they were more legible. The information written in Lakota were accounts of undocumented happenings over hundreds of years ago. How was this not in history books, because if it happened, then it happened, didn't it? I read and understood. These narratives are too far-fetched. It read like *Aesop's Fables*. No one would believe this to be true of our people, or our history. Magic, time travel, time warps, spirits moving from one dimension to another to fix time and space. This was craziness, it had to be. I could've dismissed this information as not part of our people's history. However, the facts would stand later, and before long I'd have to rely upon these very secrets guaranteeing the lives of many, including my own.

I put the books back where I found them. Funny. It'd been the other way around. The books found me. I hadn't been searching for them. I'd been searching for some old family photos in the attic. Photos my mother wanted. Did my mother play a trick on me? I supposed it didn't matter because what was past was past, so I kept this news to myself, not telling her or asking questions. A sly smile crossed my face. This could drive her bananas. Oh, I hoped so.

I slept in spurts dreaming. Tall and magnificent, I'd seen him on the hill, and standing by his side an impressive-looking buffalo. In my dream, I walked to him. He awaited my approach. The closer I came, though, the more distant he grew. Once I stood where he had, his image was all but a wisp of air. Next to my feet, I found what he'd left for me. A thin braid of rawhide, three feathers attached on one end, on the other an arrowhead of steely flint rock. This lay at my feet and the tip of the arrowhead pointed in the direction he'd disappeared. I picked it up, closing my eyes, grasping the arrowhead, holding it in my fist.

The leather strap dangled, the three feathers blew in a sudden wind gust, and I gasped, as a whirlwind of images, words, and voices flowed through my soul, fitting pieces of history into tight-knitted frames. This generated a wonderful yet terrifying saga.

When I woke, my skin was wet with perspiration. My heart beat to the point I could hear the *thump-thump-thump* sounding in my ears. I was out of breath, like I'd just run a mile without stopping.

I stared at the shadows on the ceiling as the moonlight danced from corner to corner. The curtains on my window parted. I saw the night sky and turned on my side, staring into the darkness. Out in the country, on our ranch land, without city lights to dim the stars, I saw millions twinkling and flashing. Shooting through the skies not one, not two, but several shot through bursting into small flashes then disappeared. Covered with bare wispy clouds, yet the stars shone so bright. My breath caught in my throat. I felt as if I might suffocate. With force, I breathed air into my tight lungs. I drifted back to sleep to dream again.

They'd chosen me to make the journey to flit between worlds. Mending a crack draining people of life. The Sioux with a lifetime of heritage. But this also included the Cheyenne, the Crow, the Comanche, the Cherokee, and the Whiteman.

In my imaginings, the changes occurred in stages. I was powerless to stop it, my destiny in motion. My world as I'd known it was about to fade, albeit bit by bit, into shadows. As if clouds covered the stars without warning, our future might forever change if I didn't set it back on course, ensuring the same outcome to keep the world from being flung into a tailspin to plummet and burn.

My impending task was to rewind history to stop it from imploding, and align back to yesteryear. I would form allegiances with descendants from other tribes. Our worlds, rebuilt with the courage of those called together by ancient magic and hearts of the fearless.

While I slept, my brow crinkled, and I tossed and turned until then I stilled. I would find love in an unusual partner who appeared, yet I saw no face. A man once my foe would fight alongside me. In unison with the others, we'd put the future back to rights, repairing the cracks within our worlds.

My flights of fantasies continued, and in a magical moment, the clouds dispersed, unveiling a sky filled with a million stars that set the night ablaze with their brilliant glow. The nobleman stood atop the hill and I at the bottom. The buffalo seemed grander than before. He wore the bonnet of a chief and in his hands he held a book. His head nodding, his face wore a pleased countenance. His lips moved to speak, yet I heard nothing until the wind carried his words to my heart. Words telling me that through these events I'd grow a woman's heart and fall in love to continue my strong ancestral line. My courage would prove my value and my worthiness of life and love. It was my birthright to travel the realms of time to save the legends of the Real People, the First People.

Chapter 1

"It'll be soon." At the breakfast bar, she'd been reading and rereading the *Book of Dreams*. Blaze looked at Dakota. Worry filled her eyes. She understood firsthand the fear she'd felt in a world not her own. Her daughter...well, her daughter wasn't her. Raven was part her and Dakota. A force much stronger than she'd been. Aunt Meda's book told her nothing as she flipped through the pages, in search of a sign of what Raven may face. Even in her written words, Aunt Meda was a mystery. With her own special talents, Raven might understand its craziness. Blaze didn't interpret visions. Dreams told her a story, yet she didn't comprehend any deeper meaning. For her, visions were one-dimensional. With a hefty exhale, she reread one particular story, and it saw a dark-haired maiden in travel. The journey was her daughter's quest and she wouldn't be there to guide the daughter whom she loved. This was Raven's chosen path, not hers, for she'd completed her quest twenty-three years ago.

Dakota nodded. "I feel it too, and you're aware our daughter is strong, right?" Over the rim of his coffee cup, he winked.

A tinkling laugh, the one he loved so much, slipped out, and she smiled. "Of course, who do you think her mother is, my love, my Wind Dancer?" Blaze tried playing it off, but he saw she worried.

Dakota leaned in and kissed her, tasting the sweetness from her lips.

Once the kiss ended, Blaze sighed. "Our baby will face many things, but we won't be there for her."

"Ah, but you forget, my beautiful She Cougar. You were also alone when you journeyed back in time. Our daughter is the same age you were. Raven's strong. I hate to say it, but she's stronger than you were and don't forget she's my daughter, too," Dakota remarked.

Her smile not reaching her eyes, she nodded. "You're right, but I'll still worry. Like Aunt Meda worried about me, I'll worry about Raven. There are differences, though. She's aware of her journey. But not completely prepared."

He studied the tabletop. "Raven knows something will happen, sure, but not when nor what. Although she has advantages, you didn't, because she can speak the language and knows her people's history."

Blaze's lips curled into a bittersweet smile, contented by her daughter's understanding, knowing something was about to occur, but also filled with unease, unsure of the obstacles ahead. Even the elders weren't privy to what or when her daughter's journey would start or end.

LIFE AS WE'D LIVED it, past and present, shall disappear as the world's axes reversed, erasing important moments no one ever suspected were important. Raven's task was to make sure those moments didn't vanish. Crucial past events that could cease to occur were solely dependent on her to ensure they happened as they should, keeping the world righted at all costs.

Together, they will unite to revive a world that may have never existed without them. Years before into the future, forever lost, and many important people shall cease to exist, thus changing the world. It was Raven's birthright to prevent this catastrophic calamity.

A SHAWL AROUND HER hunched, frail shoulders, she rocked with ease. Her wrinkled hands no longer nimble pulling the shawl tighter, she smiled. Meda 'Soft Dove' Clark, a tribal sooth-sayer, understood it was time for her grandniece. Raven's life journey was close at hand. In Meda's heart, she knew that Raven possessed a strength even greater than her mother Blaze.

Sounds of steps on the wooden stairs brought her out of her thoughts. A slight creak squeaked out as he emerged on the top step. Meda turned to see Blackie 'Black Crow' Kangee step on her porch, making his way to her. Bending, he kissed her cheek.

"Blackie, it's been too long since you've visited."

He patted her hand. "It's been a while. Pete, Sam, Paytah, and Wakanda will be here soon. The others are coming?"

"Yes."

He stood against the porch railing in a relaxed pose saying nothing, as they enjoyed the midmorning sunlight. Blackie not-ed her house and the area for the umpteenth time. It suited her. He loved this area. It felt like family. The house, smaller and old-er, made of wood, set on a pier-and-beam foundation, draped with lattice. Latch doors set in four various spots around the foundation as crawl spaces for plumbing repairs or other needed work. The front wraparound porch made of wood—sanded and treated with water-resistant materials, painted the color of light oak faded with age and overlapped around the sides, appearing to encircle the house. The porch, large enough to host a gathering of twenty adults, with kids amassing underfoot, running in and out. Over the years, there'd been weddings, birthdays, funerals, or other tragedies their clan endured held on their massive vestibule.

Ready to embark on the next stages of her life, as a wedding gift, she'd given all her land and her house to her niece, Blaze. She and Dakota built onto the farmhouse before Raven was born, including a new barn, a tack room, and a small cottage for a ranch hand. Over the years, they'd done well raising cattle and a small herd of horses.

Meda then moved in with Silver Moon, her Siouan Spirit sister. Silver Moon had decided long ago to never take a Christian first name or surname. The US government gave her a Christian name, yet she refused to acknowledge the name or answer to it. Long ago, the US government tried to eradicate the American Natives, pushing them into the Whiteman's world. The old woman never wished to be known as Mary, Sally, or Abigail Washington. Silver Moon, a pure Sioux woman, born Sioux, would live and die as a Sioux. No government could ever change this fact, so no reason for her to change her name.

———— ⚶ ————

THOSE TWO OLD LADIES in one house, a frightening thought. Meda nearing eighty and Silver Moon possibly in the latter part of her nineties, but only a guess. She'd never shared her age.

Had it not been for Silver Moon's unfathomable knowledge of the past and its secrets, the mystery of Blaze Clark Kangee's journey would never have been known.

So much more transpired in our past than what we read in books. The facts you thought were true concerning your history, or any history, were lacking. Certain people knew things never written in a book. Silver Moon was such a person. Blaze had concluded this was a secret for few, and she'd been one of the few. If anyone ever told you some of this history, you'd not believe it to be true. Blaze and Dakota lived within a small circle of those who knew and believed.

In time, Blaze learned her delightful daughter Raven was another special soul who shared this magic within this elite circle. Raven was destined for something unknown, and soon it would come to pass as Silver Moon had foretold.

———— ∙∙∙ ————

"THE SCREEN DOOR OPENED—GROANING and squeaking—and a diminutive woman, with long graying hair pulled into a braided ponytail, stepped onto the porch, and ambled toward the second unoccupied rocker. Blackie jumped up helping her into the rocker.

"*Pilamaya Sapa Kangi.*" (My thanks, Black Crow).

"*Tanyan Yahi Maza Ska Hanhepi.*" (You are welcome, Silver Moon), Blackie responded.

The language kept them in touch with their inner Sioux. They'd never forget who they were and how far they'd come as a people. What pained the Elders was their youth. Those who no longer understood the days of yore, younger members who'd discarded the tribal ways, losing even the language of their people. For the Elders of the tribe to hear the younger generation talk the way kids spoke these days in what they referred to as jive, slang, or gangster, wasn't English, but foreign. Its youth massacred even the English vocabulary and, over time, not only Lakota, but proper English disappeared.

Members of the top council and diehard tribal members, those who took pride in their Siouan roots and heritage, never forgot the people's language, and they spoke daily to keep it alive.

Through the years, the tribe's four Elders learned other tribal languages. It would seem necessary as other Nations and their people moved into adjoining lands, forming friendships along the way. The Sioux clan lost members of their community to better jobs, new opportunities, and marriages, and it mattered not what Sioux Tribe you originated from, be it Lakota, Dakota, or Nakota, they welcomed everyone into what they considered only as the "land of the free."

Two generations later, tribal members, such as Blaze and Dakota Kangee, and his brother Paytah and his wife Wakanda, enjoyed the old ways, the language, and the customs as did their peers.

How refreshing to have Raven, the youth of today, the old spirit she was, in the young, vibrant body she lived in, embrace the Sioux ways, keeping it alive for her generation. As a born leader, she embodied the Siouan spirit using her uncanny ability to speak the language, understanding the ways, immersing those around her in the thick culture, making it come alive in others.

Having her in their tribe was a blessing, for young people flocked to her as a moth to a flame. Young Raven was destined to create the glue to put two worlds back together again.

Paytah (Peyton) and Wakanda (Kanda) Kangee's only son would also fulfill his destiny, joining forces with his cousin to restore the stars and bring balance to both realms.

Soft Dove and Silver Moon realized the time was close. Soon, certain worlds would fade—into the winds as never being. Life would spin not only for the Sioux, but for Native Americans in totality. Various tribes would cease to have certain powers unless these events were reversed. The two worlds needed to run parallel, but at no time should they touch. Blaze and Dakota couldn't be there to guide their daughter. They had to relive their own past one last time to keep the world balanced so Raven's journey could begin. At no time could they meet or it would trap them in a never-ending time loop. Unless their daughter succeeded in her journey, anyone involved in this magic would continue to live in a past which would fade, then finally never exist.

Chapter 2

"No one's here." My heart rate quickened as I led the gray mare out, shutting the gate behind me.

My best friend followed me with his pony, Moon Beam. He was also my cousin, Chayton Kangee.

"You reckon they all went into town"? Chay asked. He was the sensible one of us most of the time, but he'd heard my panicked tone.

"Nope. There's Dad's truck and Ben's. And Mom's Suburban is in the shop. Hold Gypsy's reins while I run into the house, see what's up."

I slithered off my favorite mare sprinting up the front porch steps and into the house. "Mom, Dad, you guys in here? Ben?" My voiced echoed throughout the house.

Chay sat, shaking his head. Raven was excitable and acting weird, weirder than normal, never leaving the house, never seeing friends. In truth, having no fun anymore.

For the past two months, we'd repeated this conversation:

"Rave, come on, there's so much of the world to see."

"No, Chay, here, this land. This is all I need. I love it here and never want to leave."

"At least go into town once in a while."

I was too stubborn, but then who was he to talk? He still lived at home, too. But I was different because it was all about my

Sioux heritage—the life, the culture. Chay, also proud of his heritage, told me I needed to embrace the new world!

My excuses for not having a life were thin, nonexistent. No real reason to keep myself shut out from the rest of our group.

"I can't explain it, but I need to stay close to home. It's what my gut says." I'd repeated this for the past two or three months.

"Yeah, I know. You're an all-powerful Siouan witch who knows things." Chay poked me in the gut. "You need to spew out that feeling and start living."

Chay was bigger than me, but if I got mad enough, I could whip him. At five foot five, around a buck ten dripping wet, I was in top shape, not a sissy girly-girl, either. At twenty-four and working hard on my father's cattle ranch, I was muscular, plus, I was smarter and more cunning.

"Well?" Chay asked when I jumped off the porch, avoiding all the steps to grab my mare's reins, hauling myself up.

"Nope, nobody's home and no note. That's not like Mom. Dad and Ben, yeah, but not Mom."

I turned Gypsy's head and for a split-second the back forty flashed into my head.

"Follow me." I headed toward the back pasturelands at a gallop. Chay followed without question.

❧

Two-hundred head of cattle grazing on this section were gone. Vanished. Before me was empty land and an old shack I'd never seen before.

Chay was confused. "Where're the cows? I just helped you and Ben herd these cows back two days ago after we'd vaccinated 'em. Hey, and what's up with the old shed? Why did someone haul it up here?"

I eyed the shed. If a wind blew, even a breeze, it'd come tumbling down. It looked to be a hundred years old.

Unsure what was happening, I tapped Gypsy's flanks, moving closer. The windows were boarded, with a few cracks wide enough to see inside, but we'd have to get down to see.

A new, but old twenty-by-twenty wooden shed stood flat-dab in the middle of my dad's north pasture.

I circled the small shed again, and fear riveted through me. Panic rose in my throat. First, how had this gotten here? Second, why was it here at all? Then something in my mind's eye snapped, telling me I'd seen it before, and the knowledge I'd buried deep within fought to get out.

A loud whistle sounded, bringing me out of my deep reverie, and turning I looked at Chay who pointed and following his finger, I saw where he was drawing my attention. My mouth opened, but I didn't utter a sound. I couldn't.

Back on a distant hill stood one lone buffalo, and next to the beast stood a man. No ordinary man. He was dressed in full headdress, feathers flowing, painted face, with a spear in his hand. Next to him a large chestnut-colored stud, to which he held the reins.

My mind raced and when I saw Chay move his pony forward. I cried out, "*Stop! No! Stay!*"

Chay pulled back on the reins. "Whoa, Moon Beam, the boss says stop." He guided her backward until our horses were side by side, his eyes still on the vision we saw in the distance.

"We can't just sit here. I am so, so, so and a million more so's, curious, aren't you?" His gaze met mine, and it sent a chill up his spine.

"Rave, you'd better talk to me, oh, mystic girl," Chay said, snapping his fingers, bringing me back to earth.

I broke my stare with the old chief on the hill, but before I looked away, he smiled and gave me a slight nod. Something passed between us and I was no longer afraid, but troubled knowing something big was happening and I didn't feel as if I were ready.

"Chay, let's get back to the house."

I raced toward the house on Gypsy, not slowing down until I arrived. Chay hadn't argued and was close behind.

Once inside, Chay sat on the overstuffed chair, propping his feet up on the ottoman watching me pace, my waist-length hair in a braided ponytail, flapping as I turned, walking back and forth, in deep thought, mumbling. Stopping, I placed my pointer finger and thumb against the bridge of my nose, pressing inward to relieve the tension causing my head to throb.

"You got a headache from all that thinking and muttering?" Chay averted his focus from the loose thread on his t-shirt, to gaze at me. I stared at him like a ghost.

"Listen, Rave, there's always an explanation for everything. There's gotta be a logical one, right?"

I faced him, hand on my hips. "Logical to you, no, but logical to me, yes."

"Is that a riddle? What does that even mean?"

"Let's start from the beginning." I pulled the ottoman out from under him, letting his feet hit the floor with a thud, and sat down, then looked him straight in the eye. "You ready for this?" I was a little less frazzled, but a trace of anxiety laced my voice. Chay knew me well; I never could hide any emotions from him.

Chay might not be all-knowing, mystical, or as gutsy as the stories of his ancestors. To tell the truth, after all these years, we'd figured they'd embellished the stories. He was a here-in-this-century kind of person, preferring to refer to himself as The New Sioux Breed, and sometimes he'd mock me and my old soul.

"Yeah, okay, tell me, my warrior maiden, what gives?"

"If you're not gonna listen with an open mind, then when the feather pillows hit the fan you'll be on your own!" I huffed.

"Alright, already. I'll give it my best shot, make a believer out of me. I'm all ears." He waved his hands with an exaggerated motion, giving me center stage.

Chapter 3

"Well, that's not news to me. I've heard this same story about a million times. Geez, you remember who my parents are, right, you know, Paytah and Wakanda Kangee? Your aunt and uncle?" Chay snorted.

He'd heard the story of how the old chief's journal sent my mom and dad back in time before they became Mom and Dad, and how his mom and dad performed some voodoo spell from an ancient book and the whole pile of baloney.

"You gonna spin that old tall tale again? Come on, we're not kids anymore."

"Now, you listen to me, Chayton Star Kangee."

"Awe, now you gotta start using my full name? Crap, you know I hate my middle name. Geez, Louise!"

Why had they given him the middle name Star? Chay's mom told him the night Blaze traveled from the past back to her present world a shooting star appeared in the sky over their house. It had been a sign for her to use the name Star for her firstborn child. His father, ever so much more ginger in his explanation, said it was because the night he had taken his beloved to the stars was the night Chay's conception occurred. His mom smiled at his dad, explaining Star Gazer was his Sioux name, and this he liked, for it meant he'd never fear getting lost, because he could follow the stars.

"Can I just finish the story?" I rolled my eyes in aggravation.

"By all means, please." Once again, he motioned with his hand, giving me the floor.

"So, this is gonna sound nuts..." I inhaled, before resuming.

Chay almost said, "*What's new about nuts? Our whole family is nuts.*" But he held his tongue.

"They selected me to go search for our people and make sure changes don't occur in the past that would upset the balance of nature."

"That's it? I'm a tad disappointed. Isn't there more to it? " He huffed. "So, where are the cows? How did you do it?"

"Moreover,"—I stopped at the expression I saw on his face—"what?"

"I can't stand when you begin a sentence with *Moreover*."

"Anyway." I clenched my teeth. "I'm the selected one to fix what's broken in our world and make it whole again. Chay, will you please be serious? This isn't a joke, I promise, so please trust me."

"Fine, I'll try, not gonna promise I won't laugh an itty-bit."

For now, that'd have to do. I gave him a lopsided smile with the realization he soon would learn he had to trust me.

"Get knapsacks and bedrolls out of the loft. I'll get canteens, then search for any nonperishables. Wait. Get all the knapsacks you can find. We'll use them for other things like toothpaste, aspirin, antacids, ointment, you know, and other stuff we might need. Dig through the bunkhouse and get some of Ben's clothes. Y'all are about the same size."

I was talking a mile a minute.

"Rave, hey, *Raven*," Chay shouted. "Holy moly, girl, slow down and wait a minute. What in the fruit juices are you talking about?"

"Humor me; make believe we're going on a long camping trip via horseback. Pretend with me, because we don't have a lot of time." Something in my eyes said, *don't argue*, and he touched my arm.

"On one condition."

"What condition?"

"Explain more to me while we ride?"

"Absolutely." This was my reply as I hurried upstairs, shooing Chay to the barn and bunkhouse.

I GATHERED BEEF JERKY, peanuts in bags, dumped dry cereal out of boxes into large ziplock bags, and grabbed a box of granola bars—anything I thought might last on a long trip. After, I pulled out all the bottled water from the fridge. I was glad to see Mom purchased a fresh case which sat on the floor in the pantry. As an afterthought, I took a large box of powdered milk and laughed. You had to have milk with cereal. As I rummaged through a large junk drawer, I found a few packages of rubber gloves, and for some odd reason, I stuffed them into the knapsack. I continued to dig for matches, lighters, anything to start a fire with. Then made a mental note to get the small kerosene lantern from the tack house, then discarded that idea. We'd have to cart kerosene. Two flashlights rolled from the rear of the drawer, and I grabbed them. Flashlights, better bet. With a smile, I dug around in the junk drawer for extra batteries.

Packhorses. I ran to the front door and collided with Chay who'd run in with four backpacks, one filled, and three more that were empty.

"Crud, sorry," Chay panted, out of breath from all the scurrying around in the barn and bunkhouse. He bent to gather the flashlights and batteries he'd knocked out of my hands after we'd collided.

"It's okay. I was coming to tell you to bring Sadie and Jumper. We're gonna use them as packhorses. You find Ben's clothes?" I nodded to the one filled knapsack.

"Uh-huh, but I ain't using the old guy's toothbrush. Y'all got new ones for visitors somewhere?"

"Guest bathroom, over there." I thumbed. "We gotta hurry. We need to ride out to the back forty before we leave. Once we get this stuff gathered and loaded, it'll be after three, and won't be long before dark."

He didn't understand. Ride back for what? Chay thought this was stupidity on his part for following along with this foolishness. Hey, though, what was a cuz-slash-best-friend for, if not to follow in the craziness of the other? One day, if and when it ever happened, he hoped his wild and yet extraordinary cousin would follow him—if he ever was the one leading. He raced out heading to the barn to get Sadie and Jumper ready to haul whatever his cousin had been stuffing into the other backpacks.

I grimaced. We'd need more supplies, but we had no more room. Ascending the stairs three at a time, I ran to my mom's room, yanked the desk drawer open, and pulled out her diary, the ancient diary of Chief Black Raven and Silver Moon's undocumented history book. Rushing to my room, I pulled open the top drawer of my bureau and I freaked. Aunt Meda's *Book of Dreams* was gone.

Chapter 4

Chay found me in a mess of clothes and shoes, with boxes from my closet covering the floor of my once nice, neat room, my hands covering my face sobbing.

"Hey, what's going on in here? Looks like you tossed the joint, Bugsy?" He snorted, but I persisted in weeping into my hands and hiccupped. "I can't find the book, and I've looked everywhere." Wailing, I sniffed up more tears.

"What book? I'll search for it," he offered.

In between the sniffing and hiccups I explained, and Chay looked through the mess but didn't see what I'd described.

His brows furrowed, then a light came on over his head, and he sniggered to himself because he could see the cartoon bulb pop on as he snapped his fingers.

"It's not funny." I sniffed, blowing my nose on the nearest t-shirt laying on the floor.

"No, not laughing about this. I was, well, never mind." Deciding to forgo the cartoon in his head, he said, "I know where the book is. Your mom had it out in the kitchen this morning. She was looking at it and I saw it after she went to get your butt outta bed."

I jumped up and wiped off my teary face. "Thanks, Chay, you're tops." I hugged him.

He shrugged it off as nothing, sliding down the banister and out of my sight, heading to get the book I'd been boo-hoo'ing over. Following him I realized my mom had been looking through it—this in itself might confirm I had to have her book.

I took the book Chay handed me, along with the other books, and slipped them inside the smaller red-and-yellow-flowered backpack, then slipped it on. These books could never leave my sight.

He watched her, hoping she had a tale for all this rigmarole. He loved his cousin like a sister, but she was a loon! When she took a rifle off the gun rack and a handgun, he gave her a stare of caution.

"Really, Raven? Guns and stuff, you think we are in danger? Come on now." He gestured his disapproval.

"I'm not sure we'll need guns or ammo, but I won't take any chances and be unarmed. I'd rather have and not need, then need and not have. Chay, I'm uncertain what we're facing. Besides, like you asked me, I'll try to explain when we ride into town, but we gotta get finished up. Please, trust me."

She was unruffled, yet frightened, acting as if they were heading into a war. She knew it worried him because he knew her and she wasn't joking around.

With guns in play, I had his full attention now, if I hadn't before. We got the gear packed on Sadie and Jumper and the saddlebags stuffed with extra things, tucked both rifles into the scabbards, and I tucked a small handgun into my waistband. When he saw me do this, he nodded, tucking one into the back of his waistband, even though I'd yet to explain.

"Leave Sadie and Jumper tied here at the house. Let's go to the hill where he is."

"What do you mean by 'is'? You think he's still there?"

"I'm not sure what the exact sequence is. He might be there, he might not. I need to go see something."

Like before, I took off and Chay followed me, no questions asked.

THE OLD BUILDING WAS still there. It looked like it'd been sprayed with white paint. There were white blotches in random places on the roof and around the bottom. Out of nowhere, trees sprouted, growing in areas of the once empty acreage. Weeds grew next to the shack and bushes had piled up on the corner by the front door.

I'd stopped to gaze at the shack with notable changes, and Chay almost crashed Moon Beam into Gypsy's rump. His eyes on this unfamiliar sight, his mouth hanging open, not believing what he was seeing.

"What the devil sort of voodoo is this? I mean, what the—" He pulled the reins back to keep from bumping Gypsy, then turned his head to say something and he saw it, too.

The older man with the war bonnet had vanished and only the buffalo was there at the top of the hill. The massive beast stood, his head stooped to the ground, as he grazed. A lone buffalo, and I wasn't afraid.

Dismounting, I held Gypsy's reins looking on the ground searching for something, but not what I was seeking.

Chay watched, then he turned to glance at what now looked like a country wilderness amidst flat pastureland. Where there had once been nothing but pasture sat a ramshackle shed. Land that had been cleared now filled with trees, bushes, and weeds. He shivered in a shimmy, recalling me telling him I'd heard when you shivered it meant someone was walking on your grave. Why was he spooking himself? He was getting worried, awaiting my explanation, or to hear me say "ta-da!" then tell him how I pulled this hoax off. However, he watched me knowing this wasn't a trick, and the hairs on his neck bristled.

I squatted running my fingers over a patch of taller buffalo grass, finding what my fingers sought, and with care, I collected the old beaded, long leather braid, which had three feathers attached, and on the other end an ancient arrowhead. I smiled.

"*Pilamaya, Tunkasila, wana sota hanyewi, ehangini, Egogshan,*" I said loud enough for Chay to hear, my words carried into the wind, to the ears of the ancient past.

He hadn't understood a word because he only knew a smidgen of Lakota, but I was fluent. I'd begun learning to speak it at an early age, amazing everyone.

"Uh, Rave, you wanna translate?" he called out.

"I said, thank you, Grandfather, one of many moons ago, until we meet again."

Again on my horse, I tucked the feathers in my pocket. They were the sign I'd searched for. Straightaway I knew what the old rickety structure was and why it appeared.

"Let's go, Chay." I turned Gypsy around.

"Now hold on a minute. You wanna explain, please?" He pointed to the old shed. "Where did all the shrubbery come from? What's the white stuff? Looks like paint."

I exhaled. "You know the story, Chay; you said you've heard it a million times. Think."

It took him all of five seconds. "You mean, this was where Aunt Blaze was? That's the mill shed? You gotta be joshing me. It can't be true, that shed was in South Dakota, and you're telling me it's here now and with snow appearing on it? Shut the front door. That's preposterous. Shi...uh, stuff like this doesn't happen, ever!"

"Go ahead, you can say it. This is stupid and you think I am batshit crazy, but hey, it's there, and you see it with your own two googly eyes. Up to you what you want to believe. You'll be a genuine believer later. Wait and see. Let's go get Sadie and Jumper. Need to get to town, if we can, before dusk sets in."

I turned to leave, knowing Chay would listen once we made it to the township. There may be things he needed to see first. Afterward, a long explanation would be due.

SOON I WOULD CALL Chay, Star, or Star Gazer. Some would refer to me as Little Bird, or Black Bird throughout this amazing journey. I am Raven Maka Clark Kangee, conceived long ago, in an older era, but born in the twenty-first century. My preordained destiny: Save the mothers of heroes or the hero, not just for the Sioux Nation, but for the nations of the Real People and for those who would save many.

Chapter 5

"Why are we stopping? It's only about two more miles to town." Chay surveyed the area.

He hadn't pressed me for the story, trying to comprehend what he'd just seen. Chay knew in time I'd tell him, so as he'd done his entire life with me, he waited, and unexpectedly, I felt his impatience.

We found ourselves facing an abandoned farmhouse which had seen its last days of human habitation and a barn no longer the red barn of yesteryear which sat back off the main road, on a narrow dirt path, overgrown with brush, trees, and weeds. This place was where we'd hung out when we were teens. Played music and enjoyed peace away from our chores and our parents. The old barn had plenty of room and held tons of teenage memories. Memories our parents never needed to learn about.

I got off Gypsy, walking her and Jumper toward the barn.

"Chay, bring Moon Beam and Sadie. We're gonna keep them inside, let them rest. "

"Rave, we might want to make sure the barn doesn't cave. It looks worse than it did five years ago. Don't want the wind to topple it on top of our horse's heads, do we?"

"It looks stable. Don't be a pansy."

Sometimes following his girl cousin was a big fat P-A-I-N, he thought, sighing, but followed anyway.

"We'll be inside, and it's off the road enough for hiding, plus it still has doors and we can shut them." I looked around inside and saw a loft and a ladder, then checked it out, making sure the wood hadn't rotted. I climbed up to peer out and see beyond the small farmhouse to the road. This place had sat empty for fifteen years. The owner died and his children never wanted this life, or to embrace the Sioux heritage, which had been their birthright. It saddens me thinking how at one time in my mom's life she hadn't wanted to know about her history, who she was, or where she'd come from. Had it not been for magic, I wouldn't have been born.

"How's the view up there?" Chay asked. He ascended the ladder, hoisted it up, and set it to the side.

I frowned.

"Just making sure we can get down, in case the ladder falls while we are up here." He scooted on his backside to where I sat, still frowning at him. "Also, making sure my weight doesn't cause the floor to cave in. This barn's old, could have wood rot. Both of us up here, not good if we fall through." Chay puckered his brow when he heard boards creaking. "See?"

"Old wood creaks, doesn't mean it'll give way." Sometimes my cousin is a scaredy-cat.

I kept looking beyond the house and the trees, to the road. This paved two-lane county road was the main road for everyone who lived here. Today was Saturday. Most Saturdays or week-days, a truck, car, tractor, or flatbed would usually be coming or going. I thought it way too calm.

"You gonna just sit there gazing or you gonna talk to me?" Chay disturbed my thoughts.

"Chay, don't you think it's odd there's not one truck, tractor, or flatbed on the road? We didn't see a soul on the way here, either. Nobody's working in the fields, no kids riding today, or outside playing, nothing?"

He pondered for a half beat, then shook his head.

"It's strange, but hey, we're not always out and about, either. There are times we're at your place, riding or herding cattle, or in the barn or whatever, and no one sees where we are, and we don't see anyone else...so what?"

I didn't answer, but I crawled over, dropped the ladder, then slipped down. Chay followed.

"Let's go," I said and headed to the open barn door.

"Walking, are you serious?" he asked, standing beside Moon Beam, ready to mount.

"Jiminy Cricket, Chay, it's only two miles into town. You're a healthy man. Stop being a crybaby. I told you we're gonna hafta stay in the shadows until I see something. Lord have mercy!" I rolled my eyes waving my hand for him to come on so I could shut the barn doors.

"This way," I instructed. "Keep close to the fence line. We're gonna walk through the pastures."

He complained several times—his feet ached, the sun beat down too hot, whatever he could complain about to annoy me. Only I didn't rise to the bait, staying silent. This was punishment for him. He loved to talk, and he was tired of hearing his own droning voice.

"Fine, okay, if you talk I'll shut up. Tell me a bit more about what all this crap is, would'ja?"

I couldn't help but laugh.

"Uh, before you do, can I ask a question? Why don't we just walk on the road? Especially since you feel no traffic is gonna drive in either direction."

"Because," I said, "if we have to, we can jump a fence or run for cover in these side fields. I am not saying we will, but we should stay alert."

Chay was aware he still had the handgun tucked into the waistband of his jeans, taking note I had mine tucked in as well.

We didn't have to run. All we had to do was pull out guns, but right now, he didn't want to remind me of this. He blew out a big, long, overdramatic breath.

"Okay, spill." Chay became silent, waiting for me to tell him something plausible, only I knew he'd have to wait a long time to hear something believable—because what I was about to tell him he'd never believe.

"It was in the books my Aunt Meda passed along to my mom. Chief Black Raven's journal and a dream book Aunt Meda wrote. See this." I pulled out two chains from under my shirt. Each held an amulet. I fiddled with both, trying to decide if I should just tell him everything or wait.

"Well, what is it?" he pressed. "And if you don't quit dropping into la-la land, I'm going to shake you until your teeth rattle. Got me?"

"Let's keep walking," I said holding one charm to show him, tucking the other one back under my t-shirt. This could wait until later; one thing at a time.

I showed him the amulet. It was significantly larger than a silver dollar, however, smaller than a coaster, with a solid backing and a Plexiglas cover to keep it protected.

"This is a replica of the feathers of power," I said. Eagle feathers, once worn by Chief Swift Eagle, the dark-colored Raven feather, worn by Chief Black Raven, and finally, the hawk feather, worn by Warrior Dark Cloud. These feathers, added with the powers of our tribe, create a vertical line to the powers of each man. You know what I found on the hill? Where the old man stood with the buffalo?"

"No, what?"

I stopped walking to fish into the front pocket of my jeans pulling out the braided leather band, showing him the feathers which dangled on the end.

"This."

"You sure you're not trying to pull a fast one and you already had it in your pocket?" He gave me his *are you kidding me* stare.

"Chay, with serious things do you recall me, ever, and I do mean, *ever*, lying to you?"

"You've pulled pranks, I gotta admit, but never ones this elaborate." He searched my eyes for a glimmer of a joke and saw I wasn't kidding.

"Alright then, you're serious. What does this mean, do you know?"

I stuffed the braided leather strap into my pocket and slipped the chain under my shirt, shaking my head.

"Not sure. Only I've an idea we're getting ready for a journey, one which might be dangerous, one our people will depend on us completing for the sake of our existence, as well as the continued existence of others." My tone firm, my jaw set, and I must've had an expression he'd never seen before.

Chay nodded, and I knew he wasn't one hundred percent sure this wasn't a ruse.

Chay's eyes darted over to see her as they walked in silence. His cousin acted serious, and he'd give her the benefit of the doubt for now. He didn't know what he was walking into because he knew she wasn't telling him everything, but no matter, he'd stand with her. If need be, fight alongside her for the sake of what he too loved—the Sioux.

Even without knowing what he faced, I knew Chay would stay by my side, seeing our journey to the end.

Chapter 6

It took us fifteen minutes to go behind the shops and down a path. A fresh path of regular dirt leading us back to the farm-to-market road. The area looked the same, yet different. The old tree at the city limits sign was still there but smaller. No longer the hulking oak it had once been, but a younger sapling. But the telltale sign was the large boulders stacked a few feet from the shrunken oak tree. Same place it had been for years, more years than they'd been alive. Chay stopped. He stood on his toes, climbing up so he could see on the other side.

"The vein's still there," Chay remarked, satisfied he knew where he was, still in this world.

"Yeah, the tree appears to have shrunk. It makes the boulders seem like a mountain."

The boulders, stacked by nature, were big enough for two or three kids to sit on top of, and they'd called it the Rock of Dracula. A thin line ran across the top rock, which they thought resembled a blood vein stained with a bluish hue with two dark spots, where they imagined Dracula had sunk his fangs. They'd made up stories for years, saying it had been a pile of petrified bodies the Count had killed after drinking their blood. Stupid stuff, Chay said rocking back on the balls of his feet, but Dracula he no longer feared because these newer occurrences were scary, and I didn't blame him. I was both eager and nervous. We'd seen movies about time warps and make-believe time machines.

Movies such as *Back To the Future* or *Somewhere in Time, Kate and Leopold*, even *Avatar* had these fairytale elements, but honestly, neither one of us thought we'd be living in a real one.

"Let's go," I said.

Chay looked around and nodded. "Okay, which way?"

I looked around, squinting. "That way, I think." I pointed. "It looks different now, though, doesn't it?" My right index finger at the tip of my mouth, I chewed on my fingernail. My nervous habit Chay always scolded me about, but I feared we'd gotten turned around with all these changes and was unsure of myself and my prowess with directions.

Chay Star Kangee stood up straighter, feeling something inside of him he'd never felt before and in the beginning, it scared him. Something took hold filtering through his every being. His skin, his veins, his head, and his heart; it ebbed in and out of him. As if someone was cleaning his spirit and refilling it with something. He shuddered and then went still.

Chay stared at me and I was still in deep thought. "Raven," he said, "I'll show you the way. Follow me."

In slow motion, I turned when he spoke. I heard something. Something different from the Chay I knew. The clown, the forever doubting, always playing around, zany cousin. What I'd heard was the voice of Star Gazer, a Sioux spirit of the stars, the pathway of the people.

I stared at him, my jaw dropping, and I snapped it shut smiling.

"What are you smiling about?" he asked, pointing which way to go.

"You, Chay, I'm smiling at you. You're Star Gazer, really."

"Don't get mushy about this stuff, but yeah, I felt a...a change inside. But never think I'm not the same Chay you've always known. Maybe I just got indigestion and smart simultaneously," he kidded.

I laughed, and we walked, him directing me over new lands which popped up in our pathway. A dense treed area appeared which was not there when we'd passed earlier. It amazed me, the land had literally changed. Even now, the town behind us was still changing, moving backward to yesteryear.

Chay led me over a stream which mystifyingly appeared. It had never been there in our lifetime. His voice took on a sudden, urgent sense of concern. "Do you think the barn and our horses are there?"

"Yes, I do. Don't ask me why, though. I picked this barn because there has been a barn here since time began. Well, not since time began, of course. That's not possible." I held in a laugh.

"From what I learned, there'd been a structure since around 1815, or it was 1825. I can't remember the date. Anyway, it wasn't always a barn, but it was something. I read about it in the dream book my Aunt Meda gave me."

"Your aunt dreamed about the barn?"

"Not the barn, Chay, the land. The Sioux once occupied this area before the settlers came. In her visions, she said the Cheyenne tribe lived in this area, or at least frequented the area when they hunted buffalo. She was told a Raven would leave supplies and means of travel stored there, and hunt for a town. Weird, huh, because my Aunt Meda had this vision before I was born. She dated some of them, so I'd know when she dreamed them."

"Oh, yeah? When we get to the barn you might want to, uh, enlighten me about some of these fantasies, you think?"

I ponder this. Chay may need to be knowledgeable about what could happen. Although I wasn't even sure what was going to happen. All I knew was changes were imminent, changes spinning both of us around in a million directions, and it would be dangerous.

Chapter 7

IT'D TAKEN US LONGER to get back. The path wasn't as easy, nor as simple at it had been the first time. It surprised Chay how the land could change over what he was sure was a hundred or more years. He'd never considered himself a tracker, but he was tracking and guiding, something he never knew he could do, and full of himself.

Our light was dissipating. Just past dusk with a full moon rising, and with so much land without towns or structures obscuring them, the stars were bright and in hordes of thousands, lighting up the darker skies.

There it was. The barn we'd started in, but now the structure was crudely built, the wood rough, and the doors held shut with a sliding rail. I lifted the rail tossing it to the side to let the door swing open, and Chay rocked his head back and forth then grabbed the rail and tossed it inside.

"Wow, weird. When we left, there was hardware keeping the doors shut, not a rail. And I wanna keep it fastened when we're inside. Besides, we don't wanna get trapped inside in case someone's out here."

He had a point.

What a relief to find all four horses and unharmed. What we weren't prepared for was the very pregnant Native American woman who came out of the shadows, and behind her a larger-than-life Native American man. Both dressed in authentic clothes of the period, very real-looking.

We stood there, four sets of eyes boring into each other, the interlopers sizing up the situation, me in total awe and Chay needing a clean pair of boxers.

Time stopped. I'd been holding my breath for what felt like a lifetime. Then I relaxed enough to breathe. Chay, had I not touched his arm, might have keeled over for lack of breathing.

The man, spear in his hand, a scowl on his face, gave me pause before speaking. I had to make sure not to irritate or scare him. I knew this woman was his woman, and she was carrying his unborn child.

He spoke first, "*Nit'uwe hwo?*" (Who are you?)

"*Kangee, emaciyapi yelo.* (My name is Raven Kangee. In Lakota the word Kangee is the word for crow/blackbird.)

He gestured with his head at Chay, and I said he was my relative; his name is Chay Kangee, known as Star Gazer.

He nodded at Chay and looked back, asking me if I were Cheyenne or Lakota.

"Lakota."

"I am Cheyenne, but I understand your tribe's words. My woman, She Who Sees Truth," he said. He gestured to his woman, who had taken a very short step back, hiding behind the foreboding man. "I am called *Matsenestse* (Kingfisher)." He stood straight, proud, and not afraid. Chay and I dressed in modern-day clothes should've scared him; it would have me if I were him.

I smiled, and Chay, still speechless, took a step forward, which wasn't a bright move on his part.

"*Stop!*" His words were screamed in Cheyenne. The man called Kingfisher lifted his spear and aimed it at Chay, who froze, one foot still in the air.

Speaking in rapid-fire Lakota, I told Kingfisher we meant no harm.

Then I addressed Chay. "Step back before you get us both killed. He's scared for his wife."

"What! He's scared? Holy cow, I just about peed myself," Chay said between clenched teeth as he stepped backward, standing beside me. His eyes were on the man with the spear. He asked, "What do you suggest we do? Man, this guy is going to think we're evil spirits. What are you going to say? Our clothes and how we're dressed, we don't fit this time era, not a smidge!"

My hand on his arm to ease his qualms, I spoke to Kingfisher in Lakota, happy we had no communication problem.

"Your *Wee-yah* (woman), when does your *hoksicala* (baby) arrive?"

His gaze moved to She Who Sees Truth, and I saw tenderness in his eyes which had shown my cousin threat.

"One full moon."

The woman nodded.

Wow. This would be weird. I'd never seen a human baby born. I'd seen calves and a foal's birthing, but this would be more amazing.

"Is good? We help?" I asked.

"No, no man see, not even me."

I looked at Chay, then Kingfisher. Holy cow, I'd have to help, or She Who Sees Truth was going to have to bear this baby alone. Jeepers Creepers, this was a nightmare! Then I wondered if they'd still be here. A moon was a month. How long would we be here, and what about Kingfisher and his wife?

"You wanna fill me in, and can I move? I feel like a statue and my bones are aching." Chay did a sideways talk out of his mouth, like Clyde talking to Bonnie in a gangster film.

"Come, sit so She Who Sees Truth can rest." My hand gestured to the center of the barn, encompassing the hay and straw scattered around in places on the dirt floor.

Kingfisher nodded and took a confident step forward, unafraid, leading the woman to sit behind him. He protected her, which I admired in him.

I acted as the protector, while Chay sat behind me, his eyes never leaving the other man's face.

I tried not to laugh but couldn't help it, which caused Kingfisher to raise an eyebrow in curiosity. "Why do you protect the man? Has he no courage?"

"What did he say about me? I know you two are talking about me," Chay huffed.

"He wants to know why I protect you because you're the man," I cackled again, this time with too much mirth, or so Chay thought because he poked me in the side and I jumped.

"Chay, stop poking me."

"You can tell him what's going on and that I'm not his enemy. Tell him I'm part of your tribe even though I don't speak Lakota, even though I *am* full-blooded Sioux, because this is pissing me off. And..." His voice rose a notch. "I'm due a freaking explanation, don't'cha think?"

I nodded. Chay had never spoken to me that way, especially regarding the issue of being pure-blooded. It stung to a small degree, but I'd get over it.

"How about I explain it to you both, but it will take me some time, since *you* can't speak Lakota nor Cheyenne, so I'll need to tell the story *twice*, " I ground out between gritted teeth.

He ducked his head. "I'm sorry about the full-blooded thing, Cuz, honest, I didn't mean to piss you off. I'm, well, yeah, I can say it, I'm scared because I don't even know what's going on or why."

With a nod I patted him on his knee. "It's okay, I understand. I would be too if I were you. Heck, I'm me and I'm scared too because I still don't get it either. So, come up here, sit beside me, be the valiant warrior I know you are, Star Gazer."

He conceded and scooted up. Then, crossing his legs he stared at the other two, trying not to look defiant or threatening, or like a scared bunny rabbit, twitching to run down a rabbit hole and hide.

~

I had them spellbound with my tale, and several times, King-fisher's jaw dropped, but he snapped it shut just as fast. The woman, whose mouth had dropped open, stayed open in a full-on "catching flies" expression. Once I'd finished, I turned to Chay. "I've caught them up to where we are."

"Which is where?" Chay asked miffed.

"I told them a shortened version of my mom and dad, you and your parents, and Aunt Meda's book, the old chief, and the buffalo on the hill, and how it was my ancestral grandfather from many moons ago, and how things are reverting to the past before our eyes, and I don't know why. Also, I told them I don't know why we're here."

Kingfisher stood. "Horses safe, hidden in thicket; we come to rest. Our hunting party camped near Tatanka, but many White-men come; they hunt Tatanka too, but for hides and sport, not for winter survival, food, and clothing. Not prepared for Whiteman to fight, not afraid, but we are few, and I fear for our unborn child." The proud Cheyenne looked at his wife. "She Who Sees Truth traveled with midwife in case her time comes, but we separated from the others and here we stopped so she can rest before we go back to camp near Black Hills." He looked down on the top of his woman's bowed head.

Chay, now no longer afraid, thought he was an amazing-look-ing man. The Cheyenne man called Kingfisher was six-foot tall, lean and muscular, with a rough etched face and a squared jawline. The man's nose was long and sloped downward into a slight point, and his complexion a smooth brown, with long black hair pulled into two tails and bound with leather, keeping it from flying about. His eyes were piercing black, and he wore leggings with fringe down both sides, boots made of the hide of a buffalo, and a leather slip-over-your-head shirt lined with fringe from the same hide. Kingfisher carried a large knife in a leather belt with a pouch dangling from it, and a sling of beads. Chay wondered about their horses.

"What'd he say? And where are their horses, or are they on foot?" Chay eyeballed me.

"They have horses, two of them. They left them hidden in the back thicket. Seems they were heading to a new winter camp and Whitemen were out hunting. As far as I can translate it, they were only a small group that had been the last to leave. To avoid a skirmish with the Whitemen, they left the area and somehow became separated from the rest of the small group, including the midwife. They're on their way to the winter place in Montana, and he claims it's only a four- or five-day ride from here."

Chay let this seep into his brain. Then he had the look on his face I'd been awaiting.

"Uh...I...what the...well, hell! All I can say is we're not in Kansas anymore now, are we?"

I shook my head. "I know, I know. When we started out today, we were forty-five miles outside of Standing Rock Reservation on the South Dakota side; now we're in North Dakota, near the Montana border? Did the earth shift and dump us North, because we aren't even close to Kansas, Toto?"

"So," he leaned in whispering, and I sucked up a laugh.

"What's so funny?"

"Uh, we're speaking English and they can't understand, so why ya whispering?"

"Oh, ya, right. The old mill shack in the back forty was in South Dakota, the one your mother had hidden near the day they used a mystic spell and she went back in time, right?"

"Yeah, and she ends up in North Dakota, and that's where—"

He cut in on me, "Yeah, it's what I was getting at."

"So that's how we got here. It sorta fits, I guess." But neither of us passed out and woke up in a different time like my mom had. This sorta just happened to us while we were awake. We sat whispering to each other, trying to piece it together when She Who Sees Truth said something to Kingfisher in Cheyenne. He helped her up, walked her to the back where there was a single door, then he turned to stand guard, his eyes driving into Chay.

I pinched my lips together to keep from laughing because I'd understood just enough to know what was happening. Even if someone didn't speak the language of the Cheyenne, any woman would understand a pregnant lady's needs, at least some of them.

"What?" he asked eyeing the Cheyenne, then me.

I lifted my hands in a shrug and twittered. "Nature calls and Kingfisher doesn't want you calling on her as she calls on nature, I think."

"Well, I would never in a mil—oh screw it, this sucks. I need to communicate too, be a lot easier if I could!" This frustrated Chay.

I agreed and then thought about it. Black Raven's journal had magic. And perhaps that magic traveled with us and I could find the words to help; then I thought, nah, I wasn't magical. Even my mom had the elders helping her; were they at work helping us? I did know that after today's occurrences, anything was possible.

www.ingramcontent.com/pod-product-compliance
Lightning Source LLC
Chambersburg PA
CBHW011341010726
47493CB00009B/2906